"The book for which Bausch will be remembered. . . . A fine, fat collection of forty-two tales . . . distinguished by characters whose complexity is simply and economically suggested."

—*Kirkus Reviews* (starred review)

"In the small firmament of American writers who're both superb novelists and eloquent short-story practitioners Richard Bausch's star shines more brightly now than ever."

—Richard Ford

"Richard Bausch is, simply, one of our greatest short-story writers."

—Andrea Barrett

PRAISE FOR

Hello to the Cannibals

"Ambitious not only in its historical and geographical sweep but also in the author's choice to confine himself, with admirable conviction and credibility, to the consciousness of two women. . . . Bausch writes some of the most gripping dialogue [in American letters]. . . . Beautifully balanced between comedy and hopelessness."

—*New York Times Book Review*

"Long one of America's finest writers, Richard Bausch has surpassed even himself in this wise, brilliant, expansive novel about two very different women—explorers both—whose parallel lives intersect in beautiful and unexpected ways. *Hello to the Cannibals* is a fiercely original love story as big as the world."

—Lee Smith, author of *Saving Grace* and *Fair and Tender Ladies*

About the Author

RICHARD BAUSCH is one of his generation's most cele-
brated fiction writers. He is the author of nine novels and
five volumes of short stories. His work has appeared in
The New Yorker, Atlantic Monthly, Esquire, and many
other national magazines and has been featured/antholo-
gized in numerous "best of" collections, including the
O. Henry Awards and *Best American Short Stories.* He is
the recipient of an American Academy of Arts and Letters
Award, a National Endowment for the Arts grant, a
Guggenheim Fellowship, and many other prizes and
honors. He teaches at George Mason University and is
the coeditor of the esteemed *Norton Anthology of Short
Fiction.*

ALSO BY RICHARD BAUSCH

Wives & Lovers

Three Short Novels

RICHARD BAUSCH

Perennial

An Imprint of HarperCollins*Publishers*

WIVES AND LOVERS. Copyright © 2004 by Richard Bausch. All rights reserved. Printed in the United States of America. No part of this book may be used or reproduced in any manner whatsoever without written permission except in the case of brief quotations embodied in critical articles and reviews. For information address HarperCollins Publishers Inc., 10 East 53rd Street, New York, NY 10022.

HarperCollins books may be purchased for educational, business, or sales promotional use. For information please write: Special Markets Department, HarperCollins Publishers Inc., 10 East 53rd Street, New York, NY 10022.

FIRST EDITION

Designed by Jamie Kerner-Scott

Library of Congress Cataloging-in-Publication Data

Bausch, Richard.
    Wives and lovers : three short novels / Richard Bausch.—1st ed.
        p.   cm.
    Contents: Requisite kindness—Rare & endangered species—Spirits.
    ISBN 0-06-057183-7
    I. Bausch, Richard, 1945– Requisite kindness.   II. Bausch, Richard, 1945– Rare & endangered species.   III. Bausch, Richard, 1945– Spirits.   IV. Title.

PS3552.A846W58   2004
813'.54—dc22

2003063245

04 05 06 07 08 WB/RRD 10 9 8 7 6 5 4 3 2

for Karen

Requisite Kindness

AFTER

THE AFTERNOON BUS from Newport News was twenty minutes late, and the first five people who got off were Navy men. Brian Hutton's younger brother Norman was the last of them, looking leaner than Brian remembered him—though it had only been a little more than a year. Twenty-four years old now, sixteen years younger than Brian. Life at sea obviously agreed with him. His skin was tan, his eyes clear; the musculature of his upper arms showed under the uniform. Everything about him made a contrast to the older brother, whose frame had begun to sag.

Norman said, "Hard times, Bro."

They embraced. "Hey," Brian said. He felt heavy and awkward. He stepped back and reached for his brother's duffel bag.

"I got it," Norman said, shouldering the bag. They stood gazing at each other. "Somehow I'd talked myself into thinking this day wouldn't come."

"Almost ninety-five," Brian said. "A good long life."

Norman nodded. "I still hate it."

"Dad and Aunt Natalie are at the funeral home. You want to clean up first, or go straight over?"

"Whatever."

"It's your call, Norm."

"Let's go see them."

They headed across the open lot of the station with its borders of freshly plowed snow piled high. They had to shield their eyes from the sun; the air was crisp and cold. All along the highway beyond the end of the station lot were telephone poles festooned with bright Christmas ribbons and tinsel. You had to enter the terminal building to exit out onto the street, and inside, a thin-faced smiling man in a dark business suit stood next to a large cardboard box of pocket-sized Bibles. The box was sitting on a plastic chair. "Praise the Lord," he said, nodding deferentially, offering Norman one of the Bibles.

"Beat it," Norman muttered.

"Pardon?"

He walked on.

"Pardon?" the man said to Brian.

"Excuse me," Brian said.

Norman was waiting, smiling, by the door. "Check out his face, man. He's a confused evangelist now."

Brian let him pass through, then turned to look at the man with the Bibles, who was staring after them. He thought of going back to apologize.

From out on the sidewalk, his brother said, "Forget something?"

He stepped out and they walked along the street, toward the public parking lot up the block. "Just out of curiosity, Norman, what do you think Gram would've said about that particular exchange?"

Norman hefted the duffel bag higher on his shoulder. "Guy giving Bibles away in a bus station. I guess I'm home, all right."

"It's Bibles, Norm. What harm is in that?"

"I don't like it shoved in my face like that."

"But really—what do you think Elena'd say?"

"I know," Norman said. "Okay? I know."

They walked on a few paces.

"So, you were there for it," Norman said. "What was that—what did it—" He halted.

"I was only there at the very end. It was Dad mostly. The whole eastern seaboard was snowbound. Aunt Natalie was down in Florida with a tour group, stranded at the airport. Dad and Gram were alone and they went through it that way, the two of them."

"Jesus."

"She feels awful for not being there when it happened."

They crossed the street and entered the municipal parking lot. Norman shifted the duffel bag to the other shoulder. "God, I feel bad now. I don't know what gets into me. I can't help myself when that Bible stuff gets thrown at me, like it's a snack food or something. Gram never did that. Not once. I've got a roommate, man—spouts Bible and chapter and verse all the damn time. You should see him— he doesn't have pictures of his family or a girlfriend in his wallet, he's got pictures of Jesus and the saints. Most of the time it's like I'm the devil, because I want to drink a little whiskey now and then and go with the girls."

"Gram probably would've loved him."

"I said, 'I know,' okay?"

For a few minutes Brian couldn't recall where he put the car. He stopped and turned slowly, looking for it among the glaring shapes. The sun reflecting off the snow was brighter than it ever seemed in summer.

"Is Mom coming back?" Norman asked.

"It's too far. Um, she says. Under the circumstances."

"I figured. Christ. What about Tommy?"

"Tommy's with her."

"Well, it's a long way to come for a funeral. But Gram would come to theirs."

"It's having to be anywhere around Dad, isn't it?"

"I wasn't going to come out and say it."

Brian found the car, and opened the trunk. Norman threw the duffel bag in, then decided to retrieve something from it—a small metal flask.

"My ration of vegetables," he said. "Corn. Can't be without it." He twisted the cap open and took a swig, then offered it to Brian.

"Thanks anyway," Brian said.

"A lot of nutrition in an acre of corn."

"I'll have some later."

"What about Tillie?" Norman asked. "Will she be there?"

"What do you think?"

"So the marriage and divorce are off."

"Funny," Brian said.

"She and Gram got along though. Gram liked her."

Brian said nothing. They got into the car. His brother took another swig from the flask and offered it again. He waved it off, starting the car. "Damn," Norman said. "I'd like to see Tillie."

"Tillie's gone," said Brian. Then he took the flask and drank from it, feeling the burn as it went down. Handing the flask back to his brother, he rested both hands on the steering wheel. "I'm not built for this shit," he said.

Norman smiled at him, holding up the flask. "That's what you keep saying, there, bro. But you keep getting yourself into it."

THEY DROVE STRAIGHT TO the funeral home, which was on a quiet residential street in Point Royal, twenty-three miles down Highway 29, toward Charlottesville. The road was wet from melting snow, though you could see that in the shade it was not melting; it was encrusted there, stone solid. Several of the tall spruce trees surrounding the funeral home had broken branches from the weight of the snow, which kept thawing and then freezing again in the nights. The storm had come through three days ago. One of the spruce trees in the yard was garlanded with white Christmas lights, and the lights were on, though it was still day.

The only other car in the parking lot was their father's. Norman paused outside the car and adjusted his uniform, using the passenger side window as a mirror. The funeral home had an ogee roof, like a meeting hall, and a front portico supported by white columns. A long gray limo was parked in the shade of the portico. They made their way inside, and were met by a squarish, silver-haired man in a gray suit. "Elena Hutton," Brian said to him.

The man nodded, seeming faintly standoffish—perhaps he smelled the whiskey on them. He led them through the hall and to the left, past heavy stuffed chairs and facing couches.

At the end of a long, narrow, dimly lit room, Henry Hutton and his sister sat side by side on two straightback chairs. The casket was mounted to their left, in the corner, beside a massive array of flowers. Norman was first to reach them. Aunt Natalie gave forth a little cry, standing to throw her arms around him. Henry stood, too, and glanced Brian's way before concentrating on the younger son. There was something in the old man's expression—an obscure, brooding aversion—that made Brian feel inexplicably walled out. It had been this way since those last hours of his grandmother's life. He watched his father talking to Norman about the bus ride north.

"First time I took that ride I was on my way to Washington and my first job—as an office clerk over at the Department of State. The country's all shopping malls and suburbs now. Back then it was farms. Nothing but fields and hills and trees. Beautiful country back then."

"Henry," Aunt Natalie said. "Please, no more nostalgia."

He ignored her, putting his arm around Norman and staring off, as if he were looking at the remembered landscape. "It was beautiful country right up to the mid-sixties."

THEY HADN'T EVER BEEN a family that was very good at telling their feelings: Brian had always been the one who spilled everything, and his two younger brothers often teased him about it. Though he was by far the older and more experienced brother he felt, as they grew into men, increasingly insufficient around them, so much in need of their approval. And he had never found the way to seek it except through a kind of disclosure of himself, to which they invariably responded with a sardonic remark or a joke. Of course, his personal troubles had given them so much to talk about—the havoc of four failed marriages, all of which had ended in acrimony and sorrow. And this latest relationship, not a marriage, with Tillie, who had, no doubt, understood just in time what she might have let herself in for, and was gone. Gone.

The other three were talking about Gram; and abruptly he felt selfish, standing there with his own concerns.

He walked over to the casket and waited with his hands folded. The casket was closed, with a spray of flowers at the head: Elena had always said that when her time came she didn't want a lot of people staring at a corpse. There was a place to kneel, but he didn't. He murmured her name. "Elena Townsend Hutton." Then he whispered, "I hope you're somewhere you can hear me, Elena."

Henry, Norman, and Aunt Natalie approached, and they did kneel, and he saw that Norman's eyes were brimming. He walked back to the chairs and sat down, hating his own unquietness of mind.

He hadn't called Tillie to tell her what had happened—he was afraid she would think of it as a ploy on his part, to get her to come back. But it was true that Tillie had always liked and admired Elena. He confessed to himself that he had at times felt restive in the old woman's presence—wanting to be away from her worries about him, her grave consideration of him, her interest. She wasn't the kind of family member who made demands, yet one felt the force of her hopes like some exacting requirement. During his growing up, when his father had gone off on one of his binges or his flings with other women, or his mother, Lorraine, had suffered one of her own lapses with alcohol, Elena had cared for him. There had been periods when she was both father and mother to all three boys.

With Brian, of course, this history went back the furthest, and included several of the worst periods of his parents' chaotic first fifteen years.

Elena had remained engrossed in his life, in how he was leading it, and she had shown a knowing, exasperating tolerance for his failures. A forbearance that troubled him more than censure might have. It was her religion, she joked. And though she rarely spoke of that, she had kept her faith, and she assumed that the members of her family had done the same. It was practical to her. A matter of reasonable expectation and design: one observed the rituals and paid attention to the details of worship and piety, and faith took care of itself. She believed this to be true of married life as well: one observed the rituals faithfully, and everything took care of itself. Brian's troubles with marriage were the image and reflection of his father's, though Henry had remained married for thirty-six years and Lorraine had forgiven him over and over. Forgiven him after squalls and scenes, and with a lot of reflexive retaliation: excesses with the bottle, mostly, and Brian often wondered if there hadn't been one or two with other men as well. They had all come to Elena again and again for solace and for something else, too—some indefinable element of kindly disapproval that reminded them while it absolved them. He had often felt as if he were starting fresh after spending time in her company, and once, at the end of his fourth marriage, he had actually put his head in her lap and wept.

Now, sitting in the quiet, flower-heavy air of the funeral parlor, he saw an image of his mother sitting in the ash-colored light of a winter dusk, smoking a cigarette and staring out at the street. There was a glass, and an ash tray on the table, and she was crying. How old had she been then? Thirty? Certainly not much older than that. He couldn't place it. He sat there and pictured her, and remembered wondering what might happen next. He had been nine or ten. The only child in a scary unhappy place, the only true refuge from which was Elena. Thinking of this, he had a pang of realizing again that she was gone. The others had their backs to him, kneeling by the casket.

After an interval, his father stood, with some trouble, and came over to sit down.

Brian said, "No one else has come by, yet, I take it."

"Not yet."

They watched Natalie and Norman stand, and begin the walk across the room to them.

"Tillie stopped in for a while," Henry murmured.

Brian experienced a throat-closing thrill. "She—she did?"

His father nodded. "Said to say hello."

"She—did she—she didn't want to stay—"

"She said to say hello, son. That's all."

The two of them were quiet for a time. Without wanting to, Brian imagined how they must look from across the room: two men trying to find something to say to each other in the freighted quiet of a funeral parlor. Two failures. He had the thought. He looked at Henry—unfaithful, selfish, reckless Henry, whose wife of thirty-six years had left him at last.

Henry said. "Stop staring. Christ."

"Is there something—are you unhappy with me?" Brian asked him.

"What the hell are you talking about?"

"Nothing—never mind."

They were quiet a moment.

"Listen—" Brian began again, looking at the side of the old man's face.

Henry turned to him, and then stared down at his own hands. "Tillie said to say hello. Hell, your mother didn't even do that."

The funeral director came in with another spray of flowers and put them in among the others. The only sound was the soft susurration the cloth of his suit made as he moved. He went out of the room. There was a hushed stirring beyond the door, people arriving. Henry cleared his throat, then took out a handkerchief, wiped his forehead, and put it back.

Brian said, low, "I thought Mom and Tommy might come—" He stopped.

"Hell," Henry said. "Tom's with her." He leaned slightly toward Brian, as if he were about to offer a confidence, and whispered out of the side of his mouth, "You smell like a distillery. Go wash your mouth out, for Christ's sake."

Brian straightened, then stood and moved to the entrance of the room, where visitors were starting to gather—they were mostly people from Elena and Aunt Natalie's church, and from the neighborhood where Elena had lived for thirty-five of the ninety-four years. In the confusion, Aunt Natalie appeared at his side with a small plastic box of breath mints.

"Don't be ridiculous," he said.

"I know. I'm following orders."

"I won't breathe on anyone."

People were moving in a procession past them now, and Aunt Natalie hurriedly put the mints in her purse and took someone's hands, "So good of you to come," she said.

"Such a beautiful person," one woman murmured to Brian. She looked older than Elena had been. She put her hand in his, and kept it there, a small, bony, blue-veined softness, surprisingly warm to the touch. "I used to have a donut with her on Sunday mornings. Donut and a cup of coffee. She always had a way of noticing the best things to talk about, and she could be quite wicked, too. Yes," the woman said, almost talking to herself now, trailing off, "very funny. She made me laugh."

"Thank you," Brian said.

"How's Miss Natalie holding up?"

"Well, she's hanging in there."

"Pardon? Where?"

"She's a trooper."

"Who?"

"It's an expression. I'm sorry. It means she's tough."

"Yes, I'll miss her."

"*Natalie's* fine," Brian said, loudly.

"Nine?"

"We're going to miss Elena," he ventured, speaking even louder, and feeling trapped.

"Elena made me laugh."

"Yes."

"Natalie's bearing up, is she?"

He nodded, for lack of anything else to say.

"It's a good thing your father moved in with the two of them when he did," the old woman went on. It bothered Brian that he didn't know her name. "Poor Natalie. She deserved a vacation. She shouldn't feel bad. You know in the beginning we thought Elena would come with us."

"I think she wanted to," he said.

"Pardon?"

Aunt Natalie had gone to the other side of the room.

"That was all we talked about for a while," the old woman went on. "Going to Disney World. Elena said she liked the idea of a visit to the kingdom of vulgarity. She was very funny and—well, you know."

"Yes," Brian said, nodding at her.

Others were coming in, more elderly women. People stood talking quietly in the middle of the room, and when the priest arrived they parted for him. The priest was a young, sallow-looking man with a five o'clock shadow on his chin; he carried himself with a faint air of having been put upon by the afternoon's ceremony. A tiny piece of tissue paper adhered to the heel of his shoe. In a thin, apathetic voice, he led them all in a rosary, then offered Henry a few perfunctory words of consolation while putting on his overcoat. He had another appointment, he told them, and hurried away.

"That little sour son of a bitch," Henry muttered. "Who the hell was he, anyway? Who the hell asked for him."

Aunt Natalie said, "We asked for someone to lead us in a rosary. Be quiet."

"You know him?"

"No. Please."

"I'm gonna find out who he is. Who his superiors are. They need to be apprised of the fact that he's in the wrong line of work. The little stain."

"Keep your voice down," Natalie said, "Please."

Brian took him by the upper arm, and Henry shook loose. "Don't grab me like that."

"Will you please," Natalie said.

"Goddammit," Henry said, low, beginning to cry. "That's my mother."

"Henry," Natalie said. "Elena would want you to stand straight."

He took the handkerchief out of his pocket again and dabbed at his eyes, then folded the handkerchief square and kept it in one hand, occasionally wiping it across his forehead. People began, tentatively, to come over and pay their respects, and talk about how it affected them to know Elena Hutton. Brian sat against the wall and watched everything. Henry decided, as everyone began to leave, that he wanted the casket opened, and no one could dissuade him. Brian moved to the entrance of the room while this went on—he wanted no part of it, did not want to remember Elena lying in that narrow satin-shiny space. Aunt Natalie and Norman stood with Henry and gazed into the open box, and Aunt Natalie sobbed. From where Brian stood, he could see only their backs and the open, padded lid of the coffin. He went out into the foyer, where the funeral director stood, quietly waiting to be of service. For some reason Brian felt sorry for him, so eager to help, so strangely apologetic in his motions. But neither man spoke. Outside, the sun was going down in a coal-colored nest of clouds. The weather reports were calling for more snow. Norman appeared in the entrance of the room, looking pale and shaky. He crossed to where Brian stood. "Jesus," he muttered. "I don't think it was quite real to me until I saw her there."

"I don't want to talk about it," Brian said. "Please. For Christ's sake."

The funeral director moved to the office on the left side of the foyer and entered, closing the door quietly behind him.

"Look," Norman said. "She led a nice rich lucky American life. She had more and saw more of life than most of us will ever get or see."

"Like you said," Brian told him. "I still hate it."

Here were Aunt Natalie and Henry, teary-eyed, holding on to each other. Norman went to them and took Natalie's other arm. They all walked to the doorway and Henry stopped, put his hands in his face, and wept. For a few seconds, no one moved, and then Norman put his hands on his father's shoulder.

"Dad," he said.

"I know, son," said Henry. "I know. I wish Tom was here."

No one said anything to this.

Henry looked back into the long prospect of the room, with the casket flanked by its escarpment of flowers at the far end. "I hate leaving her alone there."

"She's not there," said Natalie. "For God's sake, Henry. Remember your catechism."

Henry shook his head, without looking at her.

"That's right," Brian said to them all. "She's not there. That isn't her in there."

HE WALKED OUT INTO the cold with Aunt Natalie, holding her by the arm. There was a wind, now. Where the already fallen snow lay crusted, there had been some melting, and rivulets of water had come from the base of the mounds, forming ice in the cold twilight. They made their way unsteadily across to the two cars. Norman got in with Henry, and Aunt Natalie said she'd ride with Brian. When she and Brian were inside the car, she said, "I've heard from your mother."

Brian turned the key in the ignition, then looked at her.

"She called from London."

"Dad didn't talk to her?"

"I asked if she would speak with him. No. That's out of the question."

"Jesus Christ."

"As you know, she has her reasons, Brian."

He backed out after his father and followed him along the winding entrance road to the highway. The sun was below the stand of winter-bare trees to their left, and the branches looked like fretwork on the sky just above the dark line of the hills. "You don't understand," he told her. "I know more than you think I do. I was with her once, we were on our way into town to take me back to the dentist. I'd had a wisdom tooth pulled, and it ended up getting inflamed, and she took me back into town and we saw Henry with some woman, standing out in front of Littleton's Tavern."

Aunt Natalie stared at him for a long time. He could feel her gaze on the side of his face. "How old were you?" she said.

"Thirteen."

"You knew, at thirteen?"

"Hell, I knew at six and seven. I didn't understand it, maybe. But, Aunt Natalie, he was kissing that woman. I'd seen that kind of kissing in the movies and I knew what it meant."

"So," she said. "You learned early."

He knew how she really meant this: Tillie was someone with whom he had cheated on his fourth wife; and the time with Tillie had been spoiled by that, as much as it had been spoiled by anything else. When a relationship begins in and is soaked in dishonesty, the dishonesty seeps into everything else. That was how it felt. Tillie had distrusted him from the beginning.

He watched the tail lights of his father's car, and realized that his Aunt was crying quietly there next to him in the dimness of the front seat. She fumbled with her purse and brought out a handkerchief.

"Men," she said.

She had never been married. She had spent most of her adult life, the years which constituted her own passage into old age, working for the university and living with her mother—watching over her, really, and being watched over by her. And like her mother, she was devout; she was also straightforward. "I guess you can't help it, coming from that house."

"Believe it or not," he said. "They were actually pretty good together sometimes. When he wasn't out catting—" He stopped himself, and reached over to touch her wrist. "Sorry."

She nodded.

"When he wasn't cheating on her and coming home drunk and

she wasn't drowning her own sorrow over all of it, they actually had fun. They enjoyed each other. And *we* had fun. When we were together, all of us, and sometimes it—well, it didn't seem like anything could be wrong, you know."

"And you were learning at your Daddy's knee."

"Please," he said.

"Well?"

They rode on in silence for a few moments. She folded her hands on her lap and looked out the window.

"Mom stayed with him, remember."

"She did a good job hiding her pain a lot of the time."

"No," Brian said. "I knew when she was suffering. We all did. So did you. But there were times when she wasn't suffering, whether she admits it or not."

"Are you angry with her?"

"Most of the time," he said, "I'm angry with both of them."

Aunt Natalie didn't react to this. He thought of Elena, and reflected that this elderly, friendly presence at his side was becoming more like Elena all the time.

Once, at a family gathering, Brian had been talking about the work of Richard B. Leakey in the Olduvai gorge, the theories about the killer ape that had evolved into *Homo sapiens,* and Elena had interrupted him to say, "How does this square with your belief in, say, the immaculate conception or the transubstantiation?"

"Gram," he had said. "This isn't about religion."

"I wasn't asking you a religious question," Elena said. "I was curious."

"I'm almost thirty," he told her. "And I'm still waiting for things to come clear."

"I'm seventy-four," she said. "Think what *I'm* waiting for."

Remembering this, he looked at Aunt Natalie, and then reached over and touched her wrist again. "You okay?"

"Just thinking," she said with a little sobbing sound.

Presently, she said, "I saw Tillie."

"Dad told me she came by."

"Such a beautiful young woman."

"It's all over, Aunt Natalie."

"Poor boy. I am sorry."

Another few moments passed. He turned the radio on, wanting the news; he got static, decided that this was not the time, and turned it off.

"Are you still seeing this other person?"

"No."

"Does Tillie know that?"

"I don't know whether she does or not."

"What was the other person's name?"

"Rose."

"Rose."

"Look," Brian said. "Forget her, all right? Rose is gone. I haven't seen her for weeks. Rose is the person I ruined this particular relationship with, but she's gone."

"Did you make her leave?"

"It was mutual, Aunt Natalie, if you must know."

"I'm sorry," she said. "It's just that I like Tillie."

"You didn't like Tillie at first."

"No," Aunt Natalie said. "I liked Marian." Then she laughed. It came from her with the suddenness of a spell. She tried to talk through it, and failed, though he could hear that she meant to say she couldn't understand why she was having this reaction, why it wouldn't stop.

He kept saying, "What? Tell me. What?"

Finally she subsided, and managed to speak: "I know it's not funny. But it—it just struck me that way: you weren't even married to Tillie yet. Struck me funny." When her voice hit falsetto on the last word, she burst into laughter again, and she went on for another minute. They were on Clooney Street before she could get control of herself. Finally, she cleared her throat. "You. And your father."

"He's acting strange with me," Brian told her. He hadn't known he would say it. Something about her laughter had made him feel that he could confide in her.

"I feel awful for him. He's lost. He's like a lost little boy."

"That's how I feel," said Brian.

"I know." She reached over and touched the side of his face. "Poor dear."

He pulled in behind his father's car, and they got out. The porch lights were on, as was the spot light. The smoothness of the snow in the lawn made him think about the fact that this was a house where no children lived. Christmas candles shone in each of the upstairs windows. Elena had put them there two weeks before she died. Henry had paid some neighbor boys to shovel the sidewalk and part of the driveway. As at the funeral home, the shoveled snow had melted at its base, producing pools of water, which were all solid ice now. Henry led the way in, followed by Norman, with his duffel bag, Aunt Natalie, and Brian. On the porch, Brian turned and looked at the lawn. Norman stood next to him.

"Look how undisturbed it is."

"Yeah."

"I used to love to run out and make my own trail in it. I still feel the urge. I swear."

"Nobody loves snow like you, Norman."

"Do you notice how the world seems—I don't know—like it's quieter?"

Brian waited a moment. There was wind clicking the branches of the trees, and murmuring in the eaves of the house. "I guess."

"I mean there's a quiet under all the noise."

"I know what you mean."

"That hurt—seeing Dad like that."

"Me, too."

They stood there.

Norman said, "Did you catch hell for smelling like whiskey?"

"Yeah."

"Ironical, huh."

Their father called from the lighted foyer. "You guys just gonna stand out there in the cold?"

They went inside. Aunt Natalie had put coffee on, and Henry was pouring small glasses of whiskey. He poured two. Norman gave Brian a look, then took his and drank it down.

"You're supposed to sip it," Henry said.

"You do it your way, and I'll do it mine."

Henry laughed, and Natalie said, "I don't suppose anyone wants coffee."

"I'll have some," Brian said.

"I poured you a whiskey," said Henry. "You don't think this is for me."

The three men sat at the kitchen table, and then Brian got up and brought cups and saucers out of the cupboard. Henry and Natalie were drinking coffee. Norman poured another shot of whiskey for himself, and this time he sipped it. For a long time, they were quiet. Finally all of them were seated, with their coffee and whiskey. Aunt Natalie blew across the surface of her coffee and set the cup down. It clinked in the saucer, a tiny flourish announcing her intent to speak. "Well, it was a triumph of a life," she said. "Somebody ought to say that."

She was the eldest, twelve years older than Henry, and almost seventy now herself. She looked around the room. "It's going to be so strange." She was on the verge of tears again.

Henry put his hand on her shoulder, then took it away.

"The best and kindest and most gracious soul I ever knew," Norman said.

"When I was nine or ten," said Henry, "She broke her ankle. We were playing baseball in the yard, and we didn't have a third baseman, so she volunteered. I must've told you all this story. She got a hit. God knows how. I mean she'd never swung a baseball bat in her life. And when she tried to slide into home, she broke her ankle. There were some guys working on a construction site nearby, and they took her to the doctor. What year was that? She had to be in her late forties or early fifties by then. Natalie, you'd gone away to school."

"If you were nine, it was 1951 and she was fifty-two."

"Good Lord. Fifty-two."

They were all quiet.

"I never thought of her being older," Henry said. "When my father met her, she was playing piano in this little movie house, for the silent flickers. Seventeen years old and she was doing it on the sly, telling her mother and father she was taking lessons. She was good on the thing, too. Natalie, what was that song she used to play that made you cry?"

"'I'll Be Seeing You.'"

"That's it. Natalie would get tears in her eyes every time."

"When did she stop playing?" Brian wanted to know.

"She never did stop, completely," said Aunt Natalie. "I could still get her to play a polonaise now and then."

"I remember that," said Norman, pouring more whiskey for himself. "Sure."

"Aunt Viola used to get her to play all the time," Henry said. "Though Viola didn't like a lot of different kinds of music. Remember how angry she'd get, Natalie, when Elena would hit the boogie woogie?"

"Or the movie stuff—the music she played when the villain was chasing the hero. Doodily-oo, doodily-oo, doo-doo, like that. That used to send Aunt Viola up the wall."

Henry laughed, his eyes brimming. "She used to do those notes just as Aunt Viola walked across the floor. Aunt Viola would tell her she ought to be whipped with briars."

Norman poured still more of the whiskey, and offered it to Brian, who refused. He was worried about the drive home. But then he changed his mind and poured his own. His brother nodded at him, smiling. Brian drank the whiskey down.

Their father was talking now about *his* father, whom he never knew.

"Elena used to tell me stories about him, you know, but there were things I guess she never told anybody about him. She never got married again, and there were a lot of men who wanted to over the years."

"Nothing ever seemed to scare her," Norman said.

"Oh," said Aunt Natalie. "There was plenty. Believe me. She just dealt with it."

"She knew how to contend with it," Brian began. "I'd have a health scare and I'd think of her, and somehow—"

His father interrupted him. "There isn't any bravery without fear. Fear is what the coward and the hero have in absolutely the same amount."

"Now is when Elena would tell us—with that sly smile, remember?—to open up our hymnals."

"She'd agree with what I said," Henry told him. "She wouldn't make light of that."

Aunt Natalie turned to Norman. "How long can you stay?"

"Oh, I've got to go back after tomorrow."

"That was a nice turnout today."

Brian poured himself another whiskey. "Dad."

"Not for me," Henry said.

"I wanted to ask you something."

Henry simply stared back at him. Then: "Well?"

"I just wondered—I wondered if I've said anything or done anything wrong."

Henry said nothing.

"I have this—something's not right, Dad."

"I lost my mother," he said, simply, no expression at all in his face. "What—what the hell're you talking about, Brian? Why the hell can't you leave it alone."

"Then there is something. You're angry with me about something."

"You're both dealing with this in your own way," Aunt Natalie told them. "And it's a little difficult to accept it that Tommy and Lorraine aren't here, either."

"Tommy sure ought to be," said Norman.

"Let it alone," Henry muttered, pouring himself more coffee.

Brian looked at his father and waited for eye contact. Aunt Natalie and Norman started talking about some of the people who visited the home, and when they got to the priest, Henry joined in. Henry was adamant that something should be done about the little shit of a priest.

Brian said, "Dad."

Henry went on talking: "The son of a bitch is probably a pedophile."

"Dad," Brian said.

Henry looked at him and then looked away as Aunt Natalie remarked that she saw the priest say Mass once or twice a month. "His sermons are always so dry and academic. And I don't think he believes democracy was the best development in the world's history, either. The freedom of humankind doesn't seem to interest him much."

"Dad," Brian said, louder this time.

Henry said, "What? *What,* Brian?"

"Look at me. I want to get this taken care of between us—whatever it is."

Henry only glanced at him.

"What's this about, anyway?" said Norman.

Henry looked across at Norman and said, "You've got me." Then he turned to Brian, and the two of them were simply staring at each other. "Well?"

"Nothing," Brian said. "Forget it."

"You've had too much to drink."

"No, actually I haven't."

"Look. Have you got a grievance, boy? I just came from my mother's wake."

"I'm not a boy, Henry. And yes, as a matter of fact, there are one or two grievances."

"Okay," Natalie said. "Well, this isn't the time."

"Why don't you tell me what your grievances are, there, Brian, while you've got enough liquor in you to do it."

"Both of you stop it," Aunt Natalie said. "For God's sake."

"What's going on?" said Norman. "I thought we were remembering Elena."

"We were," Henry said. "I'm not the one calling up crap."

"Who's calling up anything?" Natalie said.

Henry turned to Brian. "You want to call up something, let's talk about you fooling around on your fiancée, for Christ's sake."

"Okay," Brian said. "*Let's*. Let's talk about fooling around."

"Stop this," Natalie said. "I want you both to stop it."

Henry ignored her. "What was her name, there, champ?" His voice had taken the tone of casual sarcasm that Brian was always receiving from his younger brothers. It angered him, while it hurt and depressed him.

"Her name was Rose," he said. And with a shaking in his chest, went on: "Do you remember *your* last girlfriend other than my mother?"

"Don't get cute, boy."

"Hey," Norman said. "Come on, guys. Let's cut this out."

"The woman's name was Rose," Brian went on. "That was her name. She's gone now."

"Rose," Henry repeated. "And you say she's gone?"

"That's right. That's right, there. *Champ*. Like Lorraine."

"Whoa—hey. Look what are we talking this shit for?" Norman said.

Henry, without quite looking at him, muttered, "Watch your mouth."

Norman brought out his flask and drank directly from it, then offered it to Brian, who refused it with a gesture.

Henry turned to Natalie. "You'd think she would at least call. You'd think Tommy would at least want to talk to his brothers."

"Lorraine did call, Henry."

He seemed not to understand the import of the words at first. Then he looked at his own hands, cradling the cup of coffee. "She did?"

"I spoke to her, yes. I asked if she wanted to talk to you and she said she didn't. There wasn't anything I could do. I wasn't going to tell you—but then—well, I wasn't going to tell you."

He sat there shaking his head.

Natalie poured whiskey into his coffee cup. "There. Have a drink. Have ten drinks and calm down."

He pushed the cup away with a gingerly motion, then leaned back in his chair.

"What the hell did Brian do that you haven't done, anyway?" Norman said to him. "Why are you mad at Brian?"

"You're perfectly right. Forget it."

"I started it, I guess," Brian said. "I felt like there was some—hell, you're right. Let's forget it."

"We're supposed to be remembering Elena," said Norman.

Henry made no response. For a brief space they were all unnaturally quiet, not making any eye contact at all. Brian filled his glass with whiskey and drank it down.

"Well," Natalie said. "She'd be so *proud* of all of us."

Henry poured coffee into the whiskey in his cup, concentrating on it, muttering to himself. He lifted it to his lips and drank, then put it down and buried his face in his hands. "I've been through it," he said. "Forgive me. Just please, if you can, forgive me, all of you."

"I'm sorry," Brian said.

"No, no. It's my fault. All of it. I don't have a right to judge anybody."

For what seemed a long time they all waited for him to gain control of himself. Natalie stood at his side and held him, tears running down her cheeks. The two brothers drank their whiskey and kept their eyes mostly averted. When the spasm was over, Henry took some more of the whiskey-coffee and wiped his face with a dish towel. Natalie blew her nose, and spoke of the good fortune of a long life. "This ought to be a celebration. Elena wouldn't want us moping around."

Brian took hold of his father's shoulder and felt the slightest tensing of the muscles there. He took his hand away. Norman had begun talking about the Navy, being on a submarine under the ocean. He chattered, going on in the silence, looking from one to the other of them. "I'm always thinking I hear music in the walls, and there's no music, of course. Just the hum of that thing under all the miles of water. We went under the polar ice for six weeks in one run. I thought I'd go out of my mind. And that phantom music playing the whole time. The same song over and over. I didn't mind hallucinating the music, but I would've liked being able to change the station, you know? Put a mental quarter in and choose some other song. You know what the goddam song was? "Anchors Aweigh." Can you imagine that? "Anchors Aweigh." I almost went to see the shrink about it, except he was crazier than the rest of us. He was on about six different medicines for high blood pressure, and he had this look about him, like a guy who is about to break into gibberish and start posing as Napoleon."

Brian stood up and pushed the chair in under the table.

"Where you going?" Henry asked. "You didn't finish your whiskey."

"Norman'll take care of it. I've got to get home."

"You okay to drive? You can stay here, you know."

"I'm fine."

Aunt Natalie came around the table to embrace him. "I still say it's nice having this much of us together."

"Brian, I'm gonna stay here," Norman said. "If that's okay with you."

"It's fine with me."

Henry stood, and took hold of Brian's arms above the wrists. "You sure you're okay to drive, now."

"I'm okay, really."

The older man nodded, but didn't let go. "We okay? You and me?"

"I hope so," Brian said.

His father nodded, letting go and turning away. "It's all square, then." He moved to the kitchen sink and, retrieving a glass from the cabinet, filled it with water.

"See you tomorrow," Norman said, and took another long pull of the flask.

"Tomorrow," said Brian.

ON THE PORCH, ALONE, he looked at the frozen lawn. He walked into the crust of snow, out into the light from the porch, and on to the limit of the light, turning in a wide circle and coming back, trudging along.

When his father had called him at the height of the storm to tell him that Elena was dying, he tried to get the car out of the driveway. He shoveled the snow and put pieces of wood down from the stack along the fence, and it kept snowing and there was no getting out, and finally he went back inside the house—the place where, in the nights, he had lain awake and thought of suicide, Tillie gone, everything falling apart yet again—went back inside and knelt by the empty bed and prayed for Elena not to suffer. Soon he was crying, head down between his outstretched hands. It seemed to him then that it was all one loss, Elena dying and this latest failure, a chain of hazy evenings being drunk in a bar and playing little sordid games, Tillie talking about leaving—for months she talked about it—and he had gone into the thing with Rose telling himself, with the old booze-blurred conviction, that he would make up for everything later, would deal later with whatever happened, whatever price there was to pay for it all. *Elena was dying.* Elena, whose accepting and humorous eyes always looked into him and knew him for what he was, what he had been—a boy ten years old, seeing his father with another woman—understood the fear and weakness out of which so much of his repeated troubles came, and she loved him anyway.

He drove into the old part of Point Royal, to a side street, across from the tall row house flanked by an antique store and a law firm, where Tillie was staying now. Lights glimmered in the upstairs windows. He got out of the car and walked up to the end of the block, then turned and came slowly back down. It was so cold; the air stung his face.

He went up on the stoop, rang the doorbell, and waited. No one came. He rang it again, and waited again. Nothing. The wind moved the bare treetops on the other side of the street. He knocked—once, twice. In another moment, there were footsteps on the other side of the door. It opened, and a woman he did not recognize looked out.

"Is Tillie here?"

"Who wants to know."

"Tell her Brian."

The other stared at him with an uncomprehending frankness. Then she closed the door and he heard her on the stairs. In another moment, he heard someone coming back. The door opened again, and the same face looked out at him. "She was in bed. Wait there."

The door closed. He walked to the edge of the stoop and looked out at the night. Stars, a partial moon, no clouds, a beautiful snow-laden scene. In a little while, the door opened again, and Tillie looked out at him. "She didn't ask you in?"

"No," he said.

Tillie stepped out. She had put a robe on, and held it closed at her throat. "I went by the funeral home today, did Henry tell you?"

"Yeah."

"I'll miss Elena. I already do miss her. Above everything else she knew how to be kind."

"I guess we talked ourselves into thinking she'd always be here," he said.

"I'm sorry I couldn't stay longer today."

"I had to go pick up Norman at the bus station."

"How's he taking things?"

"He's okay."

A car went by on the road, and they heard the radio blaring through closed windows. The car went on up the icy street and turned.

"I'm cold," she said.

"I guess—" he began. "Would you—can we go somewhere and get some coffee maybe? It's not that late is it?"

"I have to get up early and go to work."

"But it isn't that late."

"Brian."

"It *isn't*."

"Oh, what're you doing here?"

"I—I was sorry I missed you. I wanted to talk to you."

"Okay." She waited.

"Tillie," he said.

"Yes?"

All he could think to say was, "I love you." His voice broke.

She said, "Brian."

"No," he said. "I do—and that has—look, I know I screwed up—I've screwed up everything I've ever touched—" His voice broke again. He took a breath. "And—and I know I don't deserve your forgiveness, but I do love you. And that—that has to count for something, doesn't it?"

She looked at him a long time, and her eyes shone. "You're still such a little baby, do you know that? And the odd thing is—that's what drew me to you in the first place."

He took a step toward her, then stopped because she had retreated. She seemed to recede into the shadows of the porch, moving to the doorway. She stepped up into the frame of it and turned to look at him. "It's late."

"I know you still love me," he said.

She nodded sadly. "Yes."

"We still love each other."

"No. I no longer believe *you* do. What is her name? Rose?"

He looked down. "That's over. I told you—I don't know what that was. But it's over."

"Until the next time."

"No."

"Oh, come *on*, Brian. That's the pattern, isn't it?"

He said nothing.

"You know, Elena said something about you and Henry—and Norman and Tommy, too. I thought it was so shrewd—it was when I knew I wanted to be close to her. She got that look she used to get when she knew she was about to say something startling. You remember the look."

He nodded.

"She gave me that look and said the men in this family use each other's sins as excuses—like there's—how did she put it—like there's some kind of innocence in collective guilt."

"Tillie, I'm freezing here. You're freezing. Can't we go somewhere and talk about it?"

Tillie gazed at him a moment, almost as though she were trying to remember something she had meant to let him know. There was a faintly confiding element in it. But then she stepped back and held the door open for him to enter. In the room it was warm, and he breathed a powerful odor of cooking cabbage and cigarette smoke. He heard the roommate cough in the kitchen, the shuffle of slippers there. Tillie indicated the couch, and he went to it and sat down.

"Drink?" she asked.

He shook his head. She crossed to the small portable bar on the other side of the room and poured herself a glass of sherry. She called into the kitchen. "Renata? Sherry?"

"No, thanks."

She stood there and sipped it, and appeared to collect herself.

"Is he gone?" Renata's voice from the kitchen.

"No, Renata, he's not gone."

Silence.

"Renata, you remember me talking about Brian. Brian, that's Renata in the kitchen."

Renata came briefly to the entrance of the room, someone unprepared for company. "Nice to meet you, Brian."

"Hello, Renata in the kitchen," Brian said.

Renata was not amused. "Heard a lot about you," she said.

"It's only half true."

She had gone out of the doorway, but she called back. "Even half true's pretty terrible, there, Brian old boy." They heard her laughing to herself.

"Renata thinks she's a comedian," Tillie said, loud enough for the other woman to hear.

"I'm an observer of the human comedy," Renata called back. Then, as if to preclude any rejoinder from Tillie, began to hum to herself.

Brian looked at the room—most of the décor was apparently Renata's: a regulator clock on the wall, several large department store prints, and two tall particle board bookshelves stuffed to overflowing with paperbacks and coffee table books and stacks of paper. Between the bookshelves was a computer on a desk crowded with more paper and books. The screensaver was a slow floating of fishes in green water along a coral reef.

"Renata's a graduate student," Tillie said.

"What's she studying?"

"Gender issues in popular culture."

He nodded.

"You don't have any idea, do you?"

"Actually," he said, "I think I do."

"Well." She walked over and sat down on the love seat across from him, crossing her legs, pulling the gown tight over her lap. She sat there, holding the glass of sherry, and regarded him. It seemed evident that she was enjoying having the upper hand. He felt himself give over to the thought, and then tried to reject it.

"Tillie," he began.

But then Renata came into the room in her robe and slippers, carrying a plate of cabbage and ham. Her hair was stringy and unhealthy looking, though her face had a pleasant flawless quality and her features were sharp, intelligent, and rather attractive. Her eyes were the antithesis of Tillie's: cloudy blue, and wide, as if she were in a state of unexpressed excitement. "There's food in there for anybody who wants it," she said.

"I'm fine," said Tillie. "Brian?"

"Nothing for me," he said.

"Sorry to hear about your grandmother," Renata said.

He glanced at Tillie, who shrugged.

"How old was she?" Renata asked.

"She was very old," he said.

"I'd hate to live past sixty."

He left this alone.

Renata sat at the computer, with the plate on her lap. She touched the keyboard, and the screensaver dropped away, revealing a page of text. Staring at this, she squinted, spooning cabbage into her mouth.

Brian gave Tillie a pleading expression, and Tillie shrugged, as if to say that there was nothing to be done. So they sat there and watched Renata and her computer and her plate of cabbage.

"What do you call the French knot we used to have to tie our hair in at the back?" Renata asked. "My mother was always doing my hair like that."

"A chignon, isn't it?" said Brian.

The other woman was silent, and hadn't moved. Finally she turned and looked at Tillie. "Well? Is that it?"

Tillie nodded.

"Why didn't you answer me?"

"Brian answered you."

"Okay."

They watched her eat, and peck at the keyboard. Tillie finished her sherry, and got up to pour some more. "You sure you don't want some of this?" she asked Brian.

"Not me," Renata said, chewing.

Tillie poured another glass and sat down.

Brian leaned across and said, low, "Let's go get some coffee or something."

"He's asking you for a date," Renata said.

"No," said Brian, and he heard the defensive note in his voice.

"I don't want to go out," Tillie said, concentrating on her sherry. "It all looks threatening outside now."

Renata said, "You're depressed."

"No, I'm not depressed. I'm sad. There's a big difference." Now the defensive note was in Tillie's voice.

"Do you think it would be all right," Brian said to Renata, "if Tillie and I had a little time alone?"

She gazed at Tillie. "You want to be alone with him?"

Tillie didn't answer right away.

"Say the word," Renata said.

Tillie spoke to Brian. "I asked Renata not to leave me alone with you."

He could think of nothing to say in response. He couldn't even look at her.

"Good night, guys," Renata said, rising. She carried her plate into the kitchen and they heard it clatter in the sink. Then she came back through and went down the hallway toward the bedrooms. They heard her door close.

After a moment, during which Tillie merely sipped her sherry and averted her eyes, Brian said, "There must be something we can do, Tillie. Some way to save it."

"Oh," she said. "Like I said, until the next time? It was cheating when *we* were first together."

"It's been my doing," he said. "It doesn't have anything to do with anything else. My failure. I'm not blaming it on Henry or Lorraine or anyone but myself. Me. And I'm asking for you to forgive me. Help me." His voice broke.

"Don't," she said.

"I'm so sorry, Tillie."

"I said *don't*."

He waited.

She emptied the glass and then held it in her lap, turning it slowly in her lovely small hands. "I can't, Brian. Not now. Maybe later but not now."

"I understand," he told her. "If I thought there was a chance."

"I don't want to talk about it now," she said.

She let a long interval pass.

"I'm sorry about Elena."

"Thanks for coming." His voice was louder than he had meant it to be. When he went on, he tried to soften it. "Elena would've been pleased."

"I didn't do it for Elena, Brian. Elena's gone."

"I thank you for it."

"I didn't do it for *you*, either. Why is it that the men in your family have to see everything all the time as being about them? Why is that, Brian?"

He said nothing.

"You said Norman got in all right?"

"I picked him up at the bus station."

"Tom?"

"He's in England."

"I didn't think Lorraine would come back for it. Your father seemed to think she would."

"He was hoping."

"Poor man."

Brian kept silent, watching her white fingers on the glass in her lap.

"I'm sorry, that sounded more sarcastic than I meant it."

"I didn't hear it that way," Brian said.

"No, of course you wouldn't."

Again, he was silent.

"I guess *that* was sarcastic."

"Today," he said, "I woke up wanting to call Elena and tell her what happened—that I'd lost her. I had the strangest sense that I should call and tell her that."

"I don't want to talk about it, Brian. I'm sorry."

For a long time, then, neither of them said anything. They could hear Renata moving around in her room, and the strains of music coming from her stereo.

"Will you be there for the ceremony tomorrow?"

"Of course."

"Norman and I could come get you."

"I'll get there on my own."

He kept still.

"Henry was there with her through it all?"

"All of it, yes."

"Poor man." Now there was no irony in her voice at all.

"I came in at the very end."

"I would like to have known her as a young woman."

He said, "I used to think that heaven would be that—we'd all be young at the same time, parents and children and everybody being kind—everybody home and happy."

She lay her head back, and closed her eyes.

"I should leave."

"I'm so tired," she said. "I'm sorry."

"No." He stood, and she did, too. They were facing each other, and he thought of kissing her, but then she moved with a kind of peremptory quickness to the door and opened it. The night air rushed in. He moved to the opening, realizing that he had been sitting there in his coat, someone on the briefest of visits.

"Tillie," he said. "I'll do anything."

"We'll see," she said. "Maybe we'll talk. I have to think it all through. I don't want to do it on the basis of feeling this grief."

He stepped out onto the stoop and then turned to face her. "I love you."

She gave the slightest nod of her head. "Good night, Brian." And then she closed the door.

He made his way back to the car, got in, and for a very long time he sat there staring at the lighted windows of the place. He saw the lights go out. He saw the snow come from the western part of the sky, out of a wide coastline of advancing pearly clouds lighted by the half-moon. He drove home. On one side of the sky there had never been a clearer, colder night. The snow was arriving, sailing in on the wind, tiny flecks of icy glittering. He let himself into the dark house and moved through the rooms, turning lights on without being quite aware that he was doing it. There had been something so sad in the way she had stood there in the doorway, and he wondered if she had only been anxious to get rid of him. The only way for him to know for sure was to put himself in the way of whatever she would do; accept whatever pain or hope came from trying again. And then trying yet again. He stood in his kitchen and made himself a tall glass of whiskey, and held it up to his mouth— thinking just to relax, just to be able to sleep. The smell of it dropped down into his soul. It seemed that he had never wanted anything more in all his life. But then he poured it into the sink, turned the kitchen light off, moved totteringly into the darkened hall, and made his way to the bedroom. There, he lay down, still in his coat, in the quiet house. He was not drunk. She could not have supposed that he was drunk. And he had turned down having a drink with her. And she had let Renata leave the room. She hadn't minded being alone with him. He began to cry, and lay crying quietly for a long time. There was, in all of the confusion, terror, and sorrow of the last few weeks, still, after all, some perdurable sense of helpless hope. In his mind's eye, he saw his father sitting wakeful and ashen next to the sofa on which Elena Hutton lay half-conscious, a bundle of sticks under a blanket, a skull framed with wiry hair, dark eyes staring out.

BEFORE

December 16, 1994

HENRY HADN'T DECIDED easily about the move. Having been through the upset and rancor of the end of his marriage, he longed for some sense of order and symmetry. With Lorraine gone, he had found himself rattling around in the house alone, and the days had begun to run together. He had suffered a couple of lapses with the bottle.

So he had come home, and been taken in.

Natalie was doubtful about the change, worried that his presence would be a strain on their mother, since Elena continued to concern herself with every aspect of the house's management: though the old woman had slowed down over the past several years, she still insisted on cooking the dinners and doing the laundry, still bustled around the table while Natalie ate, making sure of Natalie's comfort and refusing to listen to Natalie's demands that she be more careful, that she stop worrying about everyone else and take it easy a little.

"You're the one doing the worrying," she said.

"Somebody's got to do it around here," Natalie said.

"Oh, well, if it's a job . . ."

Natalie sometimes called her Lenie, because that was what her Aunt Viola had called her those years ago, when Natalie was a little girl and Viola would sit in the kitchen, the whole great bulk of her under an apron, complaining to Natalie's mother about the aches in her old bones and the heartbreak of having children who refused to listen to her. Viola had lived to be a hundred, and now Natalie's mother was almost that age.

"Lenie," Natalie said. "Please sit down. You'll make yourself sick. Don't let Henry do this to you. He's a big boy. He can fend for himself."

"I never said I couldn't," Henry said. "I can get my own dinner."

"No, you say that but you don't do it, and we end up doing it. We end up cleaning your messes for you. It's always been that way with the men in this family."

"We've left the subject of dinner, haven't we?"

"Both of you be quiet," said Elena. "I'd like it if you talk to each other at some level beyond the fourth grade, if you don't mind. I'd like to see a little kindness between you. Humor me, if it has to be that. But do it."

She was indeed an impressive woman: completely self-reliant, intelligent and active, erect and still relatively youthful-looking, with her clear blue eyes and straight shoulders, her sculpted features and white, white hair. She was the one Henry had come home to. He could admit this fact to himself, as he could admit it to Natalie, who finally stopped making her objections in Elena's presence, but continued, when alone with him, to voice them. "You've come back to be nursed by her and don't think it isn't obvious," she said, as if he were not aware of this and as if knowing about it might have some bearing on his decision to remain.

"Natalie," he said. "Do you want me to leave?"

She couldn't go that far. "That's for you to decide."

"Elena says she's glad I've done this. I was over here a lot anyway, wasn't I?"

"She'll work herself to death taking care of you," Natalie said.

"We won't let her do that," said Henry. "Besides, you know she'll outlive us all."

"Don't be glib," his sister said. "She's not as strong as she looks. You haven't been here long enough to know what you're talking about."

"I don't want to make you unhappy," Henry told her. "I wasn't aware you felt quite this strongly against my being here." Before she could answer, he went on: "No. That's not true, really. And there's no reason not to tell the truth. I've known how you felt about it."

"I know you're hurting, Henry. But you have to lick your own wounds. You can't depend on Lenie to nurse you."

"I'm not going to have anything to drink, if that's what's worrying you."

"That isn't all that's worrying me. I don't want your unhappiness in the house. I won't have you wallowing in it."

"Well, I promise that Elena won't hear a discouraging word."

"And you needn't be flippant about it."

He'd meant no such thing. "Really," he said. "I'm serious."

"I'm worried about her, that's all."

"Natalie, I won't get in the way."

"Oh, for God's sake, Henry. I don't think you're in the way."

Part of the trouble where Natalie was concerned was that she knew too many things about his marriage, the unhappy facts of life in his house—having had, all along, the confidence of Lorraine.

Often, in his sister's insistent green gaze he could read the subtle darkness of remembering; the signs that she was inwardly calling up his periodic unfaithfulness and neglect—his old weakness for alcohol, his failures as a father; all the rages and excesses of the last thirty-six years. But in the end Natalie never alluded to anything of this. She fretted and worried about Elena's stamina, and nagged him about his general untidiness and lack of organization as though he were a teenager. And she bristled at the slightest indication, however unintentional, that he might begin to depend on her for any of the practical domestic things that he had once depended upon from Lorraine. He attempted to keep from irritating her and took up some of the chores that Elena had been paying neighborhood boys to do: cutting the grass, weeding the garden, making sure of firewood for the coming winter. He washed the cars, trimmed the rose bushes, painted the trim on the porch, and gradually his sister seemed to accept the new situation. There had even been moments of a kind of understanding between them.

She had been there when, in the dim light of the foyer, he opened the first letter from Lorraine's lawyer, reiterating in the coldest terms her demand for a divorce. Natalie stood looking over his shoulder and she murmured, "She means it this time." Lorraine had waited until the youngest son, Norman, left the house to join the Navy. "I wouldn't have thought she could be so cold about it," Natalie said. "After so many years."

Henry understood this as something his sister meant to give him: her sympathy, her plain family loyalty. "No," he told her. "I guess I earned it. I'll tell you—I—I've just never been able to find any peace. I spent thirty years working for the university, and the whole time I was clenched tight as a fist. I'd go home and I couldn't stand the noise of my own house."

"Don't ask me for sympathy."

"I wouldn't dream of it, dear."

Natalie said, "As long as you know." And then she kissed his cheek. A benediction.

Life had settled into a pleasant routine: in the evenings, she would come home from her job at the courthouse to find him cutting the grass, or tending the flowers, or working in the house. Their mother would be sitting in her favorite wing chair in the family room downstairs, watching television, reading, or listening to music. She would have put something in the oven, a roast or a casserole; baking, which she had learned from old Aunt Viola, and after all these years she still baked her own bread.

For Henry, these evenings ran together and became the memory of a single evening, an image of himself in the cool shade of the house, clipping the tall weeds from the base of the porch steps, concentrating only on the task at hand, feeling, at last, almost quiet inside, basking in the satisfaction of knowing that Natalie was due home, the anticipation of seeing her come down the street, driving slow, like someone looking for the right address. He heard the crackling of tires on gravel as she pulled into the driveway, mingled with the other late summer sounds—the shouts of children up the block, the soughing of wind in the tops of the softly shedding trees—and it was all so calming, this tranquil music of a September sunset. Natalie got out of the car, shut the door, and called to him. "Hello." He waved, then watched her walk through leaf shade and sun, up to the house and in. The smell of fresh bread drifted to him, and he went on with his work.

What is it about this one memory of a September evening that distinguishes it from other memories, and suffuses it in the light of peace? Is it part of some pattern he couldn't, at the time, see? It seems possible that something, some element of goodness he hadn't dared hope for adds up to this picture of himself in a sweet dusk.

How deep his despair had been, to be coming home, almost sixty

years old, having failed at almost everything. And what a beautiful sur-
prise, to find a cessation of his pain, here. . . .

He thinks of this now, almost grasps at it, here where he now is—
the badness of a deep winter afternoon, a fearful cold, sitting with
his mother on the living room sofa, facing the big picture window
with its jagged borders of condensation and ice, looking out on the
snowy street, the desolate street. They are alone, now. Natalie's a
thousand miles away, in Disneyland, of all places. The snow swirls,
tiny flakes; the whole outside is agitating with it. He's been spooning little cooled teaspoons of tea into Elena's mouth because her
free hand shakes too much to hold a cup of liquid without spilling
it. Her "good" hand, the left, is bound up in a cast. Her bony fingers jut from the end of it and are an unhealthy bluish-yellow.
There are small places in the skin of her face that are of the same
shade. Between sips of tea, she murmurs her gratitude; but she's
shuddering with something inside and is attending to it.

She sighs and stares. "Ah, Henry."

"I'm right here," he says.

"I remember saying that to your Aunt Viola. I was fifty-something.
She was two years younger than I am now. And frightened, you
know—lying in the bed. She couldn't move. I said, 'I'm right here,
Aunt Viola.' My God, she lived another six years."

"Yes," he says. "That's right." It's all he can think to say.

"I've become like you now," she says, and smiles. "Dwelling on
the past a bit."

"I've stopped that," Henry tells her.

"It's cold in here."

"I'll turn the heat up."

"No," she says. "Never mind. I was somewhere else."

"Elena?" he says, looking at the extraordinarily fragile bones of
her hand—thin as the bones of a bird.

"I don't feel so good, Henry," she tells him. "I feel very strange."

When he moves to support her she makes a gesture as if to stop him; it's as though they're listening for some sound out in the blowing snow.

"It's easing off, now," she says.

"Should I call the doctor?"

"I just felt a little faint," she tells him. "Be still."

Last weekend she broke her shoulder in a fall on the stairs. One day after Natalie had departed for California with the three women she works with and the neighbor, Mrs. Eberhard—a package tour sponsored and paid for by the university. The day of the accident, Henry assured Natalie over the telephone that things were all right. The break was not serious. And when she called back, two days later, he told her their mother had come through this as she had come through everything else, and seemed to be mending as well as could be hoped for. "You go have fun," he said. "We're fine, here."

He didn't mention that in the hospital Elena had begun to experience difficulty keeping solid foods down, because the doctor had said it could be part of the healing process—her body adjusting to the shock and to the medicines they'd given her to ward off infection. The doctor seemed fairly confident that the problem would correct itself, though he had talked about putting her on an IV and keeping her for a few days more.

Elena wouldn't hear of it.

She was her own law, now, she told them. Excluding Aunt Viola, there hadn't been much longevity on either side of the family, and to be still alert at her great age was to have graduated from any requirements others might wish to impose, for whatever reasons. She wanted to go home; she was in a tremendous hurry to do so. If this was to be her death, then she deserved the choice, at least, of where it would happen. "I don't want to die in a place like this," she said. "Please, son."

He said, "Who mentioned anything about dying?"

"I want to go home. That is my wish. Can I not be granted that after ninety-four years?"

The doctor shrugged. He was the family physician, and he would do what the family wanted under the circumstances.

So they came back to the house, Henry and his mother. They spent two days getting used to living with the injury, and with Elena's new inability to keep down anything solid. They had been doing all right, and though she spoke of death now and then, Henry had marked the signs that her appetite was improving. He had in fact already begun thinking about life beyond the winter months, when the bones would heal enough and the cast could be removed, and her appetite would return to normal again. He could not believe that she wouldn't make it through to another summer. He had been thinking about the snow as something in the way of the coming spring—warm weather to take her out in, flowers for her to appreciate once more. Work for him to do around the house. She had always been so healthy. He'd read of a woman who was a hundred and thirteen. Nineteen years older than his mother.

But her appetite grew worse, and the snow came, the winds, the biting cold and ice.

Now she turns to him and seems to search his face, as though wanting to see, if she can, the change in the set of his features, the thing that might betray him, give forth the answer to her own unasked question.

HAVING GROWN UP IN this house, as the only boy in the house, he had been coddled and spoiled by the women in it. Aunt Viola's words: coddled and spoiled. Viola was his mother's great-aunt, who as a young girl living in northern Virginia had looked upon Robert E. Lee, and had grown up to write a book about manners, customs of entertainment and propriety for a lost country, a place that had already changed utterly before she was old enough to write. But it took people so long to recognize that what they had valued and thought was true was in fact no longer valuable or true. Aunt Viola's book was an old embarrassment by the time Henry was born, and she herself had reached that age when no one asks about future plans. She had her history; she was gruff and direct, and she frightened Henry, with her dark-spotted hands and her great bulk, sitting immovable in the kitchen, in the aroma of whatever she was baking.

"Stand here," she would say to Henry, meaning that he should approach her and be within reach of those thick-fingered hands. He was sixteen. He couldn't remember a time when she had not been there, ruling everything, the whole family. She had raised his mother alone, in a time when women weren't even allowed to vote. "Here," she would say. And Henry would stand there to be examined.

"Skinny." Her hands went over his shoulders, down his arms, as though she were judging the texture of the skin. "Too skinny. When're you going to get some meat on these bones?"

"I don't know," he would answer.

"Well, you have good broad shoulders. That's an important thing for a man to have."

"Yes, ma'am."

"And talk like this," she said, drawing her chin down into her chest and lowering her voice. "Your voice is too high. You have the face of a girl."

"I don't shave yet," he said.

And she dismissed him. "Skinny."

It seemed to him that she was always leading up to something like this conversation with him. And somehow she had a way of reading him, of seeing through him. And it was she who always led the talk, the women sitting in the kitchen listening to her, right up to the first years of his marriage. It was a standard and accepted thing in the family that Aunt Viola didn't like men: she had a visceral reaction to them, like some people have to spiders, or mice.

"YOU FEEL FAINT BECAUSE you haven't eaten anything solid in a while," he says to his mother, now.

"No. Right. I'm fine."

"Your color's good," he says.

She breathes. "I felt as though I was sailing away."

"Any pain?"

"My back's sore. My wrist under this cast. The side of my neck. I'm one ache from head to toe." Again, she's attending to something inside. Her hand tightens on his. "Talk to me, son."

He can't think.

"I know," she says. "Talk to me about Christmases."

He tries to think of something; he's fifty-eight years old and he can't call up the full memory of a single Christmas. All those Christmases with at least one child in the house, and everything is indistinct with repetition, clouded by habit; it all runs together. He can see that she's being brave, staring out the window at the snow gathering on the lawn.

"I don't remember the last white Christmas," he tells her.

"I never get tired of snow," she says. "Even now when it's so treacherous to someone like me."

"Be nice if we had a fire," he says, trying to seem calm.

"Don't go to all that trouble now."

"Do you want me to call an ambulance?"

"Talk about something," she says.

His mind is blank.

"How long were you and Lorraine married—how many winters."

"Elena."

"Think," she says.

It's a command. He hears something almost dismissive in it. "Thirty-six years." He's taken her hand now and is holding it in both of his.

"You were the most beautiful couple," she says. "I don't understand why you had such trouble all the time." It's what she has often tried to console him with. The thought comes to him that she knows so little about him, really. She knows he had some trouble with alcohol over the years; she knows his wife did, too. She knows Lorraine has left him. She's connected the two things, and has forgiven him for it, since, decades ago, her own husband had the same problem. But it's not the alcohol—it was never the alcohol—and among the things she doesn't know is that he never felt any ease in the society of his own house, his own wife and children. Something roiled in him and quailed, and poor Lorraine stood it—the restlessness and the fits of drunkenness and the periodic infidelity; the remorse and the appeals for understanding, the confusion, the daily worry over keeping some version of the family intact—Lorraine stood all of it, until the last child, Norman, was on his own with the Navy.

"It was me," he says to his mother. "I just don't know why."

"Oh, Lord," Elena says. She hasn't heard him.

"Let me call somebody," he says.

"Don't talk about it. Please. Tell me how Brian's doing."

He tells her that Brian is doing fine.

"Nobody's fine living by himself," she says.

"He's doing okay, Elena. He's taking care of himself."

"Can't understand what happens. Poor children don't even try. How long was *this* marriage. Two years?"

"Something like that. They weren't actually married. They were talking about it."

"And he was running around with someone."

"I don't know."

"What a thing."

Henry's quiet.

"I couldn't get to know so many people intimately. How does he do it?"

"Let me fix you something," he says.

"How old is Brian?"

He isn't certain about it. For the moment, he just doesn't know. In the time of Lorraine's absence, he's found all sorts of embarrassing gaps in his knowledge of his children: Henry misses birthdays; there have been hurt feelings. "You know your mother kept track of everything," he has said to his sons. "I've always been so bad at that sort of thing."

Once, Norman, calling long distance from Maine, where his submarine had put in for some repairs, said, "What sort of thing is that,

Dad? A birthday." And Henry could find nothing to say to him. That was one of the nights, alone in the other house, when he began to see that he was not going to be able to stand it by himself.

He gives his mother's hand a small shake, feeling the need to arouse her. "Do you feel tired?" he says.

She's staring off. "I'm terrified."

"Is it happening again?"

"Oh, Lord," she says. "Talk."

"Should we listen to some music or something?"

"Talk to me."

"It's nerves," Henry says. "It's natural."

"I thought I was used to the idea," she says.

For a moment, he's not quite sure what she means—and then he is sure.

She's gazing at him. "You don't fuss like your sister would."

He pats the back of her hand. He can't believe she hasn't perceived his fright.

"But boys believe in death more than anything, don't they?" she says. "They're always thinking about it. All the time."

Henry doesn't know what she wants him to say or do, now. "You sound like Aunt Viola."

She smirks. "She knew some things."

"She was wrong about some things, too."

"Yes, she was. Like all the rest of us."

He says nothing.

"You're talking about her book, aren't you?"

"That, too," he says.

She takes her hand away. "I'm such trouble. You don't want to talk about any of this."

"I don't mind talking about whatever you'd like to talk about."

"I don't want to talk about Viola's book."

"Then we won't talk about it."

"I'm troubling you."

"Just rest," he says.

"It's all right being afraid," she says. Then she sighs. "Poor Natalie. I'm glad she's not here. I make her so nervous."

Natalie hasn't taken anything like an extended trip in all the years she's lived here. She and her companions are old friends, all unmarried and unattached. Last week, when he talked with her on the phone and she wanted to call off the rest of the trip to catch a plane back, Henry thought of her out there on her own, standing in the confusion and noise and bustle of another place, and didn't have the heart to ask her to come home purely to relieve what he supposed, given the confidence of the doctor, was his own anxiety: the chance that Elena's trouble might be more serious than a simple broken collarbone.

"Every time I cough Natalie wants to call the rescue squad," his mother says.

"Why don't you let me get you something to eat."

She shakes her head, staring.

"Has it gone away again?" he says.

"Can I have some water?"

He puts the tea things in the kitchen, pours the water, and when he returns to the living room, he finds that his mother has leaned back and closed her eyes.

"Elena?" he says.

She's quiet.

"The water," he says. "You okay?"

"Sleepy," she says. "Put it down on the nightstand."

He puts it on the coffee table.

She looks at it, then at him. "Oh, that's right. This is the living room."

"Do you want the television on?"

She doesn't answer. She closes her eyes again.

"Anything you want me to do?" he says, helpless.

Her breathing is even and slow, her forehead cool. She's simply asleep.

He makes his way upstairs to Natalie's room and pulls the blanket and pillows off the bed. Natalie's room smells of perfume and hair-spray. Two of her wigs are on the dresser, along with an old Sunday missal with colored ribbons marking the places in it. On the wall is a representation of Christ, with soft, feminine eyes, small violet lips, and slender hands indicating the radiant heart in his chest.

The house is too quiet.

He unplugs the portable radio and brings it downstairs with him. Carefully, he puts the blanket over his mother's shoulders, then sits down across from her with the radio on low. Outside, the snow sweeps at the windows, and faintly he hears the voices of children playing on the hill beyond the end of the yard. He listens to them, listens to the wind. He dozes a little, dreams he's playing outside a house in southern Virginia, and she's in one of the windows, singing.

Waking with a start, he sits forward in the chair to look at her. In the shadows her features have taken on the appearance of a kind of grimace. It's just the bad light. But even so, it makes him utter a small sound of alarm. "Elena?" he says. She stirs slightly, turns her head on the pillow, and the grimace softens. Her eyes move behind the lids with whatever she's dreaming.

SHE SLEEPS ALL AFTERNOON and through the night, and she's still asleep in the late morning when he tries, unsuccessfully, to wake her. He calls the hospital. The doctor takes a long while to call back. When he does, he says it sounds as though she may have slipped into a coma. There isn't much to do under the circumstances, especially if she doesn't seem to be in distress. "You know," he says, "heroic measures, with someone that age—" He stops.

"A coma," Henry says. It just looks like sleep.

"Do you want me to try and stop by?" the doctor asks.

"Can you get over here in the snow?"

"I can try."

"She's just sleeping," Henry says.

But that evening she's awake. She sits up, or tries to, and she doesn't seem to know him. "I have to visit the bathroom," she says. Holding her elbow and wrist, he walks with her down the corridor and into the little room below the stairs. She needs help sitting down. When she's situated she asks him to please go get her a clean nightgown from the bureau in the bedroom. He does so, averting his eyes when he comes back with the nightgown. "Thank you," she says, taking it from his outstretched hand. "Now please shut the door."

He occupies himself making a bed for her by the fireplace. She takes a very long time in the bathroom, and twice he has to knock softly, worrying that she might've passed out.

"Just a minute," she says irritably.

Finally she calls to him, and there's something of panic in her voice. "I'm here," he says.

She asks him to come help her with the nightgown. She's standing in the too-bright light of the room; her arms and back look bruised to him. "Here," she says, holding out the shimmery cloth. They turn in the small space of the room; she can't raise her free hand over her head, and the other is fixed in its cast. At one point she laughs, or makes a sound like laughter. They move and grope and almost fall, and finally she has the nightgown on. It drops over her thin body like a fall of dust. "I thought you left me alone," she tells him.

"No," he says. "I made you a bed in the living room."

"I don't want you to leave me, young man."

"Elena," he says, "do you know me?"

She looks at him. "Don't be ridiculous."

In the living room, he arranges the blanket over her shoulder, kisses the side of her face. She wants to talk. She tells him how she met his father on a street in Memphis in the hot summer of 1917—a girl nearly exactly as old as the century, doing something of which her family would be appalled to learn, playing piano to the jittery pantomime of silent movies in a theater on Beale Street. "The whole city smelled of coal," she says, "and that poisonous breeze blowing in off the mountains. I loved the movies, back then. I haven't seen a movie in forty years."

"It's been a long time for me, too," he says. He doesn't even hear himself.

She talks about his father's early death, in an automobile accident in 1942, something Henry only sketchily recalls: He has an image of men carrying his father's body home, moving into the small parlor of the house in Memphis, where they had all lived before Elena brought her children north, in 1937. He still has dreams about the tall men crowding into the room, carefully laying the body out on the table.

"Imagine," Elena says now. "He was on his way home. He was only a block away. And he couldn't get through that one intersection alive. That last one. I heard the crash, sitting in the kitchen, cutting celery."

In a little while she has drifted off again.

He builds a fire, feeling oddly as though she's watching him, attending to him in some half-conscious daze. Her eyes open, then close.

"Awake?" he says.

No. She's quite still, and there's just the faint rising and falling of the clean nightgown over the bones of her chest. Outside, the wind blows, and he thinks of it as something searching for a way into the house. The snow keeps falling. Drifts climb to the windows. He stokes the fire, then sleeps in his chair in the liquid glow of it.

During the night, the sputtering of the embers wakes him, and he gets it going again. He tends it through the morning. No one calls. Everyone he knows is out there somewhere in the snowy city, grappling with the storm, heading into the weekend. Perhaps lines are down. Far off, he hears sirens.

HE CALLS BRIAN ON Saturday afternoon. "I think she's gone to her bed, son."

"Does that mean this is it?"

"I guess that's what it means."

"I'll come over tonight, if I can get out."

"The roads pretty bad?" Henry asks him.

"Awful."

"Call Tommy and Norman, will you?"

"What do I tell them?"

Henry can't think. The question seems aggressively obtuse.

"Should they make plans to come home? I mean they've got to make some plans if they're coming. Norman's got to ask for leave, and he might be out at sea right now. And Tommy's in England—well, you know that."

"I want everybody here. If it can be done."

"Did Aunt Natalie come back from Florida?"

"I told her not to. I'm going to call her now."

"What about Mom?"

"I haven't talked to anybody yet."

"God," Brian says. "Gram."

"I've got to call Natalie," Henry tells him.

There's no answer at Natalie's hotel room, so he leaves a message at the desk for her to call. He tries her again a little later on, and still there's no answer. Again, he talks to the front desk.

"She might be somewhere else in the hotel—would you like me to page her?" the clerk says—a young-sounding male voice.

"Could you?"

The clerk puts him on hold, and music plays through the wire. Strings and soft horns. Henry thinks of a tape running by itself in a room, and abruptly he feels the sense that things are in a great hurry. "Come on," he murmurs into the music.

"Sir? She doesn't answer the page."

"She was with three other women."

"Yes, sir. The four nice ladies from Virginia. They're all out somewhere, I guess. I'll try the other rooms if you want."

"Do," Henry says.

Again, he's listening to the music. Perhaps a minute goes by.

"Sorry, sir."

He thanks the young man and hangs up.

* * *

ANOTHER STORM COMES THROUGH Sunday afternoon. It snows all night, and all the next morning. And still there's no call from Natalie. Henry tries the hotel three times. No one's seen the group from Virginia.

He calls his son again.

"Do you suppose something's happened?" Brian says.

"I don't know what to think. I can't imagine that Natalie wouldn't call me—just to check up on things."

"Well, Norman's out at sea. He's on his way to Norfolk. He should be arriving tomorrow or the next day. But it could be longer, depending on the weather, I guess."

"You left a message for him," Henry says. "Right?"

"Of course I did. And I talked to Tommy. He says he can probably come if we absolutely need him. Mom wasn't there but he was going to tell her."

"He can probably come? What the hell is that?"

"He said he'd tell Mom about it. The airport's closed, Dad. They're all closed, up and down the country. From here to Boston."

Henry keeps the fire going and watches the news, weathermen trying to predict the path of the snow, the accumulations in and around Point Royal. Snows are sweeping across the plains with the jet stream, which has dipped all the way to north Florida. There'll be a deep freeze for days. His mother breathes very shallowly, but seems quite peacefully asleep. Early Monday afternoon, she awakens again.

"Henry?" Her voice is fearful.

"I'm here." He gets up quickly, moves to her side.

"Oh," she says, taking his hand. Her fingers are warm. "You made a fire."

"Will you have something to eat?" he says.

"We just had tea."

He stares into her face.

"Where's Natalie?"

"Natalie's coming," he says. There can be no use in worrying her, and even so he wants to say something, understands with a little transitory shock to his system what comfort he is in need of from her, even now.

"Talk," Elena murmurs.

"You should let me fix you some soup."

"I think something's wrong."

At first he thinks she means Natalie. But she has moved slightly; it's clear she's waiting for something to hit her, inside. She closes her eyes, and her mouth drops open slightly. But then she only gives forth a little snoring susurration, sleeping.

HE CLEANS THE HOUSE, goes through drawers and boxes of old clothes in the closet downstairs. He finds a pair of jade cufflinks, his father's. He sits in the stinging odor of naphtha and looks at photographs taken forty years ago. In one, he himself stands in bright sunlight with Lorraine and his mother. He's between the two women and is wearing his Army uniform. He remembers feeling handsome in it. He stares at the uncomplicated happiness of the photograph, and recalls the sense of being possessed of something neither of them could know about or understand. Even then, married to Lorraine less than a year, there was someone else, someone he knew in his summer job in Washington, a flirtation, and he thinks he can see something of it— some quality of amorous satisfaction and confidence—in his twenty-four-year-old face. He remembers those months of a sort of daily scheming, keeping his life in secret. Even then.

The fire has gone down—scattered red coals sending off heat. He stokes it, watches its moving shapes. There isn't anything to do but go ahead with things. He puts the radio on for the sound, tries to read. Twice he calls the hotel, and speaks with two different clerks about the fact that four women, each with a separate room, are nowhere in the hotel, and have not responded to numerous messages. Brian and Norman call, not fifteen minutes apart. They can't leave where they are because of the snow. Anyway, Henry has nothing, really, to report.

"I'm really beginning to worry about Natalie, now, too," he says.

"They probably took one of those tours," Brian says.

"And leave hotel rooms empty?"

"They probably missed your messages and went back out."

"I've been calling for two days. I've left so many messages."

"Can't they do anything to locate people?"

"Call the police?" Henry says.

"Why don't you call the hotel again and ask them to call the police. Or I could call them."

"I'm really getting worried," Henry says. "Will you see what you can do?"

Sometime after dark, he goes out into the yard to get more wood. The sky's clear now. He's shivering, cold and afraid. The surface of snow moves like a smoke in the wind, which seems to come down out of the stars. In late fall, he'd paid to have the wood stacked in a corner of the back porch, thinking about snow and rain. He remembers now the feeling of being prepared, of being ready. The snow has blown onto the porch and around the stack, has drifted high and is draped over everything, shedding a glittering dust with each stirring of air, but the wood under the first row of logs will be reasonably dry. He moves the top logs aside. Amid the sense of rising panic under his heart, it feels good to be doing physical work, breathing cold mist and huffing for breath. He brings in several logs, stacking them inside the kitchen door. Then he stands in the entrance to the living room and gazes at his mother where she sleeps. She seems completely at peace.

When he's got the fire built up, he moves to the phone and dials the overseas number. He wants to talk to Lorraine about it. He considers that she will want to be kept up in any case, but part of him is also anxious to hear her voice. When the connection is made, he finds himself unable to say anything for a moment other than to ask how she is, and to answer her questions. She tells him that she's heard from Brian. Brian calls her every day.

"Tell me how she is, Henry."

He hears the sound of her country in her voice (how quickly she's picked up the old accent!). He finds the strength to tell her that he thinks his mother is dying, that he's alone with her, surrounded by several feet of snow and ice.

"A great, dear old lady." Lorraine begins to cry. "A wonderful and lovely woman. I miss her. And I miss Natalie, too."

Then he's telling her about the fact that Natalie has gone missing. About this she seems faintly skeptical. She's so used to his capacity for alarm. Anyway, he can tell that she wants to hang up. She's settled in now, rounded by other habits, other loyalties and demands, her family, perhaps even some of her old associations. She's home. Something's going on in the room behind her; he can hear children—her grandnieces and -nephews—playing. It's morning there. No one's eaten anything yet.

"I don't suppose you can get away," he says.

She pauses, sighs. "I don't think so, Henry."

"Well," he says. "I'll let you know what happens," and he feels the pain of what he cannot ask of her, cannot say.

"We'll pray for Elena," she says.

NATALIE PHONES PERHAPS AN hour later. She's been on a weekend shopping and gambling spree in Las Vegas, and she says she called the hotel several times, asking for messages. The hotel people had told her there were no messages. Whoever she spoke to assured her of this, and she asked him (it was a man—she didn't know more) to double-check. The man put her on hold; she waited while he made sure. And so not only has the hotel failed to relay any of Henry's urgent requests that she call, but they charged all four women for the nights their rooms were not in use, though Natalie had spoken to someone (perhaps the same man) about reserving the same rooms for their return. "I should've called you there," she says. "But I didn't want to wake Elena if she was resting. I was sure you'd call and leave a message." She and her friends are changing hotels, of course. And Natalie wants to sue. In any case, she won't pay for the nights she was gone.

"Oh, Henry," she says, suddenly. "What am I talking about? It's time to come home, isn't it."

He can't speak for a moment. "I was worried about you," he says, mumbles.

"Is Elena—"

He explains everything.

She cries for a few minutes, apologizing, asking him to be patient. He listens to her as she tries to master herself.

"I was worried about you," he says.

"Well," Natalie tells him, "I was never in any other kind of danger."

He thinks of the flights crossing the country, the snow as it must look from 41,000 feet. Natalie will fly home as soon as she can make arrangements with the others—she'll leave immediately. Henry tells her of the storms; the bad roads. The airports closing. She'll try. She'll pray, and she'll try.

"I've been expecting it," she says, crying. "You know—but it still feels shocking somehow."

"Maybe it's going to be all right," Henry tells her. And then he's telling her about the woman who's a hundred and thirteen, how that's nineteen years—a generation. "Natalie, hurry," he says, finally, breathing the words.

HE CAN'T SLEEP. He puts another log on the fire, then goes into the kitchen and fixes himself something to eat. He sees that it's a little past three o'clock in the morning. When he comes back into the living room, he knows immediately that his mother has soiled her bed.

It's astonishing how the body keeps producing waste, even as one starves. She's lying on her back, and the blanket is tangled beneath her.

"Are you awake?" he says.

Nothing.

He stands there for a long time, as if waiting for something to change. Finally he gathers himself, moves to her side, puts his hands in under her back and legs, not breathing, lifting her, tottering there in the light of the fire. He manages to get her in the chair, still wrapped in the blanket, then removes the sheets from the sofa. Twice he stops to go stand in the open doorway, in the blowing cold and snow, gasping. The muscles of his back are tightening. He can feel all the connective tissues like hot strips of metal along his spine. The sofa is damp where he's washed it, and he puts towels down, and fresh sheets. She's slumped over slightly in the chair. Her nightgown is soaked. He retrieves the blankets from his own bed upstairs, and puts them on the sofa, then works her out of the wet clothes. Her body is surprisingly, disturbingly blue. There's a translucent quality to the skin, now, and the bones of her chest and hips seem about to push through. He sets her down gently on another blanket on the floor and there he laves her backside and legs in warm, soapy water, kneeling at her side and trying to keep part of the blanket over her for warmth. It all takes such a long time, and he's lost in the appalling necessity, the nightmare of it, unable to believe what's required and yet remembering that this pale, still shape is his mother; this body, with its dreadful harrowing skeletal inertness, is the body that bore him. For a terrible, inescapable, sick moment, he thinks of her in terms of sex, of all the women he has sought and wooed and dreamed of and slept with. It travels along his veins and leaves him shivering.

"Henry," she says, with startling force. "I feel so bad."

He's lifting her, hurting, in the ache of having carried the wood and of having worked with her; the pains stab him, and he's almost unable to straighten with her. As he moves to the sofa he nearly falls. She says, "Oh."

He adjusts the blanket over her, tucks it at her chin. "You have to eat something," he says.

She's looking at the fire. "I couldn't sleep."

"I'll make soup for you," he says.

"Henry," she says, kindly. "Thank you for putting me by this window so I could look out at that lovely tree."

The window, of course, is black. "Do you want another blanket?" he asks.

But she has closed her eyes again, is gone again.

He makes the soup anyway. When the metal spoon clatters against the pan, he thinks of the time of night and catches himself trying to be quiet. She doesn't stir. He eats the soup, not really tasting it, sitting by her bed, and when he's finished with it he washes the dishes, puts the sheets and blankets in the washing machine. Then he collapses into the chair across from her and tries to rest. Every bone and muscle of his back throbs, and though he's quite spent, sleep won't come. Her breathing is more ragged now. There's something broken about it— little separate gasps, as if each one were the result of great effort. He doesn't know how long he sits there in the dim light of the fire, listening to her, and perhaps he dozes some. It seems to him now that Time is measured out in little harsh divisions of breathing, heard in the half-consciousness of exhaustion.

He passes the night this way.

And has a groggy dream that Lorraine is asleep upstairs on the stripped bed in Natalie's room; it's another time, everyone visiting. The children are small. Lorraine is cold, curled on the bare bed in Natalie's room, her legs pulled up to her chest, her hands over her face.

When light comes to the windows he finds himself staring at the ceiling, listening to his mother's breathing; and when he remembers the dream he feels compelled to walk up to Natalie's room and look, knowing how irrational this is. Even so, it hurts him to find the room empty, the sun beating through the window onto the mattress.

He closes the bedroom door, pads back downstairs, and puts his hand on his mother's forehead, which gives off a low heat—not feverish, quite, though it doesn't feel quite normal, either: there's something inanimate about it, even as she moves a little, shuddering slightly, then lying still again. He goes into the bathroom and washes his face. And then he's crying.

He looks at himself in the mirror, brushes at his eyes with the heels of his palms. Finally he throws his heavy coat on, trudges outside in the cold to gather more firewood. He works furiously, sniffling and sobbing and wiping his face with the cold sleeve of the coat. He doesn't see Brian walk up. Turning with an armful of wood—he's stacked far more than he could need—he sees his son through ledges of drifted snow.

"You need somebody with a shovel," Brian says.

Henry puts the wood down, lets it drop from his arms, and then realizes his son is talking about the snow. "Well," he says. "You made it."

"The roads are miserable," says his son. "My car's stuck at the end of the street."

Henry can't look at him, accepts his clumsy embrace, and then faces away from him. "They're saying it might snow some more."

They go into the house together. Henry watches him head into the living room, and he sees the hesitation, the wariness, in his motions. Brian only glances at the sofa, then turns awkwardly.

"Go on in the kitchen," Henry manages to say. He hears the irritation in his voice. "I've got to use the bathroom."

In the little room under the stairs, he runs water again, splashes his face. He cleans his teeth and brushes his hair, composing himself.

He finds Brian sitting in the breakfast nook. Sunlight is pouring through the windows now, past noon, and the colors in the tile, the table cloth, the prints on the walls, look brighter, more vivid. "I checked on her," Brian says. "She seems okay. Asleep."

Henry sighs out the words, "Almost continuously since Friday." He looks at his own hands and is momentarily speechless.

Presently Brian says, "Can't the hospital do something? Can't they put her on a respirator or something—something, Jesus—listen to that."

Elena is breathing in small gasps. There's something almost mechanical about it.

"There isn't anything to do," Henry says. "What do you think this is, boy?"

There seems nothing left to say. For a while they both stare out the kitchen window at children riding sleds in that part of the street. Finally Brian mutters, "I don't know what I thought I'd find—"

"I don't know what I thought you could do," Henry tells him. "But thanks for coming."

They are quiet again, listening to the heedless play of the children in the snow. Brian stirs, rises, and with a kind of nervous agitation, begins moving about the house, looking at pictures, occasionally talking about what he sees, and Henry feels as if his son were engaged in a form of trespass.

THEY MAKE SANDWICHES for dinner. Henry becomes aware of the extent of his own neglect of himself: he's eaten almost nothing for days; he can't remember how he got from the beginning of the storms to here, how he spent all the hours. When dinner is over, Brian sits at the dining room table with a glass of whiskey and the bottle at his elbow.

"Pour me one," Henry says.

The other looks at him. "Wasn't much left. You want some of this?"

He sits down and rubs his eyes. "I guess I wasn't that thirsty."

"I think I saw some gin."

"No." Henry thinks of Elena on a playground with him and the other children in 1952, wearing denim jeans and a checked blouse, her dark blond hair braided and tied across the top of her head—a young woman playing baseball all wrong, with great cheerfulness and humor. "When I was a kid," he says, "she played baseball with us. I ever tell you about that?"

"A few times."

"She's lived ninety-four years, and that's one of the few things you know about her."

"No, Dad. That's where you're wrong. I know a whole lot about her."

"I'm sorry," Henry tells him. "I don't know what I'm saying."

They listen for a moment.

Henry takes the empty bottle and puts it in the trash. He stands by the sink, both hands on the counter, and behind him his son moves, makes a throat-clearing sound. Henry faces him.

Brian simply stares at the wall. "I've been talking to Mom on the phone. I don't think she's going to come back here."

"We talked," Henry says.

"Are you mad at her about it?"

"Don't be ridiculous."

"I think Tommy's going to work on her. Tommy'd like to come back now."

Henry says. "Let's drop it."

"The whole world," Brian says, then seems to hesitate. "I was thinking about the fact that I'm almost forty and I haven't understood one goddam thing."

It seems to Henry that this statement comes from some aspect of his son's recent troubles with Tillie. How badly he wants the other man to leave, how hard it is to be here with him, this soft-looking middle-aged man who is his son. His own reaction horrifies him, and he tries to compensate by moderating the tone of his voice. "There really isn't anything for you to do here."

"I'll stay."

It's evident that staying will cost the younger man.

"Natalie'll be home soon," Henry says. "Really, we're—we're fine here."

"Do you want me to go?"

He can't say it out. The tentative, half-hurt expression on his son's face catches him up. "I don't want you to trouble yourself," he says.

"That's all I do," says Brian. "That's what I'm best at."

Henry thinks of him as a child, searches for an image of him. Nothing will come clearly enough. "Brian," he says. He wants to say something definite to him, wants to clear the air somehow. But he can't find the words. He doesn't even know where to begin.

"What," Brian says.

"Nothing. I can't—I feel like there's something I ought to say to you."

"About Elena?"

"About me," Henry says, turning away.

A little later, Brian says, "I think I should probably go."

Henry leaves him there, walks into the living room and looks at his mother. Nothing has changed. She lies still, breathing in those little separate gasps. He sits in the chair, lays his head back. His son walks in from the kitchen, stands for a moment, sighing. Finally he sits in the chair across from Henry.

"I guess I'll go on home," he says.

"That'd probably be best."

"Oh," Brian says. And then, a second later: "God."

Henry's filled with wonder at the force of the antipathy he feels, looking upon his son's doughy, still-innocent, dark features and the paunchy shape of his body. Again, he wants to say something to conceal the anger that's working in him, but he can think of nothing at all.

"I wish I had her bravery—" Brian begins.

"Right, son, I know."

Brian's quiet. Henry closes his eyes, thinks of feigning sleep, and for a while he's simply waiting for his son to decide to leave. He has his hands folded across his chest. Brian sighs; the chair he sits in squeaks with his weight.

"Elena?" he says.

Henry opens his eyes. His mother's sitting up. She looks at Henry and then at his son. She sighs. "Boys. Scared as puppies. Look at you."

"Elena, it's me," says Brian.

She lies down again and closes her eyes.

"Elena?"

The breathing is slower, more shallow.

"Oh, Jesus," Brian says.

Henry says, "Shut up, will you?"

They say nothing for a long time, then. Henry closes his eyes and pretends to sleep.

"Dad?"

He doesn't answer. A moment later, he hears Brian get up and leave the room. Part of him wants to say something to stop him, but then he drifts off, and after a while he becomes aware that something has changed.

He sits forward. There's no sensation that much time has passed, but the lights are all off, and Brian is back, a vague shape, all round-nesses, snoring in the chair.

Henry's surprised by the wave of relief that washes over him with the knowledge that his son has chosen to stay. He thinks of Natalie lifting into the dawn over the curve of the earth, on her way home, and for a moment he feels something like gladness; it's the faintest stirring in his spirit over the fact that he will look upon his sister's face today. But there's something else, too, now—some random, unbidden, creaturely sense of belonging where he is.

He sits up. On the makeshift bed, his mother lies very still. Moving tentatively to her side, he looks into the pale shape of her face, and realizes with a resigned sinking at his heart that this silence, this deep stillness, is what has awakened him. Taking her hand, he holds it, kisses the veined, cold back of it, shuddering inwardly for a moment. But then something lifts inside him—a sensation so strong it makes him draw in a breath, like a sob. He puts her hand down, and very carefully, very tenderly, touches her closed eyes. Then he lets his palm rest on her cheek. Time ends. In some wordless part of his soul, this moment—the moment of realizing where he is and what he is doing—alters the flow of things: this little instant, at which it seems to him he has arrived out of all the turmoil and blur of his adult life, ex-pands, widens, fixes him in its cold, calm center, and his long, complicated history leaches out, is gone. Everything seems strangely, almost terrifyingly, immaculate. He kneels at his mother's side and smoothes a strand of her hair. He says her name. He weeps. And when he turns, when he sees in the half-light that his son is awake now, too, he has a sensation of being ruthlessly pulled from a dream.

"Oh, God—" Brian says. "Dad?" His voice is thin with dread.

And, quite gently, as though speaking to a child, Henry tells him.

Rare
&
Endangered
Species

*S*INGLE

*T*HAT MORNING, she was awake first. She lay in the pre-dawn and listened to him breathing, and after a time, being careful not to disturb him, she got her robe on and made her way downstairs. The kitchen was all deep shadows and gray light, the surfaces looking as though they'd been lined with silver. She put bacon in the skillet over a low flame, then made coffee. The room began to take on a definiteness, the shadows receding. For a while she sat in the window seat, sipping the coffee, breathing the warmth of it and feeling the chill of being awake early. The view out this window was of fog and dripping trees. You couldn't see much of the wide field which surrounded the house, and the mountains beyond were completely obscured. She remembered that when James and Maizie were small and required her to be up so often at first light, she had liked watching the fog burn off the soft green slopes, like an enormous ice floe melting away. The fog was thick this morning, and the light was a watery color.

It had rained most of the night.

The smell of the frying bacon filled the small kitchen. She knew it was traveling through the house. And now she heard him stirring upstairs.

Though for years he had struggled with insomnia, rising several times each night, restless and angry with himself, often unable to fall asleep until the small hours of the morning, he was usually up with the sun. Force of habit, he would say. Creature of habit. He padded into the kitchen wearing his robe and slippers. "Hey," he said, "you're up early." He cleared his throat, scratched the back of his head and yawned, then tied the robe tighter. "That bacon smells awfully good."

"Turn it, will you?"

He stepped to the stove. "What got you up at this hour?"

"Dreams," she said.

"Nightmares?"

"Busy dreams. Things piling up, and me trying to organize them."

"I wish I could sleep deep enough to dream."

"I heard you snoring once."

"Not me," he said.

"I'm going to go look at some antiques today with Pauline Brill and Missy Johnson and maybe some others, if they can make it."

"I wouldn't be thrilled about having more stuff to move," he said.

"I'll keep that in mind." She sipped her coffee, then opened a book which lay in the window seat, one of his big coffee table books about aircraft, the history of flight.

"You want me to finish this?" he said.

"If you want to."

"I hadn't planned on it."

She closed the book and moved to where he stood. They had been married forty-two years, and there were certain codes of speech and gesture they had developed for the sake of peace. These polite exchanges masked acts of will and contention: he wanted his breakfast cooked for him, for instance. Or he wanted her to stay home. He was not in the mood to be by himself.

"Sit," she said to him.

"I'll help."

"You'll get in the way."

He shuffled over to the table and sat down, then rose again. "Think I'll have some coffee."

"Coffee?" she said. "You? You're having trouble sleeping."

"Want me not to have the coffee?" he said. "I won't have the coffee."

"You never drink it."

He sat down again. But he was waiting for her to speak.

"I'll pour you some if you want it," she said.

He didn't answer.

She poured the coffee and set it before him, and for a little space there was only the sound of bacon frying.

"How do you want your eggs?" she said.

"Think I'll just have the bacon with a couple slices of toast."

At the stove, she turned the bacon again, put four finished strips of it on a paper towel to drain. The rain increased at the window briefly, then sighed away in the wind.

"What do you have in mind to buy?" he said.

"Probably nothing much."

"I don't know where we're going to put everything," he said, looking around the room.

"Maizie said she and Leo could keep some of it for us. And the same goes for James and Helena."

"Yeah, but why? For what? We'll never have a place for it again."

"Well then, they'll have to keep it all. We'll look at it when we visit them."

"Including whatever you decide to buy this afternoon?" He said this with a crooked smile, which she acknowledged with a shrug.

"Maybe," she said.

"If you see something nice," he said.

"If I do, yes." She put two more strips of bacon on the paper towel.

"Maybe I'll have eggs after all."

"Will you or won't you?"

"You going to have some?"

"I might," she said.

He cleared his throat. "We should've had more children."

She ignored this. The bacon was done. She turned the gas lower and went to the refrigerator for the eggs. "Scrambled?" she said.

"Is that how you want them?"

"I don't care how I have them."

"That's not like you."

She shrugged. "Make up your mind, Harry."

"Scrambled."

She poured the bacon grease into an empty coffee can, then washed the skillet and set to work on the eggs. He watched her.

"You're not taking Maizie with you on this antiques run?"

"Maizie has a doctor's appointment."

"Seems like Maizie's always running to the doctor."

"It's a regular appointment, Harry."

"I remember how Buddy Wells was always running to the doctor."

She was silent.

"Didn't do him any good."

"Would you put a couple of slices of toast in?" she said.

"I hadn't thought I would." He stood, moved to the cabinet where they kept the bread. "It's strange to think of a person like Buddy Wells now. Being this much older than he got to be. I can't even imagine him in his fifties, you know? Any more than I can really imagine myself being sixty-seven."

"What made you think of Buddy Wells?" she said.

He shrugged. "Walking around sleepless, you think of a lot."

She was breaking up pieces of American cheese and dropping them into the scrambled eggs. Then she moved to the refrigerator, brought out a carton of milk, and poured some into the mixture, stirring.

"Speaking of not being able to imagine a thing, I can't imagine living somewhere else," he said. "Can you?"

She said nothing.

"I was standing here thinking about the bread. Silly? Where will we keep the bread?"

"I suppose there'll be a place," she said.

"Seems like too much to have to think about." He dropped two slices into the toaster, then put the loaf back in the cabinet and shut it. "It wakes me up at night, but then I can't think about it clear enough. Can't imagine it. So I walk around and try to get sleepy."

"Are you going to want more coffee?" she said.

He stared at her a moment. "I guess I better not."

"Why did you look at me that way?" she said.

"What way?" He smiled, then touched her arm above the elbow. "Funny thing to be thinking about bread."

"I guess so."

"You ever think about Buddy Wells?"

"Not for years," she said.

"No," he said. "Me, too. But I thought of him last night. We're twenty years older than he got to be. Think of that. It's like we left him there and went flying into our old age. I was going over all that last night, you know, doing the arithmetic. Who was how old when. He never even got as old as you were at the time."

"Please, Harry."

"No, really. Think of it. You were fifty and he was almost forty, and he died at—what was it—forty-six? forty-seven? I know he didn't get out of his forties."

"Yes?" she said, as though waiting for him to finish something.

He shrugged. "Seems odd to think about it now."

"There are things I could mention, Harry."

His gaze settled on her hands, and she paused. "I didn't mean it as a contest," he said. "Forgive me. I got to thinking of Buddy Wells."

She took his wrist. "I'm sorry."

When the toast came up, he buttered it. She had put the plates out, the bowl of steaming eggs. The bacon. He poured orange juice and brought out a jar of strawberry jam for the toast, though it turned out that neither of them wanted any. They ate quietly, looking at the lawn and the field beyond it. The fog dissolved in the sun, which peeked through the clouds drifting over the mountains. It would be a bright, breezy day. Cool air came in the open window.

"I didn't think I could become accustomed to the idea of leaving this place," he said.

She said, "I guess you'll have to."

"You've gone past it somehow, haven't you?"

She didn't answer.

"I don't mean that to be a challenge, either, Andrea. But I wasn't speaking rhetorically."

"I didn't think you were."

"Well?"

She put her fork down and picked up her piece of toast, looked at it, then put it back on her plate. "I wouldn't know how to gauge such a thing."

"It's a simple concept. You were as desperate as I've ever seen you, and yet you seem to have made peace with it. You're not even angry with me about it, like James and Maizie are."

She merely returned his look.

"You seem almost settled about it now. I admire you for it."

She began eating again. "It's a house. I've loved it here. And it's over."

"Just like that."

"Harry, what do you want me to do?"

"No, I admire it," he said. "I'm still going through all the stages of grief. Walking around last night, I felt this pain in my chest. And it wasn't even quite physical, I could tell."

She went on eating.

"We don't tell each other much these days," he said.

"Yes we do. You were telling me you didn't know where we'd put the bread in the apartment. And you said you were brokenhearted about leaving."

"I am. If we could afford to stay, I'd stay. Besides, I think I was talking about something else, too."

"I understood that."

"You couldn't've really wondered why I mentioned Buddy Wells."

"Buddy Wells has been dead nine years, Harry. I don't understand you."

"You'd've been a widow all these years."

"I can't believe we're talking about this now."

"I sometimes wondered if you didn't wish you'd gone with him."

"No," she said.

"Not even a little?"

"It's absurd talking about something that didn't happen fifteen years ago. I didn't go with him. I stayed here."

"You never once wondered if maybe you shouldn't've left me? I could be such a son of a bitch in those days."

"Oh, Harry, I don't feel like this now. Really I don't. I know you're only woolgathering, but please."

"It's—well, I don't know. Leaving the place. You think about everything."

They finished the meal and started washing the dishes together. He remarked about the beauty of the day, and she agreed. And she let the quiet go on.

"What're you thinking about?" he said.

She smiled out of one side of her mouth. "Do you mean, a penny for my thoughts?"

"It was a question."

Again, they were quiet.

Presently he said, "James and Maizie still seem to think we'll walk into some miracle and be able to stay. The place is sold and they're still entertaining fantasies about it."

She was drying the dishes and putting them in the cabinet over the sink.

"I get the feeling James thinks it's our fault we're clearing out," he said. "I want to yell at him sometimes. It's their doing, really. They could've had it if they really wanted it. They could've gone in together and bought the place."

"You want them to pay for us to live here?"

"I thought we'd all live here."

"Well." She dried her hands and went into the next room, and he followed her. The light through the front window was too bright. She picked up a magazine from the rack and lay down on the couch.

He stood gazing at her.

"You're making me edgy, Harry."

"You know, you're still pretty," he said.

"Thank you. I like you, too."

"Like?"

She smiled at him.

"You never cease to amaze me."

She held the magazine up. "You know I could never stand compliments."

"Well," he said. "It's exactly true."

HE WAS IN THE utility room when the time came for her to leave. She called to him from the living room door. "Good-bye, Harry."

"Oh," he said. "Okay. Bye."

She went through the house and in to him. He had started work repairing a purple martin birdhouse that had been damaged in a storm last month. She put her arms around his neck and held tight.

"Hey," he said. "Sure you don't want to stay?"

"No," she said to him. "Gotta go."

In the car, she turned the radio up loud. The news was about the fighting in Bosnia. She let this play for a time, not really hearing much of it, then looked for music and found something baroque-sounding. The sun shone brightly; it would be a humid day. The sky over the mountains was milky with haze, and the mountains themselves looked almost bleached. Pauline Brill had already arrived at the Cider Press Café on Mission Street, where they had agreed to meet. They would eat lunch and then browse in the antiques stores along the block.

"Anyone else coming?" Andrea asked, getting out of the car.

"Just Missy. And she can't stay long." Pauline's voice had been made raspy with years of cigarette smoke, though she had recently quit. "I swear, all it needs is for me to plan something and it falls apart under my hands."

They stood and watched the road for a few minutes. "I can't really stay very long myself," Andrea said.

"I've got all afternoon," said Pauline. "My summer classes are done. I was supposed to meet with these people about their dreadful child, but they canceled. Kid almost flunked summer school and I have him again this fall. Dreadful. Although *I* should talk about a dreadful child."

"I don't have all afternoon."

"Have you started packing yet?"

"No."

"Some companies will pack for you, you know."

"I haven't given it much thought."

Pauline lived in a mansion off Highway 15 North. Though her husband had left her with an enormous amount of money, she continued teaching school out of what she described as a need to be earning something on her own. The truth was that she had been through hard times before her marriage to wealth, and now that her husband was gone, she felt that living off investment income and a trust fund was tempting fate. Something bad would happen to a person living off the fat of the land. Work was a relief from the daily trouble of trying to keep a stepdaughter in line, and in fact she liked to teach; it had been something at which she was skillful enough. It provided a contrast, she would say, to the failures of life at home—the war in the palace, as she called it. The stepdaughter was now nineteen and seemingly determined to find some way to destroy her reputation, if not herself; the two of them stalking through the rooms of that huge house in an ongoing battle, speaking, if they spoke at all, merely to taunt or chide or challenge each other. The girl, whose name was Pamela, had the looks of a movie star and was inclined to the sort of recklessness that caused talk. Pauline felt guilty and confused about her all the time, and often sought Andrea's advice when she wasn't trying to see what

Andrea might know, since Andrea's daughter Maizie had worked with the girl and had become friendly with her. "Does Maizie know if Pamela is on drugs, do you think?" Pauline asked one afternoon.

Andrea said she never talked to Maizie about things like that.

"But Maizie would know. They do still see each other socially."

"I suppose."

"Does Maizie take drugs?"

"Pauline, I honestly never asked her. I assume she doesn't."

"I'd ask Pamela," Pauline said, "but I'm terrified what the answer would be. She wouldn't tell me the truth. And anyway, there's nothing I can do about it. She's of age."

"I'm not sure Maizie would tell me the truth, either."

"Sure Maizie would. You and Maizie are so sweet together. Maizie would tell you."

"Maybe," Andrea told her.

"I think it's all to spite me," said Pauline. "Absolutely everything that girl does. As if I did anything to her at all except try to be there for her."

"Don't cry," Andrea said. "Please."

It was Andrea's natural reserve that had always calmed the other woman down. Pauline had said as much on more than one occasion. Now Pauline toed the gravel at their feet and asked if Maizie had visited on the weekend. Lately, Maizie hadn't had much time to spend with Pamela, and so the question was asked without any ulterior motive. Andrea said, "We talked on the phone."

"I think Pamela's been meaning to call her," Pauline Brill said.

Andrea looked at her and thought of the many strands of hurt pride, anger, and worry behind that ordinary statement. "I'm sure Maizie'll be glad to hear from her," she said.

"Of course," Pauline said with a small, pained laugh, "I'm just guessing."

Missy Johnson pulled into the gravel lot, turned her engine off, and stared at them through the windshield. "Why didn't you go on in and order something to drink?" she said, getting out.

"We just got here," Pauline said.

Missy wore a white blouse and slacks, showing off her slender shape and her long, lovely legs. Younger than the other two women by almost twenty-five years, she was nevertheless the one among them who was most anxious about her health and her appearance, as though all her good looks and happiness were about to be taken away from her. She was always imagining the disasters that might befall her, and Pauline had taken to calling her Ms. Little, after Chicken Little.

"I have to eat and run," Missy said. "My damn babysitter has an orthodontist's appointment."

They went into the café and were seated in a booth by the window. The waitress was a young woman with luminous blond hair. "If she didn't get that hair out of a bottle," Pauline said, "I'm buying lunch for us all."

"How will you find out?" Missy said.

"I'll just ask her."

When the waitress brought menus to them, Pauline said, "Honey, is that your natural color?"

The young woman stepped back and seemed embarrassed. Her hand went up to the small shimmering curl at her shoulder. "Yes, ma'am."

"It's very pretty," Andrea said.

"And this lady's buying lunch." Missy indicated Pauline with a nod. "Give the check to her."

"Yes, ma'am."

After the waitress put glasses of water down, Pauline said, "I swear it's the same color Maizie's was when she dyed it in February."

"I think Maizie looks good blond," said Missy. "Don't you like it, Andrea?"

"Maizie likes it," Andrea said. "I guess I do, too. Sometimes I don't quite recognize her. It's like she's this—this woman I ought to know and can't quite place."

"That's the thing," Pauline said. "It's so much harder when it's your daughter. I mean, I have an idea of it. I never wanted my stepchildren to change anything, even hair color. Of course, I've got Pamela threatening to get a sex change operation."

"You're kidding," Missy said.

"She just does it to upset me, and I'm used to it now. I play along. But I know several young men who'd go into mourning."

"She is a knockout, isn't she," said Missy.

"She's dangerous, if you ask me. I don't know what she's into anymore."

"I didn't mind when Maizie dyed her hair," Andrea said. "She has a different life. It's not connected to me anymore."

The other two looked at her. "What're you thinking about, sitting there?" Missy wanted to know. "You've got a faraway look."

"She's thinking about the antiques she's going to buy," said Pauline.

"I don't know," Andrea said. "This morning Harry said he didn't know where we'd put anything if I did buy it. Pauline, I wonder— what do you think of Harry?"

Pauline waited an instant. "I think Harry's a sweetheart."

"No, that isn't really what I meant."

"I do, though."

"I don't think he's accepted what's happened," Andrea said. "I don't think he grasps it yet—that he's going to be living in that little apartment, and that strangers are moving into the house."

"Well, you both really ought to have started packing by now," said Pauline Brill.

Andrea sipped her water and looked out the window. The haze had disappeared from the sky. There wasn't a cloud anywhere, just the endless blue skies of August. A moment later, the blond waitress came to take their orders. Andrea said, "I'll just have the water."

"That's it?" Pauline said.

"I had a big breakfast with Harry."

The other two ordered sandwiches and then began a conversation about Pauline's student, the one who was causing problems. "He's a sweet boy, really. Only he just can't listen when he's told to do something. It's a stepfather situation and so I have a special—you know, but I think there's some trouble in the home. You should hear the way this woman's voice changes when she talks about her husband. She's carrying some grievance. Something he did, I'd bet—and that she's chosen to forgive him for. I'd give anything to know what it is."

"Sometimes," Andrea said, "being forgiven is worse than being thrown out."

Missy wondered if the boy was on drugs. "It's so easy to get them these days. But it's worse than drugs. When kids in the high schools can get guns, where are we? And what are we coming to?"

"It could be drugs with this boy," said Pauline. "You can never rule that out. I worry about that with Pamela. She has all that money to throw around. Sometimes I feel like she's doing it to me—to get at me—and then I wonder if maybe I'm imagining everything and it has nothing to do with me at all. Hell, there's times when she doesn't even seem to know I exist anymore."

Missy said, "I read somewhere that ninety percent of the population is walking around with drugs on them of one kind or another, including the over-the-counter stuff. Sleeping pills and tranquilizers and stomach pills and cold capsules, and every one of them does something to you that nature didn't intend."

"Excuse me," Andrea said, and went out to stand in the sunlight at the entrance of the café. The other two hurried to finish their sandwiches, and didn't take long to join her. "You're eager," Missy said.

"I'm sorry."

"Well, I wish I could shop with you."

"Oh, come on," Pauline said. "One store."

Andrea said, "One store is all I can do, too."

"Well, this is certainly a bust."

"I've got fifteen minutes," Missy said. "Then I've got to scoot."

There were five stores, each in its own old house, ranged along this part of Mission Street, and they went into the first one. There, Andrea almost bought a soup tureen. Missy looked at a Tiffany lamp, and left a deposit on it. Pauline bought some turn-of-the-century postcards and photographs. One was of a large family ranged across the wide veranda of a big Victorian house. At the center of the photograph was an ancient woman, supporting herself on a cane and looking out at the world with a fierceness.

"I envisioned this for myself once," Pauline said.

Andrea looked at the picture. "Oh," she said. "Yes."

They went out to the parking lot, where Missy was waiting. "I don't know how you can be so interested in that sort of thing," she said. "Old scattered families. It's depressing."

"My family's all over the map," Pauline said. "The pictures console me somehow."

"I hope my kids never grow up," Missy said. "You and Andrea are lucky, really. You still have Pamela, no matter how much you fight with her, and Andrea has Maizie, and James is only an hour away. I'd love to be able to think my kids'll stay around."

Andrea was staring off at the line of mountains and sky. It had come to her that her friend Missy still had the unimaginable future to think about: her children growing up, her life achieving its shape, whatever that might be—its one history.

"Well," Pauline said, "I've got more stores to hit."

"All right," said Missy. "One more. For two minutes."

"Andrea, you coming?"

"I'd better get going," she told them.

"I just might get you that soup tureen, you know," Pauline said. "You might find yourself opening it for your birthday."

"That wouldn't be a surprise, then."

"We'll see."

"We have to go now, Pauline, or I can't do it," Missy said.

"Come on, then." They started off.

"Take care," Andrea told them.

SHE GOT INTO HER car and drove east, past the old courthouse and the match factory, to the base of Hospital Hill and the Mountain

Lodge Motel. There were cars parked outside two of the rooms, and the VACANCY sign was blinking. She went into the office and stood at the desk, waiting for the young man there to notice her.

"Yes, ma'am," he said.

"I'd like a room, please."

"Single or double?"

"Single," she said.

He gave her a little card, and she wrote *Andrea Brewer. Witlow Creek Farm. Point Royal, Virginia.* She looked at what she had written.

The boy took it and looked at it, too, without really reading it. He put it in a card file and fished a key out of a drawer. "That's twenty dollars, ma'am."

She opened her purse and got out a pair of tens.

"Room seven," he told her. "You need help with luggage or anything?"

"No, thank you."

Outside, she looked at the highway, the cars going along next to the railroad bed. The smell of coal and tar drifted by on the air. At the gas station across the street, two black men were shouting good-naturedly at each other from a distance, and two others were laughing. A woman came out of one of the bathrooms and walked briskly around to give the key back to the attendant. The woman's car was open, and a man sat waiting for her. Beyond this, the hills rolled on toward the dark blue eastern sky. She drove the short distance to room seven, got out, and locked the car. Up the other way, in one of the yards behind a house on the other side of the fence there, dogs barked and complained. A breeze shook the leaves on the trees and lifted the flag in front of the hospital at the top of the hill, those low brick buildings where her children were born—only yesterday, it seemed.

She went to the door of the room and opened it. A small place with brown walls and dark brown furniture, smelling faintly of cigarette smoke and cleanser. The bed sagged in the middle. A Bible was on the nightstand. She closed and locked the door, but left the chain off. Then she went into the bathroom and got out of her clothes, standing before the mirror over the sink. She was sixty-five years old, but she looked younger. It was an objective thing one could look at in a mirror. She did not look sixty-five. Fifteen years ago, she had almost left her husband for a man ten years her junior. She had not done so, and Buddy Wells was dead now, eight years or nine years—nine years. And so it would only have been six years; that would have been all. And perhaps it would have been enough. But she had chosen to stay in the house with its view of the mountains, where she had raised her children.

How strange, that she should feel so far away from them now.

She took a shower, then dried off, wrapped the towel around herself, and poured a glass of water from the tap. She brought this to the nightstand, where she'd left her purse. Dropping the towel, she got into the bed and pulled the blankets to her middle, propping herself up on the pillows. The sheets were cool and clean-feeling. She breathed deeply, closed her eyes a moment, then reached in her purse and brought out the bottle of pills. She did not think anymore, nor did she hesitate. She swallowed the pills quickly, one after another, until the little bottle was empty. There was the noise of traffic, and it lulled her. When the pills were gone, she put the phone on the floor, then lay on her side with the blanket pulled high over her shoulder. The light over the bed was on, and she thought to turn it off. It was too bright. She could feel the heat of it on her face. She saw herself rise and reach for it, and was unhappy to find that it couldn't be reached. A while later, she was disturbed to see that it was still burning. I'll have to get up to do it, she thought. I'll just have to do that one more thing. It's keeping me awake. And oh, my children, I wanted to tell you what I mean. I wanted to say why. I meant to tell you somehow, only I couldn't get around to it, couldn't get to any of it, couldn't find the way, and there wasn't time. There was never enough time, and you would never have believed me anyway, that it could be so important. A simple view from a window, my children. That it could mean so much, that it could give me back all the time you were small. That it could come to mean more than anything else. Not even love, oh my darlings. Not even that. But listen. I can tell you now, I think. At last. Oh, finally. Listen, she heard herself say from somewhere far off. And we can stop.

PATIENTLY

WHEN THEY PULLED onto Route 4, at the far end of the property, with its bright new SOLD sign and its straw-strewn field, James Brewer saw several dark shapes pinwheeling in the gray sky at what looked like the base of the driveway in front of the house. It made a disturbing sight. His mother's suicide was a little less than a month ago.

"Are those vultures, for Christ's sake?"

"Crows," his wife said. "I think they're crows."

Before them, to the left, a wide field of grass went on to the line of trees which bordered the neighboring farm. Small white stakes with flags on them were placed intermittently across the length of the field. Beyond the trees there were more fields, more stands of trees, and the soft, worn-down crests of the Shenandoahs, with dark, threatening clouds trailing along the top edges. A blue sheet fanned out beneath the clouds and blurred the treetops, the deep green swells of the hills. It all looked wild, uninhabited. The owners of the houses that were going to be built here would have a good view of the mountains. It was lovely country, as Brewer's mother had so often said. Brewer had a moment of realizing how astonishingly, painfully beautiful the world was when you thought of never seeing any of it again. As he thought this, lightning forked out of the center of the huge escarpment of cloud, and a thunderclap followed. He counted the seconds. "That's only three miles away."

"I can see the rain from here," said his wife. "See it? I've been watching it come. It's kind of scary watching it build like that."

"Don't watch it, then."

"A simple solution," she said. "Like not talking to your wife about anything but weather and vultures."

"What did you want to talk about?" he said.

"Oh, anything you want to talk about." Her voice shook.

"For Christ's sake," he said, "I've been driving for an hour. Give me a break."

She touched his cheek. "I know I've said this, but it—this thing happened to me, too, you know."

He slowed and pulled into the driveway, past still another SOLD sign. From here they could see the circling birds more clearly.

"Those *are* vultures," he said.

There were five or six of them, sailing and drifting with the motions of the wind above the creek bottom, perhaps two hundred yards away, where the property line was demarcated with barbed wire that ran along the overgrown creek bed.

"They took like crows to me."

"They're too big to be crows."

"Vultures are endangered, aren't they?"

"Why don't you stop being so goddam ameliorative," he said.

She sat back. "I don't even think I know what that means."

"I can stand the evidence of my own eyes, Helena. You might've noticed that I'm not shrinking from any of the realities."

"I'm lost. Would you like to catch me up on what this is you're telling me?"

"Those are vultures, all right? Not crows. Big, getting-ready-to-feast-on-dead-flesh vultures."

"Okay," she said crisply.

"Calling them crows won't change any of the facts."

"I thought they were crows," she said. "Jesus."

Next to the house there was a car he didn't recognize, parked beside his father's Ford and his brother-in-law's Trooper. "Somebody come here with Maizie and Leo? Who's this?"

She didn't answer.

"Now you're mad," he said. "We can't go in there mad at each other."

She said, "You mean we have to be ameliorative?"

"Okay," he said. "You want to be cute."

He turned the engine off and sat with his hands on the wheel, watching the shapes circle above the creek bed. She got out and started toward the house. The wind caught her blouse and made it flap at her middle like a flag. He waited a moment, then got out himself. "Hey," he said.

She stopped, turned into the wind to look at him.

"I'm sorry," he said. "I don't know what gets into me, Helena."

"We should go in," she said.

He walked up and peered in the window of the strange car. There were paperback books and fashion magazines on the back seat. It looked like a student's car. He left it and went on a little ways into the field. When he glanced back, he saw her standing at the edge of the asphalt.

"What're you going to do?" she said. "James, please."

His breath caught. The wind swirled at his back. Everything was vivid and, abruptly, quite terrible. Above him the birds wheeled and turned, dipped and seemed to ride suspended on invisible wires. One swooped low, no more than twenty yards from where he stood, the big wings beating the air heavily. He saw the ugly red wattle on the side of the head, and then it rose, heavy, veering off toward the creek bed.

"Come on, James. I'm getting chilly standing here."

"Be patient, can't you?"

"James, do you want to be alone a while? Is that it?"

He turned. The sun had come through an opening in the clouds, and there were two wide sections of the field now, one in shade, one in sun. She stood in sun. A young woman trying to understand and to do what was needed. She held her handbag with both nervous hands, and the sun made her squint so that her distress was exaggerated. But she looked very pretty standing there. His mind hurt, gazing at her. For no discernible reason, he remembered that people had told him she would be one of those women who got better-looking with the years, like his mother. At the funeral, people had talked of Andrea Brewer's vivaciousness and humor, her youthful appearance. Like Loretta Young, they'd said. The same definite features, the same lasting beauty. The same elegance, energy, and grace. A beautiful, vivacious, interested woman. And I can't imagine, they said. The phrase kept coming up. I can't imagine. Can't imagine. Nobody could imagine. It was all unthinkable, out of the pale of questions and answers.

He started toward his wife. "Vultures."

"Even if they were crows," she said, "it amounts to the same thing."

He had reached her, and he turned again to look at the black shapes circling. "Jesus, God. Look at them."

"You're turning everything under the same light," she told him. "Stop it."

He said, "Any other comments you want to make?"

She took his arm. "All right. But please."

"They're vultures," he said. "I could see their horrible little red wattles. I can't help what's true."

"Okay. I'm sorry I said anything. I swear, I can't say anything. What did I do, James? Will you please tell me what I did? I'd really like to know what it is that I did. I would like to know why I'm the one who takes your anger and sarcasm. Why is that? You never cut Maizie or Leo or your father or anyone else about it. Why is it me all the time?" She brought a handkerchief out of her handbag and dabbed at her eyes. "It hurts me, too, doesn't it? I loved your mother. Don't I have a right to feel it? I'm in this, too."

"Oh, look, don't cry," he said. "I'm sorry. Please—please stop."

"I'm trying," she sobbed.

"Honey," he said. "Here." He put his arms around her. "Come on. I'm sorry."

"It gets so I don't know which way to turn, which way you want me to turn. I didn't do anything. I see Maizie saying the same kind of things to you, and you don't snap at her. I don't understand."

He held her. The windows of the house reflected the folds of ashen cumulus in the moving sky. "We'd better go in," he said finally. The storm was rolling toward them, and the sun had dipped behind the biggest part of the cloudbank.

"I've streaked my mascara."

"No," he said. Then: "Here." He took the handkerchief and touched it to the corners of her eyes. "That's better," he said.

"I don't look like a raccoon?"

"You look beautiful," he said. And it was true.

Through the window of the front door, they could see his father sitting in the kitchen, beyond the far end of the hallway. On the table before him was a coffeepot and some cups.

Brewer opened the door and called, "Hey, Harry. You feel like company?" It was what he said every week.

His father nodded without speaking. Then Brewer saw that he was listening to someone else, and in that instant a dark-haired woman peered around the frame of the kitchen door. "Hello," she said. Brewer recognized her as one of the women his mother had been with the day she died. The woman's name was Pauline Brill.

"Hi," Helena said to her. The false cheer in her voice made Brewer ache, deep.

They entered the house and went along the shadowed hall. Brewer's father had put black cloth over the three large pictures here—they were all of Brewer's mother, in her days as a dancer and teacher of dance—and it was as though the cloth somehow took a degree of light out of the air. In the kitchen, the old man stood but remained where he was at the table, and in the brightness coming from the window, his face had a pallid look. Brewer walked in and took his hand.

"You're early," the old man said. Then he turned to Mrs. Brill. "You remember my son, his wife Helena."

Mrs. Brill offered her hand. Helena touched her fingers to the other woman's palm and then excused herself to go freshen up. Brewer thought of his mother working in her garden, the rough texture of the inside of her hands. This morning, getting ready to come here, Helena had sat on their bed painting her toenails, her hair bunched up in a towel, bath powder showing on her back and shoulders. For some reason, he had found it necessary to avert his eyes from her in this homey tableau, and now the image raked through his soul with the power of something taunting him.

"How was your week?" he managed to ask his father.

"It was okay. Maizie and Leo came by a few times. And Pauline here. Friday was bad."

"What happened Friday?"

"Nobody came by. It was murder. Murder."

Brewer glanced at Pauline Brill again. He couldn't help the feeling that she was here out of morbid curiosity, to look at the ones Andrea Brewer had decided to leave. "I go by here on my way to school." She smiled. "Today I was on my way back from church, and thought I'd stop in and see how he was doing. He wasn't in church."

"No," Harry said. "I didn't give it a thought on this particular morning."

"We're fine," Brewer said to Mrs. Brill.

"Yeah, well, you look sleepless," his father said to him.

Helena came back into the room, patting the sides of her head lightly. "This weather does it to my hair," she said.

"You look gorgeous," said the old man.

She kissed him on the cheek, patted his shoulder, and her eyes swam. Brewer thought of the mascara, without wanting to.

"I haven't done much around here, but I did box up some of your mother's things," Harry said. "You can look through them if you want, see if there's anything . . ." Then he seemed to drift, staring off. They watched him. "Forty-two years," he murmured with a disbelieving shake of his head.

Brewer said, "When did Maizie and Leo get here?"

The old man shrugged. "A few minutes ago. Sit down—you give me a crick in my neck."

Brewer and his wife sat down at the table. Pauline Brill remained standing. Outside, the storm clouds had blocked out much of the light. Everything was suffused in a silvery gray glow, like dusk.

"Anyway," the old man said, "I've been deciding maybe I won't mind leaving this place after all. It was your mother's, really." He shook his head.

James Brewer leaned toward him slightly, but could think of nothing to tell him.

"Are you sleeping any better?" Helena asked.

The old man looked at her. "I've been taking the pills they gave me—they knock me out. I sleep all right but it's not restful sleep. I feel like someone hit me over the head when I wake up."

There was a silence. Helena gave her husband a sorrowful look, which he could not bring himself to acknowledge. "Where's Maizie and Leo?" he asked.

"They're around somewhere. They went for a walk. Said they'd be back in a while."

"They're going to get caught in the rain," said Helena in a small voice.

Pauline Brill said, "I should be leaving. Just wanted to check on you, Harry."

"Pauline teaches school, too," Harry said to his son. He looked at Mrs. Brill. "James is a principal."

"Yes, I knew that."

They were all quiet a moment. Harry lifted his cup and drank from it. He swallowed loud, then cleared his throat. "My brain's like Swiss cheese. Can't remember from one damn day to the next. It's the drugs, I know. They eat away at your memory. I didn't even know it was Sunday today till Maizie and Leo showed up."

Brewer said, "Have you made any other preparations to leave? You said you'd call the moving companies and get estimates. And

Maizie said over the phone that Leo's got the guest room in their place all ready for you."

The old man shook his head. "They've got a baby coming. I'm still not sure I shouldn't've gone ahead with the apartment idea."

"Do you want us to call the movers for you?"

He glowered. "Don't talk to me like I'm a kid, James. I'm not some kid in that school you run. I forget things, but I'm not completely incompetent."

"We're just worried about you," Helena said, glancing at Mrs. Brill.

Harry cradled his cup of coffee with his two big hands. "You don't need to be worrying about me. There's nothing to worry about."

"Well, of course not," Helena said.

"Helena, please," Brewer said, then touched her wrist to reassure her. He turned to his father. "Maizie and Leo went out?"

"Went for a walk, I told you."

"Did they go down toward the creek?"

"They didn't say where they were going, and I didn't watch them."

"Stay here," Brewer said to his wife.

"Who're you ordering around," the old man said. "If I ordered your mother around like that, she'd have knocked my block off."

"What about the storm, James?" Helena said. "It's a lightning storm."

"I'll be right back."

"You can never tell them anything," said the old man. "That's what their mother used to say, too. The both of them. I told Maizie the same thing. You think she'd listen? They don't listen, and they never have, either one of them."

Brewer walked away from this, back down the hall and out into the leaf-, rain-, and ozone-smelling wind. Some of the vultures must have settled to the ground for their meal, because there were fewer of them in the sky. He started across the field, and as he neared the creek he heard his brother-in-law's voice: "Get away from here, you god-dam dreadful, ugly sons of bitches. You foul, coprophagous, carrion-eating grotesqueries!"

He saw Maizie first. She was standing, with her hands in the pock-ets of her slacks, on the near side of the creek. The gray light made her hair look darker. The roots were growing out of the blond dye she had used. "Hey," she said as he approached. Across the narrow creek and up toward the opposite field, Leo stood poised with a handful of stones. The big dark birds had risen at his shout, and had settled on the lowest branch of a bare tree perhaps fifty feet away.

"Bastards," Leo said. "Heartless unredeemable bags of death!"

"Leo," Maizie called, laughing with desperation. "They're just birds." She turned to Brewer. "Listen to him. Where does he get that stuff?"

"Scat!" Leo yelled.

Lying on the ground near him, its back hoofs badly twisted in the barbed wire, was a calf, eyes bulging, tongue protruding and swollen. The eyes were frantic; there was a sort of staid terror in them, and no animation at all.

It had been James Brewer who went to the motel room and, with the proprietor, opened the door upon the lifeless shape of his mother in the bed.

"I keep telling him," Maizie said. "It can't live. Its leg is broken. We worked like crazy trying to get it loose, but most of its strength is gone. It was past help when we got here, really. Even if we could cut the wire."

"Oh, Jesus Christ," said Brewer. "Let's go back to the house."

"Leo," Brewer's sister called to her husband, "there's nothing you can do."

"You go on," Leo said, without looking back. He was climbing the fence. "I'm going to chase them away. The least they can do is wait till it dies, for Jesus' sake."

"This is a lightning storm, Leo. Please."

"I can't just leave it here. Maybe the storm'll drive them away."

"You're supposed to be helping me with Dad."

"I'll be up in a minute, Maizie. I'll just take a minute."

Brewer walked with her up to the crest of the field. The wind was now coming at them in heavy gusts, and from here they could see Leo running across the neighboring field, waving his arms and shouting, his voice almost failing to reach them because of the wind.

"Mr. Quixote," Maizie said. "It's getting embarrassing."

"Was Pauline Brill around when you guys got here?" Brewer asked his sister.

She had been thinking of something, and for a moment she didn't answer. Then she turned to him and said, "What? Oh, she came in a little after we did."

They watched as Leo roused the birds from their branch. The vultures beat the air with their big wings and settled in another tree, and he was starting toward them. Beyond this, they could see the darkest part of the cloudbank moving across the open space surrounding the neighboring farmhouse.

"I found out something," Maizie said. "Pauline Brill let it slip."

Brewer waited.

"The day Mother—the day it—she—she haggled with a man over a damn soup tureen. The day it happened, James. They went back and forth about a soup tureen. She wanted to buy it and the guy wanted more than she was willing to pay, and she tried to talk him down. You know how she could be about those things. She tried to talk him down."

Brewer saw again the image of his mother lying in the motel bed. It was always waiting under the stream of his thoughts. In the movies, people walked into rooms and spoke to the dead, and minutes went by; they had to touch the bodies to make sure. It always took them a stupid amount of time to figure it out.

"Do you believe it?" Maizie said.

"Jesus Christ," he said. "I can't think about it anymore. It's killing me trying to think about it. I'm sick of everything."

She made a sound almost like a laugh. "I just wish I could make any sense of it. What in the name of God she was thinking of. How could she do it to us? How could she be so cold about it? Didn't we mean anything to her at all? Didn't this baby I'm carrying mean anything to her? How could she just lock herself away from us forever, without even a hint or a word to us about it? She must've known what it would do to us."

"I can't feel anything with Helena anymore." He hadn't known he would say this. Maizie regarded him, seemed to be waiting for him to go on. When he tried to speak, his voice broke. He took a breath, swallowed, not looking at her. "The whole thing's done something to me inside, Maizie. I keep hectoring her all the time and I can feel myself doing it and I can't make myself stop. She's trying to love me and make me feel better, and everything she says, everything she says just irritates me more. The sound of her voice—I feel crowded all the time, and when I look at her I see only a—a body. Meat."

Maizie took his arm. "What?"

"I can't explain it," Brewer said.

"Don't be so morbid. Try not to be morbid, that's all."

"I'm—I don't feel anything."

"That'll pass," Maizie said. "I've felt that way before."

"No," Brewer said, "it's not that. I do feel something. I feel like I can't stand to have her around me."

"I'm telling you it's been the same with me."

They were watching Leo walk across the far field.

"I know I love him," Maizie said, "but I can't talk to him about this. There's a man at work. A nice, quiet, dignified guy, not even very good-looking or flashy, you know, maybe forty-five. Funny and friendly and I—we got to be pretty close friends. I'd talk to him about Leo sometimes. And he'd tell me about his wife and his stepson. We were friendly and we made each other laugh. And not long ago there was a—this thing passed between us. We'd been such dear friends. And sometimes Leo's so—stiff and formal, like a kid trying to be grown-up. Everything is so self-improvement-oriented with him. Do you know he spends an hour every night with a thesaurus? And when he talks sometimes I can feel him bending the conversation around so he can say another one of his words. It irritates me sometimes, and sometimes it endears him to me in a funny kind of way. Because he wants to be better for me. He's really doing it for me."

James watched her comb through her hair with her long fingers. The wind blew, and lifted it, and she pushed it back again.

"Anyway, I got to where I was thinking about this nice man at work. Do you see?"

In the field, her husband threw a handful of stones at the lifting dark shapes of the vultures. He whooped and shouted, running at them.

"Nothing really happened," she went on. "But it could've been pretty serious. And for a while there when it was going on, whenever I was with Leo I felt—I was restless, and even a little bored. It was as if I didn't want him there, and I worried about whether or not I loved him anymore. And now Mother. I don't know. I've been talking to the guy, the one—I've been talking to him about it all. It's like there isn't anything I can say to Leo about Mother. Nothing Leo doesn't know. And he was always so gaga about all of us. You know how he's been. But I've felt the need to talk about it, and so I talk to this, this friend. It's all perfectly innocent, and I still feel guilty sometimes but I'm not letting that bother me. I'm doing what I need to do for myself right now, to get through, and I'm not worrying about why or wherefore because I know that's all just—this. You know? This by itself— Mother checking out on us. And with me five months pregnant. Just this and not anything else."

"I hate this dead feeling," Brewer said. "I feel dead."

"Maybe that's Mother's part in us. Did you ever think that? An element of her that made her do it is in us, too. And isn't that a sweet thought. Look, you just have to wait for it to pass, go about life a certain way until it passes, that's all. Wait it out and try to be as kind and gentle as possible until it goes away. And then you—you're sort of in the habit of being kind."

"And you feel that way with Leo now? I mean we always told each other everything, Maizie, and you can tell me, can't you? Do you feel like having Leo near you might drive you out of your mind?"

She shrugged. The wind lifted her hair again. The expression on her face was that of a person steeling herself against something. "At times. Haven't you been listening to me, James?"

"You feel it now?"

"Come on," she said. "You're fine."

"I'm afraid I'm losing my mind," he said.

Now she did give forth a bitter deprecating laugh. "That's apparently a thing we know for sure now. It runs in the family."

"I'm serious," Brewer said, wrapping his arms tight around himself.

"You're not losing your mind," said Maizie. "Look what we've been through. Look what *you've* been through."

"I don't know anything anymore," he said. "God. I love her. I mean I think I love her. But I keep seeing Mom in that awful little motel room, and then Helena talks to me and I can't stand the sound of her voice."

Leo had started back down to the creek. Behind him, the birds sat in their tree, all uncomprehending patience. To them, Leo was like the weather gathering and staggering toward them on the wind. He was something to be waited out. Down in the creek bottom, he bent over the trapped calf, and then he started up to where Maizie and her brother were. "I guess I look pretty silly," he said when he had reached them. He was a tall, nervous, sometimes awkwardly friendly man with a way of looking aside when he spoke, and an air of perpetual surprise about him. It was in his eyes, a way he had of staring with raised brows. As with most other people, Brewer liked him without being particularly able to describe his qualities. For the past two weeks or so Leo had been using most of his spare time to fix up a room for the old man in his and Maizie's house. He worked for the county government as an office manager, a job at which he excelled, but he knew carpentry and some masonry, having come from people who believed in the healthy practice of finding work to do with one's hands, no matter what one did to put food on the table. In fact, he knew enough and had the skills to build his own house, a thing he and Maizie were planning to do one day.

"I guess I didn't do much but make a lot of noise," he said now.

"A man railing against nature," Maizie said, and squeezed her brother's arm.

"Too much," said Leo, looking back toward the creek. "I hate the way the world works sometimes."

"Oh, shut up," Maizie said. "You're not helping anything." But she kissed him on the side of the face.

"Well, anyway, it's over. The heart's stopped finally."

"Oh, Christ," Maizie said. "Let's go inside." She took a step and seemed to falter.

"I'm sorry, honey."

She clung to him. Brewer stayed back and watched them as they walked toward the house, and then he followed. For a while they didn't speak. Brewer could feel the lining of his own stomach. Lightning flashed somewhere behind them, and Maizie said, "Good Lord," picking up the pace. They reached the driveway as the first drops of rain hit, and abruptly Brewer found that he couldn't go back inside, couldn't face the others yet. "You guys, tell Helena I'm going to sit the storm out here. I want to watch it here." He stepped to his car and opened the door. The rain was coming hard, and his sister had stopped to speak to him. "What're you going to do?" The rain pelted them. "Do you want me to stay with you?"

"Go ahead. I need a little time alone."

"Are you okay?"

The question seemed almost aggressively beside the point. He said, "Go ahead. I'm fine."

"Come on, you guys," Leo called. "It's lightning."

"You're not going anywhere, are you?" Maizie said.

And Brewer thought about how for the two of them it would always be like this. Some element of their being together would always contain a watchfulness.

"Maizie, I'm just going to sit here a while."

"Suit yourself," said his sister in the tone of someone choosing to dismiss her own doubts. She went on, and when her husband took her arm, the two of them hurried to the entrance of the house and in. He saw them go past Helena, whose gestures showed first puzzlement and then embarrassment. Helena stood in the doorway, looking out through the wind-driven rain. Brewer waved once, and after a moment she waved back. She was probably crying, worrying about him. He waved again, knowing this, and then she went back into the kitchen, where, he knew, she would try to put the best face on things, smiling and pretending that she wasn't suffering at his hands.

He simply needed the time to compose himself.

In the other direction, illuminated by a vein of lightning across the whole length of the sky, the ugly birds clung to their perch. He caught a glimpse of them, five black tears in the crooked branches. He was thinking about how they would soon enough be continuing with what they had begun down in the creek bed, because it was in their nature to do so and because choosing did not even enter into it and because they were always, always the same. Brewer watched them through the flashes of lightning. He shivered, holding his arms around himself, and the storm went on. He remembered his mother running across the lawn in a storm like this, with a winter coat held up over her head. She laughed and got in under the eaves of the porch, shaking the moisture from her hair and talking. That was not a woman who hated life. Brewer remembered that her hair made a damp place on the shoulders of the white blouse she wore, and oh, when was that? When was that? He could never have imagined it. And he could never believe or forgive it, either. The rain kept coming. The sky grew darker, but against the lightning the birds were still visible. The black hulking shapes sat unmoving in the branches of the tree.

PENANCE

PERHAPS IT WASN'T much of a puzzle after all, if you really thought about it, why a person decides that enough is enough in this life, and then acts on it. So Gehringer thought, pulling into his own driveway, home from another strained day at work, discouraged, tired, thinking about a stranger's suicide. Before him, his house shone in the afternoon sun; the sharp shade on the porch gave a luster to the white clapboards and the railing. He came to a slow stop and let the car idle a moment, gazing at the demarcations of shade and light. It was a pleasant, roomy old place, and he had always felt so much at home in it.

When his wife crossed the front window and glanced at him, he got out and made his way up the walk. Yesterday's storms had shaken some of the branches out of the trees and caused the creek to overflow, and now the fields beyond the lawn looked badly rumpled and unkempt. The grass stood up, showing the dark mud beneath. In one corner of the near pasture, in the shade of the big oak tree there, three cows stood chewing, staring at him. The sky was clear blue, and a crisp, cool breeze blew. It was all only itself. All futile, somehow.

And here he was, with these uncharacteristic thoughts. One person's refusal to go on living made others turn and look at their own lives.

He believed he understood it.

Everything in the house was discouragingly spotless. Abigail had spent another day going over the place, top to bottom, like someone trying to eradicate the vestiges of illness. Making his way through the polished, shining family room to the kitchen, he found her down on her knees, scrubbing the baseboards. "I'm home," he said, trying to take a normal tone.

She said, "I saw you pull in."

He put the car keys in their place on the hook above the sink. "The field looks like a hurricane went through." He watched her work. "Didn't you do that on Friday?"

She said, "Jason's flunking math, too, now."

He moved to the kitchen window and looked out. His stepson was shooting baskets. The ball swished through the net and dropped into a puddle of rainwater at the base of the pole. Jason picked the ball up, holding it away from himself, and dried it off with a terry cloth towel.

"Did you hear what I said?" she asked.

"I was wondering if you heard what *I* said."

"I heard you, Marty. This needs doing."

"No it doesn't," he said. "No it doesn't."

She worked on.

"Isn't math Jason's favorite subject?"

"If you were more involved, you'd know it was."

"I think I did know, Gail. I said, 'Isn't math his favorite subject?' I knew, see. And so I asked. The question was reflexive."

She said, "Math was his favorite subject."

He watched her moving along the floor, concentrating on the work. It was unnerving. "Can I help?" he said.

She didn't answer.

"I'll spell you, if you want," he said. "We could take turns. We'll eat off the floor when we finish, to celebrate having a house cleaner than a hospital. What do you say?"

"Cute."

He paused, thinking she might say more. There was the sound of the ball hitting the rim outside. "Well, what should we do? You want me to talk to him?"

"We can't do anything yet about the math," she said. "His teacher sent home a note that he'd be putting together a list of tutors for us to go through. I've set up a conference with Mrs. Brill about the English grade. We were supposed to have one with her a while back, you might remember, and it didn't work out. I want you to come with me."

He chose to ignore her tone. "Have you talked to Jason about it?"

"Yes."

"What's he say?"

"He says she has something against him."

"You believe that?"

His wife looked up at him, then went back to her scrubbing.

"Well, kids have been known to bend the truth about these things, Gail."

"Just come with me and we'll find out."

"I'd be glad to," he said. "When is it?"

"We have to leave in half an hour." She kept on working, moving along the kitchen floor.

"Gail," he said.

"What."

"Shouldn't you start getting ready?"

"I am. Just a minute."

"Everything's so clean," he said.

She said nothing.

"We ought to have people over so they can see it. Remember Celie—what the hell was her last name?—the one who was always redoing her walls. You used to make fun of her."

"I don't remember making fun of her."

"Oh, yes. You were wicked about it."

"I'm almost finished here," she said. "Are you ready to go?"

"I was asking you about Celie. Was her name Celie?"

"Yes."

"Wonder whatever happened to her. You used to have such a lot of fun laughing at how she was about her house."

"What are you telling me, Marty?"

"You don't really need it spelled out, do you?" he said.

"Look, are you coming with me or not?"

"I said I was. You're the one who needs to get ready to go."

"Won't take me a second," she said.

Outside, Jason bounced the basketball, playing an imaginary game. Gehringer saw the look of excitement and seriousness in the boy's face.

"I told him not to get dirty," Abigail said.

"He's just shooting baskets," said Gehringer.

She went on working.

"Gail," he said.

"What."

"Honey, look at me."

She did so. There was a kind of tolerance in her face.

"Nothing happened, understand? Nothing's changed. I know I keep saying that. But there's nothing going on at all."

"I don't want to think about it now," she said.

He let another moment pass. Then he went to the sink and got a dishcloth and began wiping the spotless counter. "Isn't this nice? We're cleaning together."

"I don't need your sarcasm, either," she said.

"I'm not being sarcastic. I'm saying isn't it nice, we're cleaning together, and in a little while we'll go to Jason's school together and we'll be just like a family."

"You don't have to go hold Maizie Brewer's hand?"

"Well, I thought you might not get around to saying it. And it's not Brewer. She's married, Gail. Remember? She's expecting a baby."

"Does she know whose?"

"That is a completely shitty thing to say. That's not fair, and you know it."

"I haven't had a lot of time to think about being fair, wouldn't you agree?"

"Nothing ever happened. Can you understand that nothing happened? And I swear to Christ you take us farther away from each other every day."

She went on scrubbing the baseboard.

"Stop that and listen to me."

She straightened. "You're spending time with her again when you said you'd avoid her."

"Nothing happened the first time and nothing's happening now. But I work with her, and she's going through some hell right now over the death of her mother. It's only the simple concern of a friend."

"And there's no one else she can turn to?"

The look of pain in his wife's face hurt him. "Everybody else turns to *her*. Please, honey. Don't do this. I'm telling you there's nothing going on."

She went back to her work. "I'm almost through," she said. "I won't take long."

"Gail," he said. "Really."

"These explanations," she said. "They hurt me. I don't want to hear anymore."

"No," he said. "I know. But honey, nothing's changed. Nothing ever changed."

"Please," she said.

"For Christ's sake," Gehringer told her. "You're doing this to yourself."

She shook her head.

"I have been a faithful husband," he said. "I may not have been as attentive as I ought to be, but I have been faithful."

"Will you please let me finish this?" she said.

He went upstairs to the master bedroom and got out of his suit. Then, thinking about the conference, he put it back on. The bed was made, the floor had been scrubbed and waxed, the furniture dusted and polished. The odor of the polish stung his nostrils and made him aware of his bronchial tubes. There wasn't a place to sit down and be comfortable, and anyway, he was still wearing the suit. Then it occurred to him that he might change suits. This one was rumpled from the day's work. He opened the closet door and chose a blue one, and another tie. He would keep the same shirt. As he was putting on the pants, his wife entered the room and took off her jeans and blouse. He said, "Is this okay?"

She looked at him. "Fine."

"As I recall, back in the early Pleistocene period when you were still happy with me, you liked me in this one."

"You look good in it," she said simply.

He smiled. "Thanks."

She went into the bathroom and closed the door. The shower ran. He finished dressing, then went downstairs, where he found his stepson making a peanut butter sandwich. The boy looked guilty for a second, then seemed to recover himself.

"Hey," Gehringer said.

Jason only smirked. His mother had said nothing to him, and yet he seemed to know there was trouble between his parents, and he was behaving rather badly about it.

"What's the story with math?"

He shrugged. "I don't know. I have to make up some tests."

"Tell me what Mrs. Brill has against you in English."

"If I knew that, I could handle it myself," the boy said.

"Well, how does she show it?"

Again, he shrugged. "I don't know."

"Oh, come on," Gehringer said. "There must be something."

"I don't know."

"Well, son, you can't make an accusation and then just let it stand without anything to back it up. What is it that she does that tells you she has something against you?"

"I don't *know*," Jason said. He seemed irritated.

Gehringer walked away from him into the living room, with its freshly laundered curtains and its ironed and starched doilies, its look of a place waiting for close inspection, a display rather than a room where people might be comfortable. There were newly cut rose blossoms in a glass vase in the middle of the coffee table, and the fireplace looked as though it hadn't ever been used. Sun poured in the windows onto the oriental rug. He sat on the couch and then, worried about wrinkling the suit, stood again.

"She makes me wait to go to the lavatory," Jason said from the entrance to the room.

Gehringer stared at him.

"She knows I have to go, and she makes me wait."

"Anything else?"

"There's other things," the boy said.

"Well, like what?"

"I don't know."

"You ever hear of the Salem witch trials?" Gehringer asked.

"No."

"Interesting situation. They hanged some people as witches. And a lot of it was just these—these kids making loose accusations. Standing around saying things. Without anything to back it up."

"I guess they listened to them back then."

"Oh, yeah—they hanged several innocent people as witches," Gehringer said through his teeth.

"Well," the boy said, "I'm not making loose accusations."

"I didn't say you were, particularly, did I?"

"I'm not stupid," the boy said with certainty, moving out of the doorway. Apparently he felt vindicated, and believed the conversation had been a success.

Gehringer let him go. There was no use pursuing a discussion with him in his victorious mood. He heard the front door open and close, and then the house was quiet. Stepping to the window again, he looked out at what he could see of the mountains and the surrounding fields. Part of the highway was visible through a cut in the trees at the end of the property. Over there was town, the Mountain Lodge Motel. A woman who could so systematically do away with herself had to be thinking about it for a long, long time.

HE AND MAIZIE HAD been friends at work, allies. They had laughed together about the foibles and vanities of others in the office, and they had enjoyed the times when work brought them into proximity with each other. Somehow the laughs had led to a feeling of heightened expectation. Without having to decide upon it or think about it, they had entered a zone of mutual concern that made for exchanged glances and a thrill whenever she spoke his name. Or he said hers: Maizie. Maizie. The whole thing was absurd, of course, since she was devoted to her husband, and since she also happened to be fifteen years younger than Gehringer. But the result of the few moments of awkwardness between them had been a strange unease, a nervousness, almost as though lines *had* been crossed.

Abigail, coming to pick him up one afternoon, noticed the difference.

Understandably enough, given her nature, she assumed the worst. And for all his efforts to explain the whole thing away, in her mind something had been acceded to in his heart. Abigail had once described herself as the sort of person who found it difficult to believe anyone could remain interested in her. Her confidence was too easily undermined. In consequence of this, he had sworn that he would have nothing else to do with Maizie, and he had been trying to make his way back from it when Maizie's mother committed suicide. And if he was certain that it was only the solace of an old friend that Maizie sought now, the new situation was still quite confusing and worrisome: for she was indeed beautiful in her grief, and Abigail grew daily more difficult to live with, clenched as she was on the suspicions she still held about him.

Each day felt more discouraging than the last. Abigail's face had taken on a new harsh, pinched look—the look of bitter religious anger. There had been times over the last few days when he couldn't bear to look at her.

"READY?" SHE SAID FROM the kitchen. Her heels sounded on the tile floor. He went through the hall to the front entrance and she started toward him, pausing to put an earring on.

"You look nice," he said.

She frowned.

"You do," he told her, resisting the urge to look away.

"I don't feel nice."

"Isn't Jason coming?"

"He's waiting outside."

"I asked him about it," Gehringer said. "He's pretty vague."

She went past him, out onto the porch. Jason had started the car and was sitting in the middle of the front seat.

"Maybe we ought not to go into this with an attitude," Gehringer said.

"Nobody has an attitude."

"It's just possible that this teacher is right, you know. She doesn't have anything to gain from lying about it, and Jason does."

They had come to the edge of the porch. Gehringer was troubled to find that his wife was trying to hold back tears. "Are you going to take this tack when we get there?" she said.

"Well, good God," he said. "What tack are *you* going to take? Don't you think we ought to go into this without having our minds made up? For Jason's sake."

"I'm going to try and do what is best for my son. And that means I'm going to try trusting him."

"Just blindly?" Gehringer said. "No matter what you learn about it or what anyone says?"

She stared at him. Her expression was almost satisfied.

"No," he said. "I'm not accepting that look, either. Don't give me that look. I have not violated your trust. In no way have I violated your trust."

"This is not the place to discuss it," she said, going on.

"Jesus Christ," said Gehringer. "Unbelievable."

She stopped. "Are you finished?" Again, she seemed near crying.

"Do you know how ridiculous all this is?" he said. "I love you."

"You use that like a club," she told him. "It's a weapon when you say it."

"Just trying to be heard above the roar of condemnations," he said. "Christ."

She went on to the car, and she was irritable with Jason, telling him to quit sitting there staring and to get himself in the back seat and buckled.

* * *

THE HIGH SCHOOL WAS built out of the side of a hill, surrounded by fields of grass and dark wooden fences. A stream ran along the front—clear water running over stones—and you crossed a small walking bridge to get to the entrance. Basketball courts flanked the building, and beyond these, the metal bleachers of the football field reflected the sun. Jason led the way inside and along the hallway to his English classroom. Mrs. Brill was not there. He sat at one of the desks in the front of the room, and his parents stood by the door. They had not exchanged a word since driving away from the house.

"What do we do now?" Jason said.

"Be quiet," said his mother.

"Well, she said she'd be here."

The three of them waited. From somewhere else in the building, the sound of a brass band came to them. It seemed to originate in the walls.

"Straighten your tie," Gehringer's wife said.

Gehringer walked to the window and did so, peering at the faint reflection of himself. Then he turned and faced her. After a moment, he said, "Maybe we got the wrong day."

"It's today."

Perhaps ten minutes went by. Gehringer watched school buses roll out of the lot across the way, and there were boys in the farm field on the other side of the highway, playing a game of touch football. He watched and grew interested. Then, remembering himself, he turned from the window. No one spoke. Jason leaned back in his seat, biting the cuticles of his fingers, his feet stretched out into the middle of the aisle. Abigail stood just inside the door, like someone afraid to be thought snooping. She looked tired and beset. Gehringer took his eyes from her.

And now the music in the walls gave way to something else: an agitation, a shuffling mixed with female laughter. The music started again, seemed to punctuate the laughter, which was coming closer. Gehringer's wife turned to face the door as a young woman appeared there, a dark-haired girl of heart-stopping beauty, bracing herself in the door frame. She'd been running and had just been caught. She looked at Gehringer, at Jason. "Oh," she said, laughing. A young man was behind her, and his hands were around her middle. Gehringer saw that their eyes shone with an unnatural light.

"Come on," the young man said. Then, peering in at Gehringer, "Oh, forgive me, folks. We were just leaving."

"Stop it, Ridley. This is the room."

"But there's nobody here—she's not here. Come on. Let's go find her."

"Ridley." She held on to the frame of the door, looking behind her at the young man, then she wrenched free and stood unsteadily in the doorway, her hands going through her astonishingly soft hair. With forced dignity, she said to Gehringer, "Excuse me, I'm looking for Mrs. Brill."

"Nobody here," the young man was saying. "Anybody can see that."

"My mother-figure," the young woman said. She laughed, turning. "Well, I guess I can't introduce you, Ridley."

"Come on," he was saying. "Please. Les' go the office. Huh?"

"Shhhh," she said, laughing again. "Drunk in the middle the afternoon."

They went out into the hallway, and for a few minutes their voices carried back into the room. "Should've known not to bring you here—"

"I do have hon'rable intentions—"

"—won't want to see me for that matter—"

"—marry you and—"

"—won't like you anyway—"

"You unnerstan'? I'm in love—all truthful hon'rable up an' up."

When it was quiet again, with only the faint sound of the brass band in some far room, Gehringer said, "Poor Mrs. Brill."

His wife went to the doorway and looked up and down the hall. "Gone," she said.

They waited.

Finally Gehringer said, "I don't think Mrs. Brill is coming."

"Maybe she forgot," said Jason.

Again, they were quiet. The sound of the band stopped. Gehringer stood at the window and watched the slow progress of the light trailing toward the horizon. The undersides of clouds looked like guttering coals. It came to him that these two people waiting here with him were the ones he had sworn his life to, and that in the moments they had all stood under the baldly sardonic leer of the beautiful drunken girl he had felt this acutely, like a jagged pain in his abdomen. He turned and looked at them—Abigail with her frown of concern and her nervous hands, folding and unfolding a handkerchief, and Jason staring at his own knotted fingers on the desk. Abruptly he wanted to reassure them. "Let's go somewhere tonight," he said.

They looked at him blankly.

"No matter what happens," he said, meaning it with all his heart. "Just us."

"If you want to," his wife said.

"Sure," said Jason in a tone that barely missed sullenness.

"It's settled, then," Gehringer said, understanding that nothing had been settled at all, but that he could muster the patience to wait for it. "I'm glad you asked me to come along to this conference."

"Well, how could I know she wouldn't show up," Abigail said.

"No," he told her. "I *am* glad."

"The woman sets a time and says she'll be here and then doesn't show up."

"I said I meant it, Gail. I am glad."

"Well, I don't see why."

Now he was rankled. He paced across the room to look at some pictures along the back wall—eighteenth-century men, poets and novelists. Pope, was it? Swift. The names went through his mind, and he wondered if they belonged to the staid, staring faces. Behind him, Jason stirred, and then there were heels clicking on the hard floors of the hall. Gehringer turned in time to see Mrs. Brill enter the room and hurry to her desk, apologizing for the delay, talking about a meeting she hadn't been able to avoid.

"People have schedules," Abigail said.

"Yes, I am sorry."

Gehringer moved to stand with them. Mrs. Brill offered them desks, and in a moment they were seated before her like students. "Now," she said, rifling through pages on her desk. "Jason, Jason. Here we are."

"Do you want Jason here for this?" Abigail asked.

The other woman hesitated. "Yes, I think that's fine."

"I mean, if there's something you think we should hear, alone," Abigail said.

"Well, Jason knows he's not doing well," said Mrs. Brill.

Gehringer spoke up. "Jason says you don't like him personally."

Mrs. Brill stared at him. "He does?"

"That's what he says. He says you make him wait to go to the bathroom."

Now she looked at Jason. "And how is it that I do that?"

"He says you know he has to go, and you make him wait."

"I see. And how do I know he has to go?" Mrs. Brill rested her left elbow on the desk and put her chin on the folded fist of that hand.

"Jason?" Gehringer said.

Jason shrugged.

"Son?"

"My son doesn't feel comfortable in the class," Abigail said. "I think that's the point."

"No one feels comfortable in the class," said Mrs. Brill, "because Jason keeps trying to disrupt it."

"Now wait a minute," Abigail said.

"Listen to her side of it," Gehringer said to his wife.

"You can just stay out of it," said Abigail.

"Let's all please calm down," Mrs. Brill said.

Jason sat staring at his hands.

"Would you like to say something, Jason?" said Mrs. Brill.

"Jason?" Abigail said.

Gehringer stood. "I think we're wasting time here. It's obvious, Mrs. Brill, that you're not ready to deal with my wife, who's been inclined to jump to conclusions—"

"I beg your pardon," said Mrs. Brill, having apparently jumped to some conclusions of her own. "I have been under some strain lately, yes. But I'm fully ready to talk about Jason."

Abigail stood. "Come on, Jason."

"Well," Gehringer said to Mrs. Brill, "you see? They just won't listen." He could hear the anger rising in his voice, moving in his chest. "They take it into themselves and decide, and that's the end of that."

"Mr. Gehringer, I have documentation," Mrs. Brill said. "Please sit down and we'll discuss this calmly. Mrs. Gehringer, will you please come back and sit down."

Abigail had moved to the door.

"Can we please discuss this in an adult fashion," Mrs. Brill said.

"You don't understand," Gehringer shouted. "I'm agreeing with you. I'm telling you, you can't win. No matter what you say, no matter what you do, you can't win. They've stacked the cards on you, and that's the end of that."

Now they were all staring at him. Abigail held a handkerchief to her face. Jason had come to his feet.

"Perhaps if you would all like to be alone for a few minutes," Mrs. Brill said, rising.

"No," Abigail said, moving to her chair again.

"Aw, Christ," Gehringer said. "I didn't mean for this—look. I'm sorry."

"Please tell me what my boy has done to disrupt your class."

Mrs. Brill cleared her throat, eyeing Gehringer. "Actually, I thought I'd have Jason tell you himself."

Abigail had begun to cry. She wiped her eyes with the handkerchief. Gehringer sat down, turned so that he could look from Jason to Mrs. Brill and back again.

"I'll pay attention better," Jason said, watching his own nervous fingers. "And I won't talk out of turn."

Mrs. Brill nodded, and she made a notation with her pencil on Jason's folder.

"There have been some tensions at home," Abigail said, sniffling.

"I understand," said Mrs. Brill.

Gehringer knew he was the subject of this exchange. "If I'm not needed anymore," he said, "I'll wait outside."

Mrs. Brill was writing on the folder, and Abigail was watching her.

"If you'll excuse me."

"Of course," Mrs. Brill said.

He went into the hallway and down to the end of it, where the doors were, and the brilliant late-afternoon sun. Out in the parking lot, the drunken young woman lay across the shining hood of a red sports car, one leg up, showing thigh. She held some tiny object close to her face, as if to examine it for flaws, and on the curb across from her the young man sat, his arms resting on his knees. Apparently there were no flaws in the little object; whatever she held was just the thing. It was in the way she reached over and offered it to the young man, who looked at it with clear satisfaction, admiring it. Then he put it in his mouth and smiled at her. They were perfect, Gehringer thought, their belief in perfection was all over them. They were without a care in the whole wide world.

DESIRE

"THINGS ARE WORSENING by the minute," Ridley says, meaning his own climbing panic, but knowing they'll think he means the culture—the failures of education and the depredations of the politicians, the general mess all around, the sense that nothing counts for anything anymore, the powerless, disenfranchised feeling of the whole population. This is, after all, what they have been talking about. It is always the major subject of discussion whenever he spends time with the Masons, the old couple who live downstairs, his land-lords. And he owes them two months back rent that so far nobody has mentioned. "A whole system of beliefs is disintegrating," he says, try-ing to keep them in focus. He wonders if his eyes are showing any signs of what he has ingested. He knows he's likely to talk a little faster, a little louder, and so he tries to keep it slow and as precise as possible. The Masons have been kindly, and they do not deserve this, any more than they deserve to go two months without rent. They have made meals for him. They've befriended him, and he knows they're wondering about the money he owes them.

"The history of everything," Mr. Mason says, "is a path down-ward. The study of all history is really the study of decline. And this is the decline of the West. Don't you think?"

"People get old and pass on, and so do cultures," says Mrs. Ma-son. "I think each individual life mirrors the life of a civilization, in a way. It's the natural course."

"Or perhaps it's the other way around, dear," Mr. Mason says. Then he hesitates, like someone leading a student through a lesson. "The civilization mirrors the life of the individual." He nods at her. "Don't you agree?"

"Well," says his wife, "perhaps. I think I meant it as I said it, though."

The two of them read a lot, and they like to talk about it all. It's a way of keeping up, as Mr. Mason once put it, a way of keeping men-tally fit. But they are drawn to the most negative prognosticators and philosophers. It's amazing. They've been married about sixty years, and cling to each other now, like children in a storm. Ridley thinks of them holding on in the winds of what they have been reading. There's plenty for them to worry about right here. Their savings are dwin-dling. The taxes on this small two-story house, which was paid for more than a decade ago, are more than three times what their mort-gage payment was. They rented the upstairs room to Ridley because they needed the extra money. But Ridley lost his job and got involved with Pamela Brill, and what money he had managed to save started going toward trying to keep up with her. Pamela is twenty-three, and because she's never been without money, she never thinks about it—often forgets to carry any. She lets others spend it, quite unselfconsciously.

Ridley's hopelessly in love with her.

"So," Mr. Mason says, putting his hands on his bony knees. "We're happy you came to see us. Is there anything we can do for you?"

Ridley can't remember why he's come down here. He says, "Just, ah, wanted to say hello."

"Nothing else?"

"Can't think," he says. "My brain, it's a sieve."

"Our young man is a little out of sorts," Mrs. Mason says.

"You've both been so nice to me," Ridley says.

"Would you like something to eat?" Mr. Mason asks him. "I think we can rustle up something."

"I'll help you, dear."

It's obvious that they want to go off and talk about him. He searches his mind for the reason he walked down here. He runs through it all—remembers making his unsteady way down the stairs at the side of the house, knocking on their door, looking at the sky gathering heavy clouds over the mountains, another storm system on its way, rolling over the hills. Remembers standing there on the porch waiting for them to answer, and feeling immediately the sense of guilt for what he owes them. The talk. The genuinely convivial company they make, always so eager to engage him in conversation. And they're really very interesting people.

He listens to them moving around in their kitchen. They murmur, but he can hear them. He thinks he can hear the little fibers moving in their throats; he's attuned to everything. They're not talking about him, after all. They're preparing sandwiches, cutting slices of Swiss cheese, opening jars. "Fetch me that, will you, dear?" says Mr. Mason.

"Yes, dear."

"Do we have any horseradish?"

"Should."

"Do you know where I put it?"

"Can't say I do," Mrs. Mason says.

"Why don't you pay more attention to where I leave things when I forget to put them away?"

"Guess I'm just falling down on the job."

"Now I can't find the mayo."

"It's on the bottom shelf."

"No it isn't."

"Then I don't know where it is."

EARLIER, OUTSIDE THE high school where her stepmother teaches English, Pamela Brill had offered him some small red pills in a vial. They'd already had some whiskey to drink. "Know what these are?" she said, licking the edges of her lips.

"Pills?" He hadn't meant it to sound like a question. His embarrassment was extreme. It was way out of proportion. He forced a smile and tried to seem casual. He cleared his throat and said the word again, hoping the smile was sardonic. "Pills."

She lay across the hood of her Mazda. All languid grace, and that amazing skin. They were out in the sunlight, in the school parking lot. In front of the whole world. He was half drunk. He would never do anything like this sober.

"Okay," she said with a smirk. "But guess what kind of pill."

"I don't know," he said. "A non-pharmacy kind."

She offered it to him. "Very good guess."

He was horrified. "Really?" he said.

"It makes America beautiful."

"You're beautiful," he said.

"Oh, shut up. I hate that shit. Stop it. Come on, you know what I mean. It makes everything gorgeous."

"Well," he said, "I think that depends, doesn't it?"

She seemed perplexed, considered this a moment with her astoundingly perfect features scrunched up. She was a person who could get a man to commit murder. "Do you mean like, they say an unhappy person doesn't have a positive near-death experience?"

"Who says that?" Ridley asked.

"Like if your attitude is wrong when it happens, you know, they say you suffer the pangs of hell."

"Not me," he said. "I don't believe in hell." He thought he could remember her saying that at some point.

"Is your attitude wrong, Ridley?"

"My attitude's right. I said I don't believe in hell."

"That's nice," she said.

"You don't, either," he said. "Right?" He tried to smile.

"I've never given it much thought." Again, she considered. He wanted to kiss the corner of her lips, and thought of touching her hair. Just touching it. It looked like it might burn your hand.

"Where'd you get this stuff?" he asked.

"Never mind. Let's try some. Want to?"

"I'm a bit drunk," he managed.

"You look a little pale."

"No," he said.

"That's what I like about you." She laughed. "You're such a nervous cat."

"I only seem nervous," he said, swallowing suddenly.

"You get so formal with me. It's nice," she said. "Here." She handed him the pill.

"Thank you," he said, resisting, just in time, the urge to bow. He hadn't slept well in weeks. He hadn't been able to rest at all.

"Ready?" she said. Then she swallowed hers. "Now you."

"Don't have anything to drink with it," he said.

"It's small. Melts in your mouth."

"Okay," he said.

She was right. It went down to nothing almost as fast as it touched his tongue. And then he was waiting for it to do whatever it would do. At first there wasn't much sensation at all. But then he began to wonder if things weren't changing for him in a big way. He decided that he was becoming extremely aware of time. It seemed that time broke down into slow, discrete seconds which stretched themselves out. She had stepped down off the car and was talking about driving away. He wanted to drive, and she said she wanted to ride in back with her legs over the seat. They got themselves into the front, and he saw that someone was standing in the doorway of the school. They had been seen.

"Someone saw us," he said.

She didn't answer.

"Pamela?"

"I guess we'll go to jail, then. Have you ever been to jail, Ridley?"

"Of course not."

"I spent a night in jail when I was away at school. Drunk and disorderly. I was close to death."

He drove carefully to the Masons' old house. Home. The idea that he lived there seemed too strange for words. "Jeez," he said.

They sat there breathing.

"I think we should do some more," she said. "I've got it—let's swallow some of it with orange juice. That'll be like in the best tradition. Do you have any orange juice?"

"Orange juice."

"Right. You know, the orange stuff in the little frozen cans."

"No," he said. "Orange juice hurts my stomach."

"Poor baby. What do you have to drink?"

"I can get some orange juice," he said.

"What else do you have?"

"Beer?"

"Ugh," she said.

"I've got V8 juice."

She looked at him. "Why?"

He had been using it to make up for the fact that he never ate any vegetables, and for the one gram of fiber in it. Ridley's main concern, when he wasn't thinking about Pamela Brill, was his digestive system and his health generally. This was not something he felt he could tell her, so he said nothing at all.

"Well?" she said. It was a challenge.

"I like it," he told her. "I make—I make Bloody Marys with it."

"Oh, okay. There you go, Bloody Marys. Let's have that."

They made their way inside. She was actually coming into his apartment. He stood in the doorway and thought about how it would look to her. He had become almost fastidious, living alone. As usual, he had made the bed this morning and hung up his bathrobe; his slippers were next to each other under the bed.

"It's so neat," she said, sounding disappointed. "I'm such a slob."

"Lady downstairs," he told her. "Real philosopher type. She cleans it. Comes in every day no matter what. I'm a slob, too, usually."

"I keep myself clean, though," she said.

"No," he said. "Right. Me too. It's best to stay clean if you can help it."

"I don't mean I'm anal or anything. You know, I don't mind a little dust. That's just living in a place. But mold and mildew and things like that. Things that grow. I'm pretty careful about it." She exhaled a satisfied sigh. "So the lady who cleans for you is a philosopher."

"Not officially," he said. "She does a lot of reading."

"That makes two of us. Except that nothing I've read has anything in it really about how I'm supposed to get through the days."

"Sure it does," Ridley said.

"I finished college, Ridley. I learned how to look at stuff, you know, and identify it. I learned the names of some places and some people and some wars. But nothing I read in the whole four years told me anything about how to get from one day to the next. Not really."

He searched his mind for some response. "That's not quite what it's ever supposed to do, is it?" he said.

"Then what good is it?"

"I think it's just supposed to be itself."

But she was on to something else, looking around the room. "Where's our Bloody Marys, anyway?"

He was fairly sure he didn't have the makings for Bloody Marys, since he wasn't sure what went into them in the first place. He had no gin or vodka. "I don't really feel like a Bloody Mary," he said.

She sat on the edge of his bed and leaned back on her hands. "I've never had one."

"It's a nighttime drink," he said.

Frowning, she said, "I thought it was morning."

"It's not a lunch drink."

"Brunch. And I haven't eaten."

"Oh," Ridley said. "I never have a Bloody Mary for lunch. I'm already crocked."

"Actually," Pamela Brill said, "I need a pick-me-up. That's what a Bloody Mary is, isn't it? A pick-me-up."

"No," said Ridley, "not for me. I take one, you know, before I go to sleep. Like a sleeping pill. I go right out. Bango."

She sat forward. "Don't mention that to me. Sleeping pills. Don't say that."

"I'm sorry." He didn't know why he was apologizing.

"Sleeping pills. God. This friend of my stepmother's—didn't you see it in the paper? And my stepmother was with her, too—had lunch with her—the day she did it."

Ridley watched her run her hands through her hair. Every cell of her was absolutely perfect. His chest hurt. He couldn't exhale all the way.

"You didn't read about it?" she said.

"I don't think so."

"This friend of my stepmother's. Went antiques shopping with my stepmother and another woman, then drove to a motel and swallowed a bottle of sleeping pills and went to sleep for good." She lay back. "It must be terrible to be old."

He moved to the bed and sat down at her hips. She was inches away. "Pamela," he said. "I love you. I want to marry you."

"Imagine checking into a motel room knowing it's where you're going to *die*."

"Maybe it was an impulse," he said. He was looking at the fine down on her legs, the smooth thighs, the way her shorts bunched up at the top of them and revealed the tan line. Oh God, he thought. Or perhaps he had spoken this.

"What," she said.

He *had* spoken. "Nothing."

"It makes you think, doesn't it?"

"What," he said.

"Dying like that. All alone in a cheap motel. My mother thinks she did it because she was having to give up her nice farm and everything."

"She didn't leave a note?"

"Nothing. Not a single thing. Isn't that eerie?"

He touched her knee.

"Don't."

He took his hand away as though it had been bitten.

A moment later, she said, "Do you ever think of suicide, Ridley?"

Oh, yes.

"Well, do you?"

"I have," he said.

She sat forward, so that they were side by side. "Me too."

"You?" he said.

She nodded simply. "Sure."

"Recently?" he said.

"I guess."

"Why?"

"I don't know. I think it's a kind of sickness with me. Sometimes I just don't want to be bored anymore, and I think of doing it. I actually think of it like it might be something to do. It's that sick. I've been unhappy, too. It's kind of scary that it's there, like a place you go to. Suicide. It's like there are times when I think it's waiting for me. Like I'm this little animal and everything's going extinct."

"If I was you," he said, "I wouldn't be unhappy. Ever."

"Oh, really?" Her smile was beautifully sardonic.

He was thinking of saying that if he had the luxury of living in that body, he would spend all his time in bed with someone. But then the someone he saw her in bed with, in this version of his imagined self, was her. She stared at him, and it was as though she were reading his thoughts.

"You know how to say 'Kiss my ass' in Spanish?" she said.

He shook his head.

"Hey, seenyore, come and keess my asss."

"Oh," he said, laughing. "Oh, right—I get it."

"Hey, seenyore," she said. "Come and keess my asss."

"That's good," he said.

"So, are you going to fix us these Bloody Marys?"

"I've got whiskey," he said.

"Okay." She shrugged. "Whiskey."

Neither of them moved.

"Well?" she said.

He leaned toward her, and she kept her eyes on him, watching him. He put his mouth on hers, seeing her eyes still open. He pulled back.

"What," she said.

He tried again. Her tongue was heavy; it moved with a languid, harrowing softness in his mouth. He felt his heart beating at the top of his head. His hands were on her arms, pushing her back onto the bed.

"Hey," she said, turning her head away. "Wait a minute, lover."

He could feel his weight on her.

"Get up, will you?"

"Jesus," Ridley said. "Oh, man." He got to his feet. She propped herself on one elbow and regarded him. "I'm sorry," he said.

"Hey, seenyore," she said. "You just want to keess my asss."

For a moment, he could say or do nothing at all.

She reached into the pocket of her shorts and brought out the vial of pills. "Let's ride on a cloud when we do it. I'm not high enough."

"I'll get the whiskey," he said, out of breath. In the small cabinet over the refrigerator was a flask of Old Grand Dad. He brought it down, his hands trembling. The neck of the flask ticked against the lip of his glass. He spilled some.

"I'm thirsty," she said behind him.

"Coming up." His voice caught. The word *up* had come out in a falsetto. She laughed softly, lazily; she reveled in her effect on people.

They each took another pill and sipped the whiskey, and for a time everything seemed calm enough. They sat on the bed and waited, and she talked about her stepmother's friend, who had abandoned her family and hadn't even left a note. "I know her daughter," she said. "Her name is Maizie." She laughed softly. "I worked with her and we got to be friends. That's not exactly the truth. Since she got pregnant, I haven't seen much of her at all. And I haven't even talked to her about her mother. Actually, I wouldn't even know where to begin. Maizie used to talk me out of suicide, you know? Jesus—I wouldn't know where to begin."

"Pamela," he said. "I can't stop thinking about you." He had decided that he should tell her now, before the drug took over. "I'm in love with you, and I want us to stop all this and settle down together."

She shrugged, not looking at him. It seemed as if she might even yawn. "Everybody says that. That's movie talk."

"It's true. I'm speaking the absolute truth as I know it."

"You watch too many movies," she said.

He was ready to swear off ever seeing another movie again in his life. "I know, but listen to me," he said. "I want to marry you and start a family." The words sounded oddly foolish on his lips. "I love you," he said. "No matter what else is true."

She laughed. "Stop it." Then: "Feel anything yet?"

"I feel that I love you," he said.

"Stop it."

"I do. I honestly do, Pamela."

"Here." She gave him another pill. He had begun to experience sharp pains in his left side. Shooting pains. He put the glass down with the whiskey in it, and tried to kiss her again. "Wait," she said. "Jesus."

"I love you," he said.

"Oh," she said. "Oh, wait. Feel that? Jesus. Tell me how it feels, come on. You must feel something by now."

He had experienced the pains, and now he noticed a strange tunneling of his vision; all the edges were beginning to blur and dissolve. He felt as though his eyes were bulging. He couldn't believe she would not react, his eyes bugging out of his head. "God," he said.

"Whoa," she said, opening her mouth. Her expression was that of someone flying down the steepest turn on a roller coaster, though she kept watching him, too. "Whoa," she said. "Jeee-sus. Feel that?"

He swallowed the rest of the whiskey, and the room grew liquid. She was sitting on the bed with her legs crossed, and he did not remember when she had arranged herself like that. He lay face down, arms dangling over the edge, head lolling, tongue out. He moved it, licked something—her knee. He had turned and was licking her knee.

"Okay," she said, lying back. "Ohhhh-kay."

He got to his knees on the bed, and then he was pulling at her shorts, the flimsy pink panties underneath. "Stop it," she said. "Tell me what it's doing to you."

Her hand pushed his away. Everything wavered and went up in waves of air. He lay down at her side, and his hands wouldn't work. He was tossing in a boat, riding an ocean, and she was murmuring in his ear, moving her tongue at his ear.

"Okay, lover," she said.

He couldn't raise himself up. He reached for her, felt the weight of her, and heard the laugh. They lay in a tangle of clothes. She was trying to unbutton his shirt. "I love you," he said. And then he was crying.

"Jeee-sus. What're you crying about?"

"I can't stop."

She pulled away and stood. "Where's the bathroom?"

"Pamela."

But she had stumbled away. He heard her in there, coughing. "Ridley," she said. "I have to be alone for a few minutes. That goddam whiskey."

"I'm in love with you," he said, still crying. Everything seemed so hopeless for a moment. He gathered himself, tried to clear his mind.

"Get out of here, Ridley."

"I'll be downstairs," he told her.

"Just get."

So he came unsteadily down the shaky wooden stairway, realizing that he had reached this level of intimacy with her; he had been in bed with her and she had called him lover. He knocked on the Masons' door. The world was suffused in a yellow glow, and he felt completely immutable and clean. The hopelessness had dissipated like a cloud. He was solid as a piece of marble inside. He thought of the curves of rock under his skin.

The Masons let him in, offered him a glass of water for the parched sound of his voice (he hadn't noticed the parched sound of his voice, but he took them at their word), and quickly enough after they brought him his glass of ice water, he began to feel everything shift toward fright.

HE'S ASHAMED, AND HE understands that lately whatever he's feeling seems somehow beside the point. Even so, he keeps finding in himself this little tremor of well-being, like a secret nerve discharging at the synapse. In those moments, it's almost as if, at the core of himself, he were a man standing on a boulder amidst a fast-flowing river. It convinces him, each time it happens, that things might soon take a turn for the better.

He's looking for that feeling as Mr. Mason comes back into the room.

"Well," Mr. Mason says, setting down a plate of crackers and cheese. "I myself always believed in discipline."

"Yes." Ridley looks straight at him, focusing. "And it's gone. Nobody even thinks about it." He remembers that this is the subject. And then he hopes it is.

Mrs. Mason says, "Civilizations are like arrows in flight. They arc and then fall to earth."

On occasion, Ridley thinks of her conversation as a series of captions for the pictures her husband paints. The old man has described himself as a history buff. Everybody, according to Mr. Mason, is a buff of this or a buff of that. There are computer buffs and movie buffs and radio buffs and song buffs. Ridley is a medicine buff, though it has been some time since he dropped out of college. He told Mr. Mason that he was a pre-med student when he quit. All this means is that he took one biology and one chemistry course. He failed them both, but this makes no difference to Mr. Mason. "Young Ridley here," Mr. Mason will say to visitors, "is a medicine buff." To Ridley's friends, Mr. Mason says, "Are you medicine buffs like Ridley?"

"Entropy is in God's plan," he says now. "As is our struggle with it."

Mr. Mason's views are all informed by his religious feeling. He's nondenominational, he says, with Catholic leanings. Ridley has privately described him to friends as a God buff, since all his talk leads inexorably back to God. Having read the works of Thomas Aquinas, and having once almost decided to attend the seminary, Ridley can talk the talk. Even now, with panic roiling in his heart. "When was the last time anybody asked for sacrifice?" he says. "Even the word sounds strange, doesn't it?"

"Never sounded strange to me," says Mr. Mason.

Ridley is always unnerved when something he has said that is a lie, and that he has thought would be picked up by someone and agreed with, is turned back in disagreement. It's always as though he's been caught out, the falsehood showing on his face somehow. For a second, he can't say anything else. The two people sit on their couch, their faces pleasant and empty. He feels them begin to slide out of solidness, feels the beginning of hallucination, and tries to talk again. "It's a great world," he says. He had meant to say *word*. Sacrifice is a great *word*. The old people simply stare back at him. "My eyes feel funny," he says. "I've got allergies to certain kinds of things in the air. And I hate war. I hate all different kinds of war. Guerrilla war and holy war and—and wars of liberation. Did you know that the albumen in eggs is full of strontium 90 from practicing for the war we didn't get around to fighting?"

They stare at him.

"Sometimes I think wars are like God's forest fire for people, you know?" This seems perfectly clear to him, but he can see the doubt in their faces. "My eyes sting," he says. "It's really something."

"Pollution," Mrs. Mason says, smiling to encourage him. She seems to think there's more. Out the window, behind her almost too bright bluish-gray hair, trees wave in the wind. There's a storm coming. The sky on the other side of the trees is black.

"I think suffering really comes from people realizing they're not doing what's right for their spiritual development," Ridley says. He's almost certain he got it out clearly, but the two of them look worried and nervous. "Really," he goes on. "Don't you think so? People have—they could have everything. Beautiful—you know. And they—they throw it away on nothing, a lot of empty shit like drugs and alcohol and running around like there's no tomorrow and talking about suicide that way, like it's a thing you flirt with, for Christ's sake. When a person would swear to love them forever in a minute and work to stop every bad habit just for the chance—you know. I mean if you love someone, I mean isn't that what we're all supposed to be doing?"

"Pardon me," Mr. Mason says, rising. He walks into the next room. Ridley hears the windows closing there.

"Rain," Ridley says to Mrs. Mason. "I didn't think it was supposed to." His voice shakes, as if someone has punched him. The sentence has come out all wrong. He thinks he must've said it wrong, because she's giving him a troubled look. "Rain is nice, isn't it?" he says.

She says something he doesn't quite catch, about her garden. During the summer, before things started running out of control, he helped her put the garden in. He worked all day for three days, bare back cooking in the sun, clean and pleasurably thirsty, so that water tasted better than anything, and at night he slept deep. He had not met Pamela Brill yet. He had flunked out of college and been disowned by his father for the failure, and he was unable to decide what he should do in the way of work, a career. The whole idea of a career made his stomach hurt and filled him with the dread of death.

He remembers digging in Mrs. Mason's garden, thinking about the cool water in the tin ladle from the well.

"It's terrible now," he hears, and realizes he has spoken aloud.

"Yes," Mrs. Mason says, agreeing.

"Pardon me," he says to her. "I lost my train of thought."

She smiles, staring.

"Did you hear me?" he says.

"Yes," she says in that agreeable way. When her husband isn't there, she becomes quite vague, Ridley has noticed.

"Do you remember what I said?" Ridley asks her.

"Discipline," she says, making a fist. She's watching him carefully. She's wary. "It started because we were talking about why a woman with a nice family and a husband and a lot of nice things would lock herself up in a motel room and do away with herself."

"Who?" Ridley says, more confused all the time.

"The woman. That person they found in the motel room down the street."

"Oh, my God," he says. He can't remember. He thinks of Pamela. He was talking to Pamela about this. Did they bring this up? "Did you bring this up?" he says.

"We were talking about her. She took a bottle of pills."

"We only took four apiece," Ridley almost shouts. "It just gets worse."

"Pardon?" she says.

He says, "Everything's coming apart at the seams."

"Are you all right?"

He nods, sees Mrs. Mason's features shrink. Is she frowning? She's leaned forward slightly to look at him.

"Are you sure you're all right, young man?"

"Oh," he says, "I'm just fine."

The rain hits the window with an insistence, as if it wants in now, and Mr. Mason comes back into the room carrying the box of crackers. "These are all I could find," he says. "I'm afraid the cupboard's bare."

This is a hint, and Ridley knows it. He can't put the words together in his head. "I've got a job interview," he says. But they don't seem to have heard him.

"All this makes me very nervous," Mrs. Mason says.

"She's never liked storms," her husband says. "That one yesterday really frightened us both for the lightning."

"I've never seen it so bad," she says.

"Well, I shouldn't've mentioned it," says Mr. Mason. "I can see it also upsets our young tenant here."

"Such an awe-inspiring thing," says Mrs. Mason.

"You mean the—that—the woman that—the suicide," Ridley gets out. It's as if he's solved a puzzle they've given him. "Her. I know about that."

They stare at him.

"I was talking about the lightning."

"It's a disgrace these days to tell a girl you want to get married and have a family. It's a fucking joke."

Mr. Mason draws a breath. It's clear that he's overcoming some resistance in himself.

"Excuse me," Ridley says.

"You're upset," says Mrs. Mason.

There's more talk, but Ridley can't quite follow it. Then he can.

Mr. Mason says, "I heard that she was lying in the bed with the covers pulled up, like someone lying down to sleep, you know."

"Right," says Ridley. "No note."

"A note?"

He waits. The next thing they say will give him something to latch on to.

"Poor woman," Mrs. Mason says.

Ridley realizes that his hands are gripping his knees. He tries to look calm. The Masons are changing before his eyes, drifting out of their own shapes. He almost leaps at them. "Hey," he says, too loud, and they sit forward. They have recomposed themselves. Their color is odd in the light.

"Yes?" says Mr. Mason with a faintly suspicious tilting of his head. "Where were we?"

"There's no knowing what a person goes through," Mrs. Mason says. "We should talk about something else."

"No one can ever really know another person," says her husband.

It thunders. The sound seems to move across the sky, like a heavy ball rolling on a table, and then everything is still again. The rain comes down. Ridley has a moment of believing he can hear it splattering against the leaves of the farthest tree, and then he sees that on the branches of that tree there are two large black hulking birds. The sound now seems to rise from those shapes, and it comes at him through the small opening at the bottom of the window. He can almost see the air tremble with it. His heart shakes; he breathes the odor of wet wood and ozone, and thinks of outer space. Everything makes too much noise.

"Without discipline and sacrifice," Mr. Mason is saying, "I think some people learn to start expecting perfection. And when they don't get it"—he shrugs—"why, they jump out of the boat. That's the only explanation I've ever had for it."

"Maybe it's because they think life won't change," Mrs. Mason says, emphasizing the last word. "Or else they're too afraid it *will* change."

"I would like to know," Ridley says suddenly, "what the hell we're talking about." It's as if he has barked at them. Then, softly: "It's getting dark."

They wait. There's a greenish light at the windows. Ridley is float-ing loose inside, anchorless, guilty, while the Masons sit regarding him. His vision is clouding over. The wavering light changes and ap-pears to flare up, and it seems to him that a ball of flame rolls out of the fireplace and licks across the carpet to the television set, where it flashes and makes a bright shower of sparks. It's like the Fourth of July. He sees flames climb the wall, crackling, bending and fanning out at the ceiling. It's a hallucination, the worst thing, and he grips himself, trying to smile at the Masons, who are huddled together, their faces calm as facts. He tries to think what he has said, tries to re-cover everything that led up to the moment, and the fierce heat on his face makes him fear that the fire is real, that he has not imagined it. The Masons are still huddled on the couch, apparently waiting to die. Their faces are blank.

"Come on," he says to them. "Jesus. I took something." He stands, reaches for them. "Get up," he says. "Jesus, it's real."

Mr. Mason tries to cover his wife's face. They do not move. Ridley pulls at the old man's arm, then bends down and puts his arms around him, lifting.

"What are you doing?" Mr. Mason says.

Mrs. Mason has flopped over on her side and is shouting for help.

"Here," Ridley says. "Lift her." But he can't get either of them to move. The air is burning his lungs. He can't see.

"Don't hurt us," Mr. Mason is shouting. "Please. Help. Help."

Every movement Ridley makes is doubled in his own perception, and finally, somehow, he finds himself on the stairs, tumbling down onto the lawn, with the Masons shouting at him from the stairs.

"—call the police," Mr. Mason is saying. "If you come near us again—"

Ridley moves off from the house into the rain, and lightning shud-ders nearby. When he turns, he falls, ends up lying on his back, arms spread, the black sky moving over him. The house is plainly not lightning-struck, and there's no fire. "Excuse me," he says. "I'm

sorry." Then he tries to yell to them. "I thought it was a fire. I'm absolutely sick with love."

"Crazy," Mr. Mason shouts. "I won't have it."

Mrs. Mason says something he can't hear. Ridley lifts his head in
the rain and there they are, holding on to each other, looking troubled
and afraid, and above them, on her own part of the stairs, is Pamela
Brill. He has a moment of brilliant clarity, remembering himself. She
looks at him with a terrifyingly cold curiosity. "Oh, God," he says. "I
want you. I don't have anything else. I don't want another thing in the
world."

She says nothing, steps into his doorway out of the rain, still giving
him that chilly, evaluative look. When the Masons begin shouting at
him, she joins them, screams at him, the perfect teeth lining the red
mouth. "It wasn't what you think," she says. "You with your stupid
imagination. You're drunk, and that's about all you are, too. Plain old
drunk." It's clear that she's enjoying this—that for her, it's all part of
the same fun. For an instant they are all contending with one another
and the storm, trying to be heard, saying words he can't distinguish
for the anger and the shouting and the thunder. He lies back. It's as
though the pure force of their displeasure has leveled him. Except
that, as the rain washes over him and lightning flashes in the sky, he
feels an unexpected peace. It comes to him that his love makes him
good, and for this one wordless instant he can believe it. Out of everything else, this true thing shines forth, perfectly clear. And he is reasonably certain that it's not coming from any drug. His love has
elevated him. His wishes for honorable actions and faith have made
him excellent, even in this disaster. Through the relative brightness of
these intimations, he sees the others still shouting, still gesturing, and
in his strangely exalted state, it's as though they are calling to him
from a distant shoreline, long-lost friends, dear friends, loved ones,
urging him on, cheering him, happy for him as he sets sail in search of
his unimaginable future.

GOOD-BYES

MAIZIE, MY DARLING, I'm sitting here trying to find something to say to you, and all I can think about is how it was when I was a kid and ran through the rooms of an empty house, the echoes bouncing around. I'm feeling pretty blue tonight. And the echoes are bouncing around here, of course. Every move I make gets repeated in the walls. It's so strange to have this house empty again, and maybe it's a good thing that your mother isn't here to see it like this. I remember you and James running through these rooms when we were first here, before the furniture got moved in, both of you yelling so loud I had to get after you. Tonight I feel like a little kid, and the way my voice echoes in the walls is at least partly what's doing it to me. It makes me more certain than ever that I shouldn't move in with you and Leo, and I'm sorry for all his hard work on the room. But you'll find some use for it, I'm sure.

You were so anxious to buttonhole me when we moved your mother's things out of here, and I guess I wasn't very helpful. I know I wasn't. I'm not the best man for getting things said that need saying, and there's a lot I miss, I know. James told me he was joking when he said that about how I miss so many close calls I ought to be an umpire, but I know he was serious enough, too. You both think I'm pretty dense, no doubt. And even so, you think I'm keeping something back, that I'm lying when I say I really don't have a very definite idea why your mother did what she did. You think there's something hidden, some secret we kept from you, and there just isn't. For instance, you both knew about it when she had her trouble about Buddy Wells. You both knew how close we were to separating.

I just don't have any clear ideas about it, and I wish that weren't so. I wish I could say I knew for certain what she was thinking about, or that I'd seen anything in her behavior or heard something in her voice.

To be exactly truthful, I thought she was happy.

I thought she was handling the move far better than I was. After all, she was the one who took charge, who went through all the papers with the real estate people, and showed the house and grounds. It was your mother who took us through each stage of the sale of the property and all the settlements. She wouldn't let me have anything to do with it. I had been having my usual trouble sleeping, and of course my stomach was giving me fits. The whole thing had me rattled pretty bad. But she seemed to have warmed to the idea and got comfortable with it—I remember, I even questioned her about it on that last day—at no time did she seem unfocused or despondent or indifferent.

Anyway, I refuse to believe that she could've done it just because we were leaving the house. That's a hardship, maybe, but nothing to kill yourself over.

There were, after all, things to look forward to. Being a grandparent, for instance. And having some time and money to travel a little. She always wanted to go to Rome and look at the Sistine Chapel in person. And there were all those Donatelli statues. The tombs Michelangelo did. You know me, Maizie. I don't know much about Art, but we were saving up for the trip. I'd love to have been able to give it to her. I would've let her teach me like she always said she wanted to. We'd go on one of those posh two-week deals, maybe. Or a combination cruise. Something really elegant. We actually planned it. I put extra dollars away for years, and I don't have any idea how much she saved on her own. But somehow school and work and the farm—things got in the way. She held the purse strings, of course, and she started dipping into the Italy money so she could get for you kids the things she wanted you to have. She didn't mind, either. Neither of us had any regrets on that score.

But I want to try and give you everything you want to know, Maizie. And so I've decided to tell you a story about your mother and me, and it starts with the night she told me about Buddy Wells. I knew Wells a little, enough to see that whatever else he was, he wasn't the sort of man who could've been much use to your mother. I think I also sensed that he was a little enamored of her. Wells was the sort of man who couldn't keep his own emotions out of his face, there wasn't a single subtlety anywhere in him. They began with a friendship, like a lot of people—he was bringing his daughter to your mother's dance classes, and they'd got to talking. The daughter charmed her especially. She invited him and the daughter to a party or two that we had, back when we were entertaining a lot. One day, out of the blue, Buddy made a declaration of love to her. It shocked her, apparently, though I can't imagine why. She didn't know what to do with it at first. For a few weeks she kept the whole thing to herself. She even sought ways to keep from ever being alone with him. But then she found that she was thinking about him in the nights, and wondering what he might be doing during the days. She decided she felt something for him, and on an evening toward the beginning of summer, she decided to tell me this.

"Buddy Wells has fallen in love with me," she said.

It was a Thursday evening after her spring recitals, and I had made my own dinner and settled into my chair with the crossword puzzle. I said, "Anyone could've told you that."

"You don't understand," she said.

I said, "Sure I do."

There was such a look of alarm on her face, Maizie.

I said, "What is it?"

"I feel the same way," she said.

I didn't say anything for a few seconds. It hadn't quite sunk in yet.

"I've fallen in love with him," she said.

I said, "You've—" but nothing would come.

"He wants me to move in with him."

I said, "You're joking."

"I don't know how to put this any other way," she said. "I know it sounds silly." That was what she said. Those were her words.

"You can't be serious," I said.

She stammered like a little girl in a school lesson, but couldn't get anything out.

I waited.

"Oh, for God's sake, Harry, you know what I'm going to say."

"No," I said. "I don't have the slightest idea."

"I'm moving in with him. He's in love—we're—we—"

"You mean this?" I said to her. "This is serious."

"I don't know," she said.

"Well, is it or isn't it?"

"I'm not making it up, Harry."

I didn't say anything.

"I'm not making it up," she said again.

I said, "Let me get this straight—"

She said, "Please, I told you. Don't make me go through it again."

"All right, Andrea," I said. "Suppose you tell me what you want me to say."

"I don't know," she said.

"You think you do, though," I said.

And she nodded. It was as if she were relenting somehow, as if I'd forced the answer out of her.

"Why don't you tell me instead of making me say it for you?" I said.

She began to cry.

"Have you slept with him?" I said.

Maizie, it was as if I'd thrown something at her. But a husband has the right to ask certain things. She said, "Not—not yet."

"But you're going to," I said.

"I don't know." This was said with a good deal of frustration, and again it was as if I'd been badgering her about it.

"You came in here to tell me something. Is that all of it? I don't see why I should be put into the position of a goddam inquisitor about it, since you are my wife."

"I don't know," she said again. "I know I love him."

"Well, for Christ's sake," I said, "let me know when you know the rest of it." She had her purse in her hands and was standing over by the door. I was sitting more or less right where I'm presently sitting.

She'd come through from the bedroom, where she'd been most of the evening. It'd been a normal evening. There hadn't been anything that would have led me to suspect a situation like this. I said, "Where are you going now?"

She said, "I don't know."

I said, "This is an appalling case of ignorance on your part."

"Please, Harry," she said.

I said, "If only you knew how silly you look, mooning over that open-faced kid. You're funny, you know it? A laughingstock. No, you're ridiculous. I can't believe that you, with your goddam reserve and your refinement and your book and garden clubs and study groups and Arts Leagues, could be willing to make such a public fool of yourself this way, being sluttish like this with a kid ten, twelve years younger than you are."

She started to cry.

"Really, Andrea. I think you've gone off the deep end. Look at you. This kid's in his thirties, for Christ's sake. You were nursing James when Buddy Wells was in elementary school. It's so silly. Silly and sordid. What do you think?"

She stood there crying, not looking at me. And I felt suddenly almost sorry for her. Part of me sensed that she had blundered into the whole thing, and that she was perfectly and painfully aware of how ridiculous she had become.

I sensed, too, as any husband would, that it all had to do with me. But there were other reasons for me to feel that way, as you'll see soon enough. And it was what put me over the edge. When she started toward the bedroom, I followed her. I said worse things. I was getting carried away now, and even my sorrow for her couldn't stop me. I told her just what I'd do if she left—how the talk would go among the people we knew, and what I'd make sure you and James and the rest of the family understood about it, how she had carried on with Wells behind my back and betrayed everything we stood for. And I said that if I had any say at all, she would spend the rest of her life in Buddy Wells's circle, alone, without anyone to turn to when things went sour, as they certainly would, with somebody like Buddy Wells. I reminded her of her age, and of you and James—especially I reminded her of you, and what it would mean to you, starting into your womanhood. I was shouting, letting her have all of it, things I hadn't ever said to her, and wanted to say to her. Because what I never said to you or James or to anyone was that all my married life I'd carried the feeling with me that the woman with whom I was spending my days lived her real life separate from me. Somehow, Maizie, in a way I couldn't ever understand or appreciate, I wasn't the husband she apparently needed.

I stood there watching her cry, and I had said everything there was to say, and then I almost touched her shoulder. I knew I had gone under her pride and wounded her, and even as I was proud that I'd struck some of the wind out of her sails, I felt sorry.

I felt sorry, Maizie, but as you know it didn't stop me from calling you and James and getting both of you into the fight to keep her. I believed, and I still believe, it would have been a terrible thing for her to have gone with Buddy Wells. But then, given my disappointment and my anger, I thought for a time that maybe we should separate. I have always believed that loving involves an act of will—or, really, many acts of will. In my mind, she had decided against me, and as the days went by I found that I cared less and less about keeping her. I felt that I had been right about her. I had not imagined that she always withheld something. I watched you and James fight with her, and just couldn't bring myself to do or say much of anything.

One afternoon, as she was dressing to go to her studio, I said, "Have you talked about your little love affair with any of your friends?"

"They don't know anything."

"What about his friends?"

"No," she said.

"You can trust that?" I said.

"I can trust it."

"You have my permission to go with the son of a bitch," I said. "I won't fight you."

She looked at me. She had been pulling one shoe on. "What?"

"You heard me," I said. "I'm not going to try and stop you anymore. I'll even help you put the best face on it. Just get it over with quick."

She waited a few seconds. "I don't guess I deserve you being kind," she said.

"No," I said. "I'm being practical."

"Well, maybe so," she said.

"You're free," I told her. "And that's that."

"Thank you," she said.

And I thought that *was* that.

When she told me she was staying, it was as simple as saying the time of day. I was in the kitchen late the next morning, and she came home from the studio and walked up the back steps.

"Harry," she said. "I'm home."

I had been eating a bowl of cereal. I barely looked up.

"I'm not going to go away, either." She said this peering at me through the screen in the door.

I said, "Go or stay. It's up to you."

We didn't exchange another word that day, but in the morning we had coffee together and talked about the leaves changing on the side of the mountain, how they were always the first to change every year. She wondered about you, struggling with your classes. And about James. It was very ordinary and maybe a little hollow, but it was friendly, too. It was even conciliatory, I think. And we just went on from there. It wasn't long before we'd got far enough past it that we could talk about it. And then we could forget it, too. I believe, Maizie, that we were a fairly happy couple. There are pictures. You can see it in her face. She kept herself far from me in a lot of ways over the years, but she was never devious or dishonest. It was not in her to be dishonest. And those pictures show her being happy. We did talk about Buddy Wells on that last day, but it was me who brought it up.

We bantered about him, in fact. I said something about how much money she'd have if she were Buddy Wells's widow. It seemed to me that she was amused. And later I told her that she was still beautiful, and that I loved her. Because I did. I did love her, Maizie. All the time.

And I ask you to imagine how it can feel like starvation to be intimate with someone you can't really reach—the sort of person whose love is somehow only partly there, who holds back something essential that another man was freely given, almost at the cost of a long marriage and a family.

I don't think I'm excusing myself. I wasn't the best husband a woman could have—I don't suppose James was so far wrong with his joke—but I'm not to blame, and after all, I am the one who's still here. I admit that my first reaction to the news of what she'd done was wondering what I'd done to head her there. I blamed myself, more than you or James ever could, and I know that some part of both of you does blame me—for not seeing clearly enough, for not sensing that something was so wrong.

But I refuse to accept any blame now, harsh as that sounds. If it were possible to speak to the dead and be heard, I'd tell her the same thing. I'd say, "Andrea, listen to me. No pity, Andrea. None. No excuses, no regret for anything, and no sympathy, either, for what you've done to us." And I'd mean it.

But as I won't accept any blame, I won't place it, Maizie. She did what she felt she had to do, and I can't change it, no matter how much I wish I could, and I don't blame her for it. I accept it as a fact, what she decided to do with her life. You and your brother will have to decide how you feel about it. When I close the door on this old house, I'll walk away recalling how your young voices sounded in it, and it'll hurt me exactly as it's supposed to, and I guess it'll even make me wish I hadn't finally said no to the room in your house.

But I won't entertain one regret about anything. Not one.

It's midnight now, and I just said my name aloud, and listened to the echo. Like most people my age, it's terribly hard for me to accept the idea that my boyhood memory of being fascinated with the way rooms sound when they're empty means nothing, or that thinking of it now means nothing, and I'm afraid that's what your poor mother tried to say to us—that none of it has any meaning. But that was how *she* saw things. I don't know what else to say about her now, or how else to think about it. She finally said no to everything, like a kid throwing a tantrum in a public place.

And I still love her.

I wish she was in the next room. I wish she'd chosen some other way to deny us herself. I'd like to think of her being alive and happy, even if it had to be somewhere else. Even if it had to be with a man like Buddy Wells, and even if I hated her for it.

Love, Harry

DIURNAL

WHEN MAIZIE'S MOTHER *wasn't the subject behind their talk, they found time to be easy with each other, and to be like other expectant couples. They had taken the Lamaze classes, and done the exercises at home, and they had discussed names, and made plans. He had dreamed up whole lives for this child, made of triumphs and love, and sometimes he felt as though he had cut through the carapace of sorrowing distraction and worry that encased his wife. On one occasion, lying in bed sleepless in dawn light, they had even teased and laughed about the names, trying absurd ones on each other. "How about Attila H. Kelleher?" Leo said. "No, I have it, how about Adolf H. Kelleher?"*

"I think if it's a boy," Maizie told him, "we'll call him Leo, after his very strange father."

"Not Leo," he told her. "And not Carl, either. I knew a kid in school named Carl and he was a total jerk. How about Judas I. Kelleher?"

"Stop it," she said, laughing. "Please." A moment later, she said, "Benedict A. Kelleher," and they laughed together.

"Sirhan S. Kelleher," Leo said.

"John Wilkes Kelleher."

They laughed. "Genghis K. Kelleher," he managed.

For a moment, neither of them could speak, and it was all as light-hearted as it used to be between them.

He said, "Suppose it's a girl."

She was wiping her eyes. She frowned, took a breath. "Let's talk about it later."

"I can't think of any notorious bad women," he said.

"Lizzie B. Kelleher," said Maizie, "for Lizzie Borden."

"How about some multicultural names? Retributia Kelleher. Or no, Corona. Corona Cigar Kelleher. Or there's all the nouns, right? The hippie names. How about Peace? No, too obvious. Disharmony. There you go. Disharmony Kelleher. What do you think? No? War Kelleher. Psycho Kelleher. Communist Kelleher. Thoroughgoing Kelleher. Hungry Kelleher."

"I don't want to talk about it anymore," Maizie said.

"How about Maizie?" he said to her, kissing her cheek. "A little Maizie for me to spoil."

"No," his wife said. "I mean it now, Leo. I don't want to talk about it anymore."

"There's a fifty-fifty chance it'll be a girl," he said, wanting to save the mood somehow. But she had sunk into herself, and was thinking again about her mother. Gently, he said, "Honey, we could name her Andrea, if you wanted."

"Oh, for God's sake, Leo," she said, rising, moving away from him. "Sometimes I don't believe you."

He said, "I can't very well be expected to gauge your feelings if you never tell me what you feel."

She said, "I feel right now that I want to be alone."

TODAY, MAIZIE WALKED in from the back, kicking the doorjamb to knock the snow off her boots. The snow powdered her shoulders and glittered in her hair. She glanced at her husband, breathed "Hello," then smiled, looking away, her eyes wide with the exertion of having climbed the porch stairs. There was something almost childlike about her face in this light, her cheeks rouged with the chill. She glanced at him and looked away again. Lately, whenever she caught him gazing at her like this, she seemed flustered, as if he had intruded on her in a private moment.

"Is it slippery?" he asked.

"What? Oh, not really—not in the grass. I walked in the grass."

"How far'd you go?"

"Down to the end of the block." She removed her coat, shook the snow from it, and hung it on the peg next to the door. "I guess we'll see whether the old family lore has any truth to it. If things go according to the story, we'll be parents by morning." Her mother used to tell about how walking during a snowstorm had brought about the labor that produced Maizie, two weeks after she was due, twenty-nine years ago. "This doesn't look like much of a storm, though."

"It's not bad on the road?" Leo said.

"It's not sticking to anything but the grass. We'll have clear roads for the ride to the hospital. If this has worked."

"I was thinking about James and Helena, actually. Whether they'll have trouble getting here tonight."

She smiled. "You don't believe this baby will ever be born, do you?"

"I'll believe it when I see it," he said, smiling back.

She had braced herself in the doorway to the kitchen, pushing one boot off with the toe of the other. Then she stopped and leaned her back against the frame, resting her hands on the amazing roundness of her belly. Earlier, she'd joked about not being able to button her coat, and he'd caught himself thinking about a day, sometime in the future, when she would be completely herself again; she was getting some of her natural humor back. It was true, as he had wanted to say so many times, that life insists on itself. Now she massaged the place where her navel was, with a gingerly, tentative motion of her fingertips. "I'm sore," she said. "Right here. It feels stretched to the breaking point."

"Need help with the boots?"

"I'm fine." She pulled at the remaining boot. When it came off, she made a harrumphing sound, then dropped it and leaned against the frame again, breathing hard.

"Your father called."

She said nothing.

"About two minutes after you left."

She moved to the sink and put the tap on, filled a glass of water and drank.

"He said he just wanted to know how you are."

"Did you tell him I'm fat?" she said, pouring the rest of the water out.

"When you stand there like that with your back to me, it's impossible to see that you're pregnant."

"I'm shaped like a big pear." She wet a paper towel and dabbed her cheeks with it. "I feel feverish." She walked over to him. "Do I have a fever?"

He touched her forehead. "Cool as a cucumber."

"I feel like I have a fever."

"You've been out in the cold."

Straightening her back, she put one hand at the base of her spine. "I'm going to go see if I can take a nap. Do I have time?"

"James and Helena said they'd be here about eight," he said.

She sighed, looking at the clock above the stove. "I have a little while, then. Oh, will this baby ever come."

He watched her go on back into the bedroom, and then he took a package of turbot fillets out of the refrigerator and cut them into smaller pieces for frying. From the window over the kitchen sink, he could see that it was still snowing. Gusts of it swirled under the street-lamp, but the road surface was still visible.

She called to him from the bedroom. "Did Daddy want me to call him back?"

"Didn't say so."

"Did anyone else call?"

"A Mrs. Gehringer. Asking for you."

For a while there was no sound from the bedroom, and he supposed she had drifted off to sleep. But then she spoke to him from the end of the hallway. "Did Mrs. Gehringer say anything else?"

"Just asked for you. I told her you were out, and I didn't know when you'd be back, and she thanked me and hung up."

Maizie started back toward the bedroom.

He followed her. "Who's Mrs. Gehringer?"

"No one," Maizie said. "Marty's wife. Remember Marty from work?"

"The older guy, sure."

"If she calls again, I'm asleep. I'll call her back."

"When do you want me to wake you?"

"I probably won't sleep."

He hesitated a moment, thinking she might say more. Then: "I'll come in half an hour before they get here."

She lay down on her side, facing away from him.

"Okay?"

"It's fine," she said. "I'm just really tired."

"Do you want me to call and see if I can catch them?"

She sighed. "No."

"It's no trouble, Maizie, if you don't feel like company."

"Please," she said. "Just let me be quiet a while."

HE WAS AWARE OF most of his shortcomings, and he feared that there were others. He had never been the sort of man who dealt in subtle shadings—whether they had to do with the ebb and flow of emotions during the course of an evening, or with, say, the source of light emanating from the painted sky of a Monet—and no matter how hard he tried, no matter how many books he read to improve himself, there was no getting around his clumsiness, his nervousness in groups, his old tendency to bungle things during conversation, to put his foot in his mouth, or fail to get the joke, or lose the train of thought in mid-sentence. He was not slow, nor at any disadvantage in terms of intelligence, though he often felt that way; the problem was that his nerves often made him go blank. There had been times when she teased him about these failures, but lately they only made her restless and impatient. And yet when she had snapped at him, or been abrupt with him, she seemed almost too contrite, as though there were something coming that she was sorry for. He had found it increasingly difficult to speak to her beyond the practical exchanges of a given day, such as whether or not she wanted him to call her brother and ask him not to come.

She had kept so much of the pain about her mother to herself. Nothing he had been able to say could draw it out of her. "I don't want to talk about my mother," she told him. "Please. I don't even want to think about her."

"I just wanted to say, you know, I'm—I'm here if you do want to talk."

"Please, Leo."

There was the pregnancy to worry about, and for a while there was the fact that her father was coming to live with them. He'd kept himself busy enough putting the spare room together for the old man, doing what he knew how to do best, and he took special pains with everything—even put chair railing in, and crown molding. It was a lovely room when he was finished, with its own private entrance from the outside and its own little kitchen and bathroom. All that work, and then the old man decided he didn't want it after all.

When it was first completed, Leo brought her in to look it over.

"It's beautiful," she said. "I hate it."

He felt something drop in his heart. "I'm pretty proud of it," he told her. "What do you hate?"

"I hate that it's here. That the farm is gone and that my mother— it's the place for my father to come spend the end of his days because of all that. Do you see?"

"It's a place for your father, yes. I worked like crazy on it, Maizie."

"I know you did. Can't you understand?" she said. "It's all part of this whole awful thing. The farm getting sold off and my mother checking into a motel room and taking a bottle of pills and every time I heard the hammer down here, every sound it made, it just—it's part of the same bad thing and I hate it and I'm sorry."

"Why didn't you say something?" he asked her. He was almost glad that she had said this much to him about it.

"I don't mean to hurt your feelings," she said. "Please."

"No," he said. "Listen. It's the first thing you've told me about what happened, how you feel. I would've gladly stopped—"

"It's a room for Dad," she said. "It's just that it's necessary at all."

She put her arms around him. They had been married almost six years, and her touch still thrilled him. He turned and bent down to kiss her.

"Baby," she said, "sweetheart," patting his chest with the ends of her fingers. But there was something perplexed and distant in her voice.

AT SEVEN-THIRTY, HE WALKED back to where she lay sprawled on the bed, her arms over her face. Standing in the doorway, he whispered, "You awake?"

"Yes."

"They'll be here in a little while."

"I had a contraction just now." She moved her arms and looked at him, seemed to study his face. "What's wrong?"

"Nothing," he said.

"You keep watching me."

"I'm sorry. I don't mean to. I'm trying to be here for you in this."

"There'll be plenty of time when it starts," she said. "Babies don't usually come all that suddenly. You keep hovering over me like you think I might crack open or something, like an egg."

He'd meant her grief over her mother. He decided not to pursue it. When she sat up, slowly, accommodating the heaviness of her belly, he reached down and took hold of her elbow, to help her stand.

"Don't," she said.

He stood back.

"I'm sore all over."

"Are you having another contraction?"

"Yes." She sat down again, lightly massaging her abdomen, breathing deep. "It's passing."

He watched her.

"Easing off now."

A moment later, she began to cry.

"What," he said. "Tell me."

"Nothing, honey. Really."

"I'm sorry," he said.

"You don't need to worry about me," she told him. "I don't want you worrying about me."

He nodded. Then, because she wasn't looking at him, he said, "I know."

"Going through all this, and being pregnant on top of it."

Again, he nodded. Now the situation was reversed: he had thought she was talking about the baby.

"I have to brush my hair."

"Right," he said. He walked slowly with her into the living room and helped her get settled on the couch. She wanted music, so he put the stereo on, then went back into the kitchen. He got out the rest of what he would need to cook the dinner. They'd been seeing James and Helena more often since the old man had left for Tampa, and on most of these occasions Leo did the cooking. He liked it that way. It eased him inside, and when Maizie appreciated what he had done, even when the appreciation was automatic—spoken in the middle of thinking about something else—he felt happy. It was a respite from the continual feeling that he ought to be doing more to make their lives change for the better, more to help the healing process, without knowing what that thing might be. Because of her mother, because of the pregnancy, he couldn't seek an answer from her about himself—about her feelings for him—because he did not want to become only another element of her suffering.

And maybe he was that, anyway.

He hadn't been working very long when she came into the room and crossed to the window over the sink, looking out at the snow. "Still not sticking to the road," she said.

"I saw." He watched her. "Have there been any more contractions?"

"No. It's just Braxton-Hicks, I'm sure."

A moment later, she said, "They're late."

"Probably took it slow," he said. He thought she looked tired. "I'm sure James would understand if you wanted to cancel a thing like tonight."

"You know," she said, "I never thought you'd be so comfortable with members of my family. You and James seem to get along so well now. And you used to be so afraid they'd disapprove of you."

"I guess that's—been a fear of mine." He felt his throat tighten, and this surprised him. Lately, the slightest things moved him. "I want to keep us all together," he managed. "It's a family, after all."

His own family was long gone—dead, or scattered to the winds. He had a cousin somewhere in Oregon, another in New Orleans, still another somewhere in Illinois, one or two in New York. His father's brother lived in northern California, with a wife and three stepsons. He rarely heard from any of them. He had met Maizie at college, and when she brought him to these Virginia hills to meet her family, he found himself doing and saying absurd things in an effort to ingratiate himself. He loved them immediately. They were so intelligent and attractive, so fortunate, and they seemed to contain elements of the charm and elegance of the house they lived in, as though each of them had sprung naturally from its graceful arches and sun-lighted, tall-ceilinged rooms. He was admiringly jealous of their stories, their shared history, and their happy knowledge of one another, and he envied them even their irritations and chidings and petty quarrels—all those familiar little aggravations and gibes that seem to arise from nowhere and yet are a part of the daily assumption, the lived-in confidence, that the other person's feeling for you will always be the same. It seemed to him that in order to find their way through the anguish of the thing that had happened to them, they must try to concentrate on what was good about them, as a family. To do this with all their hearts, and to take no one and nothing for granted.

Maizie looked out the window over the sink again. "The road's getting a little covering now."

"I hope they're not stuck somewhere."

"An excuse for necking." She gave him a small, sardonic smile. Another of her mother's old stories was about driving back to Virginia from her family home in Michigan, in 1951—how the car had got stuck in the snow, and how she and their father had kept warm through most of the night by necking in the back seat under a pile of blankets.

"Want to see if we can get to Michigan tonight?" Leo said.

"Don't," Maizie said. "Why do you keep calling it up?"

"Honey, you brought it up that time."

She had already begun to correct herself. "I'm sorry, you're right. Let's just leave it."

Lights pulled through the snow and into the driveway, then went out.

"Is this them?" Leo asked.

"It's a pickup truck," Maizie said. She went to the door and opened it, pushed the storm door out. Someone was coming along the walk, carefully, almost falling down in the slickness. Leo moved to stand behind Maizie, who now held the door open and said, "Yes?"

It was Pauline Brill. She stepped up onto the porch and stamped her boots. "Hello," she said. "Sorry to bother you. You're not eating, are you?" She stamped the boots again.

"Come in," Maizie said. "Leo, you remember Mrs. Brill."

Leo said he did. They moved into the kitchen, and he offered her a cup of something hot. She demurred, with a grateful smile, and said there was no time. She had not come to stay. They spoke of the weather and of the fact that Maizie was overdue to have her baby, and though they joked and smiled and seemed relaxed, there was of course the one subject they couldn't speak of, and its stubborn presence behind their talk made everything else seem produced, somehow. Mrs. Brill did not take off her coat. Maizie sat at the table and Leo leaned against the sink, and when all the pleasantries were done with, there seemed nothing left to say.

"Well," said Mrs. Brill. "I'm actually here to see if I might enlist you both in an effort to get the school bond issue put on the ballot in the fall." She reached into the pocket of her coat and brought out some sheets of paper, folded and dog-eared, water-spotted. "This is not a good night for carrying a petition around, but it was the only night I could spare this week. You know Pamela is getting married."

"No, I didn't know that," Maizie said. "I haven't seen Pamela in a while."

"Yes." Mrs. Brill nodded. "This young man she met at a dance in town. Isn't that quaint? A perfectly nice boy, too. Though he hasn't got the best prospects. Flunked out of pre-med at the university and just got a job at the car wash, if you can believe it." She handed Maizie the folded papers. "But I've long since given up any pretensions about those kinds of things, if I ever had them. After all, I was a hairdresser when I met Edward all those centuries ago."

Maizie opened the pages. It was a group of signatures, some of which were slightly smeared.

"I have a pen," Mrs. Brill said.

Maizie smoothed the pages out on the table, and the other woman handed her the pen. Leo looked at his wife's hands, the amazing creamy suppleness of them under the light, and caught himself thinking of what Maizie's family must've said about him in those first days: this clumsy, well-meaning boy from Ohio (he could hear them) with no family to speak of, and no special talent at anything. Maizie had said once that she found him beautiful, that she had chosen him on sight. She used to joke about how she had gone to school to shop, and he was what she had brought home with her. And yet when, recently, she read him her father's strange letter, sitting up in bed with the piece of paper in her trembling hand as he lay on his side staring into her dark eyes, he had heard phrases that might have been applicable to his own situation. If she hadn't been so distressed by it, he might've told her so. He'd held it in. He'd gone out into the chilly dusk and spent an hour splitting logs for the woodstove, working in a kind of fury, thinking about his wife's father—the work that had gone into getting the room ready for him—and feeling himself locked in the trap of his wife's condition and circumstances.

"Thank you," Mrs. Brill said.

"Should I sign it?" Leo said.

"Oh, sure."

He leaned over the table, taking the pen from Maizie. As he signed, the telephone rang, and Maizie reached for it.

"Hello."

Leo handed the paper to Mrs. Brill.

"This is she. Yes, Mrs. Gehringer. I—yes. Yes." Maizie looked at him, and then at Mrs. Brill. "I'm sorry, I can't really talk right now."

"I know her," Mrs. Brill murmured to Leo. "If it's the same Gehringer. I teach her son."

"Mrs. Gehringer," Maizie said in a strange, brittle tone of voice. "I'm almost nine and a half months pregnant."

Pauline Brill put the papers in the pocket of her coat. She and Leo were both staring at Maizie now.

Maizie was sitting with the phone at her ear and one hand visored across her forehead, the elbow of that arm resting on the table. "I appreciate that," she said. "It was a friendship." Then she repeated this phrase.

"Well," said Pauline Brill, "I'd better get on."

There were other lights in the drive now. James and Helena arriving. There wasn't going to be an opportunity to talk about this phone call. Mrs. Brill patted Maizie on the shoulder and made her way out the door, along the walk. She greeted James and Helena, and for a moment they stood talking. Mrs. Brill was telling them about her stepdaughter's coming marriage. In the kitchen, Maizie sat listening to whatever Mrs. Gehringer was saying on the other end of the line. Finally she put the handset down on the table and let her face drop into her hands.

"Honey," Leo said. "What is it?"

She stood with some difficulty and put the handset back in its cradle, set the phone in its place on the counter.

"Maizie?"

"I've—I told Marty some things." She seemed at a loss.

"What things?"

James and Helena were coming in, brushing the snow from their shoulders. "I don't know, maybe we ought to turn right around and go back," James said. "It's getting bad out there."

"You can stay with us," Leo said, taking Helena's coat.

Maizie embraced her brother, then led them all into the living room. They arranged themselves around the coffee table, with its art books and stacks of magazines, and Leo went into the kitchen to make drinks for them. He heard them laughing about something Mrs. Brill had said out on the sidewalk. Maizie sounded like herself. He poured the drinks—whiskey over ice for James, white wine for Helena, sparkling water for Maizie and himself—and made his way back in to them with all of it on a tray. Helena was sitting on the arm of the sofa, above the level of her husband's shoulders, and she had one hand resting on his back. James sat forward to take his and Helena's drinks.

"So," Leo said, putting the tray down on the coffee table and sitting across from them. "What's the story?"

"Story?" Helena said.

They all seemed to hesitate.

"What've you all been talking about?" Leo said.

"Where were we?" said Helena.

"We were wondering when Maizie is going to have this baby," James said.

"I took a walk in the snow tonight," said Maizie. Then, to James: "You remember?"

"Do I remember what?"

"Mom's story, about the night she had me."

"I don't think so."

"Oh, you know it, James. She used to tell it to us when it snowed." James's face was blank.

"You can't tell me you don't remember the story."

James said, "I've been thinking about that time when we were at the Fourth of July celebration out at Blue Ridge Park, summer of—what—'eighty-two? We were all there, the whole family. I don't know why we went that year. Dad was always so reluctant to go anywhere on holidays. We all went, and there was a band playing in a gazebo—this rock band, of all things. Playing in a gazebo in the park. And Mom wandered off. Do you remember? It took us the longest time to find her. We spent the whole afternoon looking for her, and we didn't find her until the fireworks started."

"I found her," Helena said. "She was sitting down by the edge of the pond, watching the ducks."

"Do you remember, Maizie?"

"I guess so," Maizie said.

"I remember," Helena said. "It was getting dark. I couldn't even make her out from a distance. It was the hat—I saw that straw hat she wore, sitting next to her. So I walked up and said, 'Andrea?' I said it two or three times before she heard me. I said, 'Andrea, what're you doing? We've all been crazy looking for you.' And she said, 'I went for a walk.' Really, she said it so simply, I wondered what I'd been so upset about."

"She was always doing things like that," James said. "You'd look up—at the parties they threw, all those people around. It happened more than once. You'd look up, and she'd be gone. She'd be off in another room of the house, or out walking. She'd just slip away."

"Let's talk about something else," Maizie said.

"We can talk about this," said James, "can't we?"

For a small space, no one said anything.

"She was my mother," James said, "and I don't feel like I ever really knew her."

"We've been going through this," said Helena. "We keep listing qualities—traits, you know. She liked elegance. She worked at it. She ran a dance studio for little girls. She had a way of looking right at you when she laughed. She was good at conversation."

"I woke up one time and she was standing by my bed, staring at me," James said. "I was about thirteen years old. She was standing there, perfectly still. I thought it was a ghost or something, and when I yelled, she moved and scared me even worse. It was like a statue coming to life. It took her a long time to calm me down that night."

"Remember how she used to be about Christmas?" Helena said. "When did that stop?"

"I keep getting these flashes of memory about her," said James. "When she and Dad were having problems, she'd leave some part of herself undone. There'd be a button loose, or a strand of hair. Or she'd forget to put both earrings on. Remember that, Maizie? It was a conscious thing she did, like a statement or something. I said, 'Mom, your eye liner's smeared a little,' and she gave me the strangest look and said, 'I know.' Just like that. Like there was nothing unusual or in need of correction. A perfectly natural thing, in a woman who was always so concerned about how people saw her."

"Please," Maizie said. "I don't want to talk about her anymore."

"Maizie, you can't tell me you're not thinking about all of this."

They were quiet again. They heard the wind in the eaves of the house.

"I keep thinking about how everything looked in the motel room," James went on. "She'd hung her clothes up in the bathroom, for Christ's sake. They were on a hanger on the back of the door."

"I've been seeing that picture of her," Helena said. "Sitting by that pond in the twilight. It's like I could almost call to her. I've dreamed it. I used to watch her standing in front of the house waving at us as

James and I drove away. She always stood there until we got out of sight. Rain or shine. She'd get so small in the distance, still waving."

"When I was a kid," Leo said, "my mother used to talk about getting out of earshot. She didn't like the feeling. I'd head off to school and she'd keep saying my name, saying good-bye. I lived a block and a half away from school, and she'd yell so loud I could still hear her as I climbed the front stairs of the school. It was like a game, and we laughed about it. But when she was serious, she'd say something about how it always hurt her—the fact that I'd be out of earshot, away from the sound of her voice."

The others looked at him.

"What you said," he said to Helena. "It made me think of it."

"No," she said. "I understand."

"Every year," James said, "for how many years, she had that party for those little kids in her dance studio. We had to help out. Remember, Maizie? Didn't she—remember she slipped out of a couple of those, too. Once I found her sitting in the office with the lights off. Sitting at her desk in the dark."

"I've done something like that," Helena said. "I used to sit in my closet when I was a kid. It made me feel safe."

They sipped their drinks.

James said, "I have this memory of her, running to get out of the rain. It haunts me. She was laughing—I can see it so clear. This young woman, this person I thought I knew, enjoying life."

"She had such lovely skin," Leo said.

"Remember how she used to get about the way we dressed?" James said to Maizie. "She gave me such a lot of grief about my hair. She was always worried about other people. It seemed to me that she never thought about herself at all."

"Oh, she thought about herself, all right," said Maizie.

Now they all looked at her.

James shook his head slowly. "I still can't—" He broke off.

"I'll be back," Helena said, rising. "I have to powder my nose."

"Jesus, Helena," James said. "Couldn't you come up with something more original than that?"

Helena bent down and showed him her nose. "I'm going to powder my nose," she said. Then she turned and made her way down the hall to the bathroom. Leo took a drink, watched for a while as Maizie tried explaining to her brother about their mother's walk-in-the-snow story, then excused himself—neither of them heard him—and went into the kitchen to start the dinner. He put rice on, and came back toward them to ask if they wanted coffee with the meal, and as he entered the space between the kitchen and the living room, he heard Maizie say, low, "I had a call from Marty Gehringer's wife today."

"Who?" James asked.

"Gehringer. The one I told you about in September."

"Okay."

"She's blown everything out of proportion, and now Gehringer's moved into an apartment in Point Royal. She blames me."

"Jesus."

"I don't know what to say to Leo."

There was a pause then, in which Leo felt as though they might have realized that he was near. From down the hall came the sound of water running in the bathroom. He braved a silent step backward, then froze again as Maizie began to speak.

"How is it now?"

"Better," her brother said.

"You gave her grief about powdering her nose."

"I was teasing."

"It's really better?"

"I've simply decided to wait until I recognize her again. She looks very beautiful tonight, don't you think?"

"I love Helena," Maizie said.

"I love Leo," said her brother.

Leo made his way to the kitchen and ran the tap—wanting some sound to place himself in another part of the house. After a moment, he turned the tap off and set the fire going under the skillet. He watched the oil corrugate with the heat. When he put the flour-coated fish in, it crackled and sent several needle-sized drops of oil onto his wrist. He turned the fire down, hearing his sister-in-law come back through from the hallway, and now the three of them were talking about a movie that Helena had seen, and liked. It came to him that the whole evening remained to get through. He looked out the window at the snow, the swirling flakes under the streetlamp. It was quite possible that James and Helena would stay the night. In the other room, someone had put music on.

He checked the fish, took the salad out of the refrigerator. After a few minutes his brother-in-law strolled in, sipping his whiskey. The women were talking animatedly in the other room. James went to the back door and looked out the window there.

"Bad," he said. "Bad, bad."

"You can spend the night," Leo said automatically. He couldn't look the other man in the face.

"Maizie had a contraction just now."

"Braxton-Hicks," Leo told him.

"What's that?"

"Contractions that don't mean the baby's being born."

James was quiet a moment. Then he seemed to come to himself. "Hate the winter," he said. "Makes me feel like things are closing all around me. You know, the early dark."

"Whatever," Leo said.

"Is something wrong?"

"Not a thing," Leo told him. "Everything's completely jake."

"Jake."

"It's an expression," Leo said.

"Okay, yeah, I remember." James sipped the whiskey. "Did I say something to piss you off?"

"I don't know what you're talking about," Leo said.

The other man shrugged, looked out the window again, and sighed. "Maizie said the old man called."

"He wanted to know how Maizie was. Is. And I really couldn't tell him much."

"I haven't heard from him," James said without much inflection. "How does he like Florida?"

"I forgot to ask. We didn't talk very long."

James was silent. In the other room, the women had also fallen silent.

"He sounded chipper enough, though," Leo said.

"Chipper."

"I mean he didn't seem to be—"

"No, I know," James said quickly.

"Maizie's still mad at him about the room. And the letter, of course."

"The letter shouldn't make her mad."

"The anger in it surprised her. She wasn't ready to have it said out like that."

"Hell, I'm angry," James said. "Isn't she angry? How can she not be angry?"

"I wouldn't know." Leo turned and concentrated on the frying fish.

"I'm mad as hell," James said. "Still."

There didn't seem anything else to say.

"Everybody's a victim," James went on. "Right? I'm so sick of that shit. And I'm *still* mad. And Dad's right. No pity. No fucking pity. A part of me hopes he's forgetting her. I hope he's got himself a girl-friend or something."

Helena entered the kitchen. "You hope who's got himself a girl-friend?"

"Who do you think?"

"Well," Helena said, "he's about to have himself a grandchild."

For a little space, no one said anything.

"Did you hear me?" Helena said. "It's started."

* * *

THE TRIP TO THE hospital was smoother than they'd feared it might be. The roads were covered with the snow, but it was mostly slush. They drove through it as though it were rainwater. "Do you need us to go faster?" Helena asked, because Maizie had abruptly taken hold of her arm and begun to squeeze; she was having another contraction. "Can you go faster?" Helena asked Leo.

"He's going fast," said James. "You want us to crash?"

"It's fine," Maizie said.

"Can I do something?" Leo said. "Do you want me to count with you?"

"No," said Maizie. "Jesus."

A minute later, she said, "It's going." Then: "Oh, that was hard."

They turned onto Hospital Hill Road and drove past the Mountain Lodge Motel. Leo glanced at the several lighted windows and couldn't help wondering which was the one. He looked at James, who had turned and was attending to Maizie. For a few minutes, no one said anything. They pulled up the hill and around to the emergency room entrance. Maizie got out on her own, then seemed to cringe, leaning against the wet car in the still-swirling snow, holding on to herself. "Wait," she said. "Oh, God."

James had run into the building, and Leo and Helena began helping her move toward the doors. They were supporting her by her elbows.

"Wait," she said.

And now an orderly came out pushing a wheelchair, accompanied by a nurse. They got Maizie into the chair, and Leo walked alongside her, through the bright open space of the waiting room, past double doors into a corridor and other rooms. He'd lost track of James and Helena.

"Oh," Maizie said. "It's bad."

He put his hand on her shoulder and she took it, holding tight. She was panting, trying to do the breathing that they had worked to perfect.

"That's it," he said. And he tried to breathe with her.

"The baby's coming," Maizie said.

"We'll take care of everything," said the nurse.

In the labor room, in the confusion of his getting the hospital gown on, and the mask, Leo heard Maizie whimper, and he realized that they had been separated. Someone, another nurse, talking in a hurried but very calm voice, told him he had to go back out and sign some papers. "We did all that," he said. "We're pre-registered."

"Leo?" Maizie's voice.

He pushed past the nurse and stepped into the little room where Maizie lay, her hands gripping the metal sides of the bed.

"Oh," she said. "Oh, help."

Leo took her hands. "What's the object," he said. "Fix on something."

"Hah," Maizie said. "Ah. Hah. Hah. Ohhhhh." She closed her eyes and seemed to be straining to get up. Then she lay back and looked at him. "I'm cold."

"It's going to be fine," he said to her.

A nurse or doctor had lifted the sheet over her and reached in. Then she stood back and snapped the rubber glove off her hand, smiling. "This your first?"

"Yes," Maizie said.

"You're doing wonderfully."

"The baby's coming," Maizie said. "I walked in the snow." She looked at Leo and began to cry. "I walked in the snow."

"You're not quite dilated yet," the nurse said. "So do your breathing. It'll be a while."

"I feel like it's coming," Maizie said.

"It is, honey. But it won't be right away." The nurse, whose hair was the color of sunlight on straw, nodded at Leo and stepped out of the room.

"I walked in the snow," Maizie said again, crying.

"I know," he said. "I know, my darling." He leaned down and put his arms around her. A contraction had started, and she was doing the breathing, trying to get it right. But then she was just gasping, and holding on. "Oh, please," she murmured. "Please, God—it hurts. Is it supposed to hurt this much?"

"Is it easing off?" Leo asked.

"There—oh, a little."

The door opened and a man looked in, a doctor—not Maizie's doctor. "Hello," he said. "I'm Dr. Moyer, and I'm on call this evening. Dr. Ransom is in surgery, an emergency. So I'll be doing the delivery." He stepped over to the side of the bed and touched Maizie's shoulder. "We doing all right?"

"It's hurting her bad," Leo said. "Can't you give her something?"

The doctor spoke to Maizie. "We're going to give you an epidural, but it'll take a little while. Can you hold on a bit?"

"I guess so," Maizie said. Tears streaked down her cheeks, and she wiped at them with the backs of her hands.

The doctor put a rubber glove on, then lifted the sheet and examined her. Then he, too, snapped off the rubber glove. "Everything's going just fine."

"Oh," Maizie said. "Oh, no."

"Try not to tense up," the doctor said.

"Oh, God," Maizie said. She held Leo's hand so tight it hurt. He leaned down close to her ear and tried to do the breathing. "Don't," Maizie told him. "You're cutting off my air."

"Remember the exercises," he said.

"I remember the fucking exercises," Maizie said through a groan. Then she lay her head back and breathed out, a long, sighing breath of relief.

The doctor was looking at Leo. "It's all right," he said. "It'll be all right." Then he tapped Maizie's knee. "Listen to your coach."

When he had gone out, she asked for a cold washrag on her lips. "They're so dry."

Leo accomplished this, using one of the rags they had brought with them. She was quiet, and he touched the damp cloth to her mouth, lightly, using his other hand to caress her forehead. When she opened her eyes to look at him, he had the sense that she didn't quite recognize him.

"Is it starting again?" he asked her.

"No."

They waited. Perhaps five minutes went by, and then five more. She asked for the wet rag again, lay back, and closed her eyes. A moment later, she opened them again.

"Anything?" Leo said.

"No."

Presently she said, "If this is false labor—"

"It's not false labor," he told her.

They were quiet a moment. "Leo," she said abruptly, "that phone call tonight—"

"You don't need to be worrying about that now."

"I *am* worried about it." Her tone was aggravated and tired.

He held her hand, and waited.

"I've been friendly with Marty Gehringer, but nothing happened. Do you understand me?"

"Maizie, for God's sake," he said.

"I could talk to him, and that was all it was."

Leo was silent.

"It had nothing to do with you."

Unable to help himself, he said, "Apparently."

"Oh, hell," she said.

"Look," he told her. "Can we concentrate on this? I'm sorry."

"It doesn't mean I don't love you," she said.

"Maizie, this is not the time."

She was silent. Another minute or so went by. He thought she might've drifted off to sleep. But then she opened her eyes and looked at him. "I have the feeling something awful is going to happen," she said.

"Stop it," he told her.

They were quiet again. Somewhere in another room, a woman shouted.

"I love the walls here," Maizie said. "I wouldn't want to miss anything."

He put the damp rag on her forehead.

"Thanks," she said.

Again, they heard the scream.

Maizie looked at him. "Oh, hell," she said, and seemed about to cry.

"Is it starting again?" he asked her.

"No."

He waited.

"Ohh," she said. "Now it is. It's—ohhh, a hard one. It's—mmmm."

Leo held her hand. Together they tried the breathing, and it went a little better this time. The contraction eased off.

And then the doctor and nurse were there. Leo saw that the doctor's hands were freckled, that his wedding band seemed to cut into the ruddy flesh of the ring finger. "Could you excuse us, please? Just while we administer the epidural."

He went out into the corridor, and along it to the waiting room. James and Helena were sitting side by side against the far wall, James reading a magazine, Helena watching a couple make their way out the door. She saw Leo first, and stood. "Already?"

"No," Leo said, and remembered, with a little unbidden rush of elation, that he was going to be a father. "They're giving her an epidural."

"But everything's all right?"

It struck him that he had always liked Helena so much. He embraced her. "She's in a lot of pain. But the doctor says everything's fine."

"The epidural will help," James said. His face looked ashen, and perhaps it was the light. When he put the magazine back in its place on the small table at his side, Leo saw that his hands shook. James ran his thin fingers through his hair, then seemed to let down.

Helena said, "Are you all right, James?"

"I'm not having the baby," James said irritably.

"You look like you're about to collapse. And don't talk to me in that tone of voice."

"I'm fine," James said. "Really."

"I've got to get back," Leo said, letting go of her.

"We'll be here," Helena said. Then she sat down and put her arm over her husband's shoulder. "You'd think James was the father."

In the labor room, Maizie lay propped on pillows. The pillows were from the bag that she had packed weeks ago in preparation for this—and now, after the rehearsals and practice sessions, someone else had put the pillows under her, and Leo felt guilty.

"Sorry," he said. "I told James and Helena they didn't have to stay. But they're staying anyway."

"Leo, it hurts me. I've had two really bad ones close together. And these people left me. They just left me alone."

"I'm here now," he said, and felt the blood rise to his cheeks. "Do you want me to get you something?"

"No."

"Do you want the rag again?"

"I'm being such a coward, Leo. But I can't help it."

"Is the epidural—"

"Nothing helps. It's going to come again and I'm so scared."

He held her hands, and when it started, he worked with her to do the breathing, but at the height of it, she yelled. It was a sound he would not have believed; it terrified him. Then she was trying to breathe again, trying to count. "Ohhhh, God," she said when it had subsided.

The room seemed to be growing smaller, all the colors in it growing sharper, more defined and more lurid. The light hurt his eyes. Somewhere off in another room, another woman moaned and then screamed.

"What is this," Maizie said. "This is where they take you."

He wet the rag again and put it to her lips.

"Thank you," she said.

"Do you want it on your forehead?"

"Yes." She gasped. "Oh, God." Then she was trying to sit up, her face contorted.

"Is it starting?" he said.

"Ohhhhh, Jesus Christ God." Her nails cut into the skin of his palm, and she was trying to do the breathing again, and failing. "Ohh, stop it. Please, make it stop."

"Where is everybody?" Leo said. "Jesus."

The pain eased, and now Maizie was crying. "I can't do it."

Leo held her. "Again?"

She shook her head. "I can't do it, Leo. I can't do it."

"Let me see if I can get the doctor," he said, and was secretly ashamed for the sense of relief he felt himself moving toward—to be out in the hall, to be heading freely away from this little room, with its instruments and its electronic sounds and its dry white light. "Do you want me to go look for the doctor?"

"No," she said. "Please don't leave me." The words were spent in a breath, and she was gasping again, trying to pant, holding his hand and looking into his eyes. "Ohhh, please. Help it—oh nooo. No." She lay back, and for an instant he thought she might've passed out. But then she had come forward again, and her hand relaxed. She rested her head on his shoulder. "I think the epidural is taking effect."

"I want to know where the hell the doctor is," Leo said.

"They said we'd be here alone for a while. I'm only five centimeters."

"I think a doctor should be here."

"I want *you* here," she said.

He kissed the top of her head. "Want the washrag again?"

"I'm dying of thirst," she said.

He wet the rag, and she put her head back. And the nurse came in. The nurse raised the sheet, paused, then moved back to the door. "Everything okay?" she asked.

"We're in a lot of pain," Leo told her.

The nurse walked over and took Maizie's other wrist, looked into her eyes. She checked the monitors and then smiled. "It's all normal.

On schedule. When you get to ten centimeters, we'll move you into delivery."

"When will that be?" Leo said.

"Just a while longer," said the nurse.

"I'm having the baby," Maizie said.

The nurse smiled. "Is the epidural working?"

"Nothing's working."

"I know it feels that way."

"Ohhh no, I can't. Leo, please."

Leo held her while she cried and groaned, and when he looked again, the nurse had gone. Beside the bed, the console with the monitor on it made a soft beeping sound. He couldn't decide if he had heard it before. Maizie panted, sweating, then slowly relaxed. "I can't do it, Leo, please."

"It'll be okay, baby," he said.

"If it would only stop."

He wet the washrag again, but she didn't want it.

"I can't breathe as it is."

The doctor came in and examined her. "Progressing nicely," he said.

"She's in a lot of pain," Leo said.

The doctor nodded and gave a small, cryptic smile. "It'll be fine." Then he touched Maizie's shoulder. "Maizie, you've got a bit of a wait. The epidural should help. Soon you'll be able to push, and that'll make you feel better. Can you make it?"

Maizie nodded, glaring.

When the doctor had left the room again, she looked at Leo. "I hate this," she said.

"They're so blithe about it," Leo said.

A few minutes later, the nurse came in again. "How're we doing?"

"Drugs," Leo said. "My wife is suffering." He was almost crying.

"Oh, God, the baby is coming," said Maizie. "Now."

"I know it's hard," said the nurse. She moved to the foot of the bed and lifted the sheet. "Good Lord," she said. "I'll be right back."

"Ohhh," said Maizie. "Leo!" She threw her head back and raised her knees with an involuntary jerking motion. Leo moved to her side, and her hands tugged at the sheet over her abdomen. For a second, she seemed to be squirming toward the head of the bed, but then the sheet was pulled back and Leo saw the baby's head push out of his wife—it had come with a slippery ease that startled him—and now it was face down in a pool of streaked blood. "Ohhhh," Maizie said with a deep, exhausted sigh. She was trying to see, lifting her head.

Leo reached down and touched the wet surface of the head, the shining, blood-soaked hair, wanting to turn the face up out of the blood but worrying about the neck. "Oh, Jesus," he said. "Jesus, help us."

"Leo," said Maizie. "Leo—please. Ohhh, ohhh."

He turned the head a little, looked at the small wrinkled mouth, the deeply shut eyes, and he couldn't move, couldn't get the face completely turned out of the blood.

"Leo!"

The baby's head had slid out of his tentative grasp and was face down in the blood again. He was watching his own baby drown, and the only choice seemed to be to pull it up, and risk breaking the neck. He reached down and took the head in his hand, and couldn't bring himself to move. In the next instant, the doctor burst in, and with tremendous urgency grabbed the baby by the head, his fingers digging deep under the tiny jaw, pulling. It was a struggle. The baby didn't want to come. At some point during all this, Maizie had got hold of Leo's hospital gown, and when a nurse looked at Leo and said "You, out," Maizie gripped the gown even tighter, so that while the bodies closed in around the bed where the baby and Maizie were being worked on, Leo was prevented from moving out of the way. "You must leave," another nurse said.

"No," came Maizie's voice, stronger than it had been in all the time they had spent in this room. "I want him here!"

Through the tangle of arms and moving shapes surrounding the bed, Leo saw his wife's face. Maizie was looking down at where they were working to free the baby from her, and she was crying, saying a word he couldn't make out. Finally she gave forth a long, sighing shout, and a nurse said, "It's a . . . girl."

"Oh, baby," Maizie said. "Little baby. Let me see her." She had let go of Leo's hospital gown, and the backs parted. The hands of these others—Leo didn't even know how many there were—guided him into the circle around the bed and toward Maizie, with the child on her belly. Leo's new daughter was gasping, the eyes so tightly shut that he could not imagine them ever being strong enough to open. But then they did open. They opened, and seemed to see, and the nurse with the straw-colored hair picked her up and took her to the clear glass bassinet on the other side of the room, to bathe her. He watched them stick some suction thing in the little slack mouth, and it seemed to him that they were handling her too roughly. But it was all just expert speed, and then Maizie spoke, still crying. He didn't hear her. He moved to her side and leaned down to kiss her soaked forehead. The doctor was gently pushing on her stomach. For a few minutes, there seemed nothing at all to do except stand still and try not to get in the way. When the nurses were helping Maizie move onto another gurney, she looked at him and said, "Leo, it's a girl."

"Beautiful," he said.

And Maizie kept crying.

"It's over," Leo told her. "It's okay. You did great, honey."

"Leo," she said. "I wish she was here. Why isn't she here?"

He put his hand at the side of her head and pulled her to his chest. "I know," he told her. "I know."

"Oh, why did she do it, Leo? Why isn't she here for this? Why couldn't she fight through it and be here? How could she do it to us?"

"Don't," he said.

The baby let out a small, fierce sound, almost of anger.

"Listen to that," he tried to say.

"I wish she'd told me something. I would've helped her through."

He kissed her cheek, and she turned and kissed him back.

A moment later, he said, "You know how it was that day when you were all looking for her, that Fourth of July?"

She leaned against his chest. "What."

"Whenever there's a big gathering like that," he said, "music, dancing, and all that, I always think about how there are all these personal lives gathered together in the sound—like the sound holds them together. I'm not explaining this very well. It's like there's all these people living their own lives, with their own secrets and worries and desires, and the music connects them. It's all part of their time with each other. And—but sometimes there are people who wander out of hearing, away from the others. The music can't reach them, and when you call their names they can't hear. Like the way *my* mother was, calling good-bye to me all the way to my school, just to keep the connection. And well, honey, maybe it's like your mother just—got out of earshot."

Maizie said nothing.

"I'm sorry," Leo told her. "I'm sure I don't make any sense."

"I've been so mad at her for it," Maizie said.

The others in the room seemed not to be there, and then they were. They spoke quietly about levels, and procedure, and already the business of the hospital was moving on, a woman moaning down the hall, the doctor talking to a nurse about what dosage of some drug to give still another patient elsewhere. Several others were working on the baby.

"Is everything okay?" Maizie said to no one in particular.

"Everything's fine," Leo reassured her, although he wasn't certain of this himself.

Maizie said, "I want us to start over—go back to the way we were. I don't want to feel this anger anymore."

The doctor moved to the foot of the bed. "She's pinking up real nicely," he said. "You did fine. Both of you." Then he nodded at Leo. "All three of you."

They brought the baby over, wrapped in a hospital blanket—dark pink, ancient-looking, with a head of black hair and small dark tufts on the lobes of her ears. The eyes opened, and they were a deep, deep shade of blue. The fingers of one tiny hand were jutting from the folds of the blanket, and they moved, closed over the edge of the cloth, and then opened again.

"Hello," Maizie said. "Oh, welcome, my little baby."

"She's beautiful," Leo said. "Isn't she?"

Maizie looked at him, soft eyes, all his, giving him everything of herself; it was in the look. "Beautiful," she murmured. Then she opened her gown and put the baby to her breast. "Oh, see, honey? She's taking right to it."

"I see," he said, and felt time open outward. It was the strangest sensation, as though he were already decades older. He reached down and touched his daughter's leathery hand, the amazing fingers, perfectly formed, almost frightening for their softness.

The doctor was still standing there. Leo felt an abrupt surge of affection for him, as if they would go on from this moment to become the greatest of friends.

"Tell me," the doctor said, "this little girl's name."

Spirits

I MET BROOKER at one of those parties for new faculty. I was just out of graduate school, after a stint in the Army, and I had just arrived, that July, to get myself ready for the fall semester. Brooker was the most distinguished member of the faculty, and I think I must've been surprised to see him. When I had come through on my campus interview in the spring, the people who squired me from place to place gave me the impression that he was notoriously aloof; there were bets among them as to who would next catch a glimpse of the creature.

But then, I was a fiction writer, the first ever hired to teach at this small, rather conservative teachers' college, and he wanted to get a look at me. He told me this in the first minute of our acquaintance, as if he wanted me to know he wasn't a regular at such gatherings: he really had come specifically to meet me. He had seen my stories in the magazines; he knew I had a book coming out, and he liked everything of mine that he'd seen. I was, of course, immediately and wholeheartedly in thrall. Remember that I was only twenty-six, and I suppose I offer this as an explanation, if not as an excuse; it could never have occurred to me then that he was merely flattering me.

The party took place on the lawn of the president's house, which was a two-hundred-year-old Colonial mansion with walls two feet thick and new, polished tile floors that shone unnaturally and made me think of carcinogens, for some reason. The president was a small, frail-looking old man with a single tuft of cottony white hair at the crown of his head, and twin tufts above his ears. His name was Keller, and he was a retired military officer with a Ph.D. in modern political history, Brooker told me. Dr. Keller was clearly delighted that Brooker had decided to attend his party. He stood in the open door to his house, the hallway shining behind him in a long perspective toward other open doors, and offered me his hand. "Come right through and get something else to drink, young man," he said. We had all been filing toward him from the lawn, which was dry and burned where there was no shade, and lush green under the willows and oaks and sycamores that surrounded the house.

"This is our writer," Brooker said to him.

"Well, and what do you write?"

"He writes stories, Dr. Keller."

"Oh. What kind of stories?"

Brooker left me to answer this, and I stammered something about seriousness that I'm sure Dr. Keller took as evidence of the folly of the English department in having hired me in the first place. His next question was a clear indication of this.

"Are you tenure-track?"

"Yes, I am."

He nodded, and then he had turned to Brooker. They stood there exchanging comments about the turnout, the weather, the long spell without rain that had killed the grass, and I took this opportunity to study Brooker. For a man of nearly sixty, he was remarkably youthful-looking. His hair was gray, but thick, and his face still had the firm look of the face in the photographs of Brooker with Jack Kennedy before he ran for the presidency, or with Robert Kennedy near the end, or, later, with Lyndon Johnson. I remembered reading that Brooker had become disaffected with public service after the riots in Chicago, and had joined the faculty of a small private college in Virginia, and I was a little pie-eyed about the fact that I too was joining the faculty of that college. Life was roomy and full of possibility and promise; and I was for the moment quite simple and happy.

"So," Brooker said to me, entering the hall where I stood, "you have met our fine old president in his fine old house."

"Very nice," I said, gazing at the walls, the paintings there, which were of Virginia country scenes of a century ago.

"Have you found a place to live yet?"

I was paying a weekly rate at the Sweeney Motel off the interstate. I had paid the first month's deposit to rent a house that wouldn't be ready until the first week in September, and I was using the advance money on my book to make it until then. My wife had remained behind at the large Midwestern school where I had taken my degree; she would make her way here as soon as things were settled. I told him all this, feeling a little silly as I went on but finding myself unable to stop; it was information he seemed glad to have, and yet I wondered what could possibly interest him in it. I wound up talking about Mrs. Sweeney, who, because I was the same age as her son, had given me the single-room rate for a double, and kept stopping by to see me in the evenings, as if to give to the general pool of the world's kindness in the hope that somewhere someone else would offer something of it to her son.

"I'm giving a series of lectures at Chautauqua Institution this August," Brooker said. "I hate to suggest that you leave Mrs. Sweeney, but I wonder if you might not want to use my apartment for the month. You'd save money that way, and you could get some work done."

I just stood there.

"It must be awful trying to work in a motel."

"Well," I said, "I haven't been working."

"I'm going to be gone right through the last week of the month, because I have to spend some time in New York City too."

The president joined us then, wanting to introduce some people to Brooker, who nodded at them and was gracious and witty while I watched. There were two women in the group, one of them not much older than I, and as the president began to talk about the lack of rain and his garden, Brooker leaned toward me and, breathing the wine he had drunk, murmured something that I wasn't sure I could've heard correctly. I looked at him—he seemed to be awaiting a signal of agreement from me—and when I didn't respond he leaned close again, and, with a nod of his head in the direction of the younger of the two women, repeated himself. It was a phrase so nakedly obscene that I took a step back from him. He winked at me, then turned his charm in her direction, asking her if she liked the president's fine old house.

"Built in 1771," Dr. Keller said, looking at the ceiling as though the date might have been inscribed there.

"I love old houses," the young woman said. "That's what my field of study is. The American house."

Brooker offered her his hand and introduced himself, and then began an animated conversation with her about modern architecture. I stood there awhile, then moved off, through the hallway to the kitchen and out the door there. Some people were still on the lawn, but I went past them, to my car, feeling abruptly quite homesick and depressed. I drove around the college and through the town streets for a while, just trying to get the sense of where things were. The place my wife and I had rented was on the north end of town, in a group of old, run-down frame houses. Sitting in the idling car and gazing at it, I felt as though we had made a mistake. The place was really run-down. The porch steps sagged; it needed painting. I had agreed to fix the place up for a break in the amount of rent, and now the whole thing seemed like too much to have to do along with moving and starting a new job. I drove away feeling like someone leaving the scene of an accident.

When I got back to the motel, Mrs. Sweeney was waiting for me, and talking to her made me feel even worse. I kept hearing what Brooker had murmured in my ear. Mrs. Sweeney sensed that something was bothering me, and she was mercifully anxious not to intrude, or impose. She stayed only a few minutes, and then quietly excused herself and went on her way.

I had showered and was getting into bed before I remembered that Brooker had offered me his apartment. I was ready to doubt that he could've been sincere, and even so, when I called my wife, I found myself mentioning that I might be spending August as a house-sitter for none other than William Brooker.

"Who's William Brooker," she said.

I said, "You know who he is, Elaine."

"I'm not impressed," she said.

We didn't speak for a few seconds. Then I said, "So, do you miss me?"

"I miss you."

"What're you doing right now?" I asked.

"Talking to you."

With a feeling of suppressed irritation, I said, "What've you been doing all day?"

"Studying."

"The faculty orientation party was no fun," I said, and I went on to tell her about Brooker's murmured obscenity. Part of me simply wanted to express what I had felt about it all evening—that while I might have uttered exactly the same thing at one time or another, in Brooker's mouth and under those circumstances it was somehow more brutal than I could ever have meant it in my life. But there was also, I'm sure, the sense that my shock and disbelief would appeal to her.

"That doesn't seem like such an unusual thing for one man to say to another," she said. "Was she attractive?"

"You didn't hear the way he said it, Elaine."

"Did he slobber or something?"

Now I felt foolish. "Elaine, do you want to talk tonight?"

"Don't be mad," she said. "It really just doesn't sound like such an awful thing to me."

"Well," I said, "you weren't there."

"Are you going to stay in his apartment?" she asked.

"I don't know—I guess it'll save us money," I said, feeling wrong now, convinced that the whole question was pointless; that Brooker hadn't been serious, or that I had misinterpreted a gesture of hospitality anyone else would have known how to give the polite—and expected—refusal to.

"Why don't you hang up and go to sleep?" Elaine said. "You sound so tired."

"What if I get this apartment," I said. "Will you come out sooner?" And in the silence that followed, I added, "You could come out August first."

She said, "I'm in summer school, remember?"

"All right," I said, "the second week of August, then."

"We'll see."

"What's to keep you from coming then, Elaine?"

"We didn't plan it that way," she said.

Later, after we'd hung up and I'd been unable to fall asleep, I put my pants and shirt on and went out for a walk. Mrs. Sweeney was sitting on her little concrete slab of a porch, with a paperback book in her lap and a flyswatter in one hand, her stockings rolled down to her ankles, her hair in a white bandanna. She glanced over at me and smiled, and then went back to her reading. I went on up the sidewalk in my bare feet, and stood near the exit from the interstate, thinking about the fact that I was married, and that tonight my marriage felt like an old one, though we had been together only a little more than a year.

2

ELAINE WAS TRYING to finish a master's degree in library science. The first time I saw her, she was wearing a swimsuit. I had just finished my first year of graduate school and was living in a small room above a garage, trying to write, and spending most of my afternoons at a lake a few miles west of the campus. There was a beach house and restaurant on the lake, one of those places whose floors are covered with the sand that people track in from the beach, and whose atmosphere is suffused with the smell of suntan lotion. I was sitting alone at the counter, eating a hot dog, and two young women walked in, looking like health itself, tan and lithe and graceful in their bikinis. They ordered ice cream cones and then walked to the back of the room to see what songs were on the jukebox. I sat gazing at them, as did the boy behind the counter—a high school kid with a lot of baby fat still on him, and with the funny round eyes of a natural clown. There wasn't anyone else in the place, and when the women strolled out finally, the boy put his hands down on the counter and let his head droop. "It's a tough job," he said, "but somebody's got to do it."

I laughed. We were for the moment in that exact state of agreement which may in fact be possible only between strangers. I got up and went out to the shaded part of the beach, where the two of them had settled at a picnic table. I had never done anything of the kind, but I was so struck by their beauty that I simply began speaking to them. I asked if they were students at the college and if they were going to summer school, and I asked how they liked the lake. They were polite, and they gave each other a few smiling, knowing glances, but we spent the rest of the afternoon together, and when I left them I asked to see them both again; it was all quite friendly, and we agreed to meet at a pizza parlor just off campus. That night, when I went there to meet them, only one of them showed up. This was Elaine. We had something to eat, and we went for a walk, and the odd thing to recall now is that I was a little disappointed that she, and not her friend, had come to meet me. I remember feeling a little guilty about this as the evening wore on and it became evident that Elaine and I were going to be seeing each other. As it turned out, her friend was leaving school, and I never saw her again; but even so, there were nights in that first year of our marriage when I would wake up next to Elaine and wonder about the friend. It was never anything but my mind wandering through possibility, of course, and yet when I think of Brooker, of the events that followed upon our first encounter at the faculty orientation party, my own woolgathering makes me feel rooted to the ground through the soles of my feet.

* * *

HE PHONED ME EARLY the next morning. I had been lying awake, thinking about calling Elaine, and when his call came through I thought it *was* Elaine. "I wondered what happened to you," he said.

I was vague. I think I was even a little standoffish. I said something about having things to do, errands to run.

"Listen," he said, "I wondered if you were still interested in house-sitting for me."

I hemmed and hawed a little, the thought having crossed my mind that I hadn't actually said I *was* interested; for some reason, now, accuracy seemed important: it was as if I might lose something to him if I allowed him to blur any of the lines between us.

He said, "I don't want to impose on you."

"No," I said, "really. I'm very glad you thought of me."

"You'd be doing me a favor," he said.

And so we agreed that I would come to the apartment for a drink that evening, at which time I could get a look at the place. His wife was arriving from New York in the afternoon, and if past experience meant anything at all she would not feel like entertaining a dinner guest; but a quiet, sociable drink was something else again.

"I could come another night," I said.

"No," he said after a pause, "tonight will be fine."

After we hung up, I went outside and found Mrs. Sweeney hanging wash on a line in the yard.

"Have you looked at television this morning?" she said. "Did you see the news last night? You see that guy arrested for molesting that little girl?"

She didn't wait for me to answer.

"That's my ex-husband," she said. Her eyes were wide and frightened and tearful. "You believe that? My ex-husband." She turned to hang up a sheet, and I thought I heard her sniffle. "You think you know a person," she went on; she was looking at me now. "You live with a person and you think you know him—know the way he is. His—all the way to his soul. You think you understand a man's spirit when you look in his eyes and he's your live-in partner for three years. Three years," she said. "Do you believe it? And he was always the cleanest, nicest man you'd ever want to meet. Quiet and easy to get along with and sort of simple about things, and a good storyteller sometimes, when he felt like it. A little slow about work, sure— but . . ."

"Maybe he's innocent," I said.

She stopped what she was doing and gave me a look almost of pity, except that there was impatience and frustration in it, too. "He confessed," she said. "He confessed to the whole thing. Can you imagine what this'll do to my boy, a thousand miles away from home, on some boat in the ocean, hearing that his stepfather did a terrible thing like that and then *confessed* to it?"

"Maybe the news won't get to him," I said.

"Oh, it'll get to him. I'll write and tell him about it. It'll get to him, all right." She put her apron full of clothespins in the basket at her feet and walked over to me. "I should be getting something for you to eat."

"No," I said, "I'm fine."

"I have a cook named Clara, but she's sick."

She had told me this on the day I registered—she'd repeated it three or four times since. I had begun to wonder what this Clara must be like to be missed so much.

"I'm fine," I told her.

She shook her head. "Do you believe it? A little girl." Then she turned and pointed at the motel office. "The paper's right inside the door there. It's on the front page if you want to read about it. My husband a rapist, for God's sake."

"It's a terrible thing," I said as she marched toward the office. I think she meant to get the newspaper and bring it out to me, but then the phone rang in my room, and she said over her shoulder that I could come see it when I had the time. I went back into the room, certain that the call was from Elaine. I said "Howdy" into the telephone, and was greeted with a silence. "Hello?" I said.

"Uh, yes. This is William Brooker. Listen, I wanted to ask you . . ." There was another silence, during which he sighed, like someone backing down from something. "Look, this is a little embarrassing. I mean I suppose it could wait until tonight. But I'd had a few drinks before I—before the party, you see."

"Yes?" I said, trying to sound only politely interested.

"Well—I said something last night—you know. We were all standing there and that extremely choice young lady was talking to Dr. Keller, and—you remember I said something a little off-color to you . . ."

"I didn't quite hear what it was," I lied.

"Oh. Well, I was wondering if you thought the young lady might've heard me. Or Dr. Keller."

"I wouldn't be able to say for sure."

"Yes, well. I shouldn't bother you with it. You say you didn't hear it at all?"

"That's right."

"I don't like to offend," he said.

And I was suddenly seized with a perverse desire to make him repeat the phrase that had so unnerved me the night before. "What was it, anyway?" I asked him.

"Oh, nothing. Just something a little—a silly little comment, you know. A joke. An impolite little aside. What I'd like to do to her—that sort of thing."

"Well," I said, wanting just as suddenly to let him off the hook, "I'm sure no one heard you."

"But—you said you *couldn't* be sure." Precision was Brooker's talent, someone had said.

"I'm reasonably sure, Professor Brooker. I mean if *I* couldn't hear you I don't think anyone else could."

"That's right," he said. "Good." I had the feeling that I had just heard the tone he took in his classroom, leading a group of neophytes through the thicket of Twentieth-Century Politics.

"So," I said.

He said, "Well, I guess I'll see you tonight." Then, exactly as though it were an afterthought, he told me I ought to wear a suit and tie for the occasion.

"Excuse me?" I said.

"There'll be one or two other people here, if you don't mind."

"Not at all," I said. And I didn't really hear him as he talked about who his other guests would be, because I was thinking about the fact that I didn't have a suit *or* a tie, and so would have to go out and buy them. I had exactly twenty-two dollars in my pocket, and there was perhaps another forty in the checking account I'd opened only that week. The next installment of my advance wouldn't arrive for days.

Brooker had hung up before I could muster the courage to apprise him of this, and then I decided I wouldn't want him to know under any circumstances. I would simply go without if I had to.

Of course I knew I would do no such thing. I would probably have been willing to steal what I needed; but as it turned out this wasn't necessary. Mrs. Sweeney's son was about my height and build, and he had left four suits behind—this was apparently his whole stock of them—along with about five hundred ties, all given to *him* by his former stepfather, the rapist and child molester, who according to Mrs. Sweeney had had a thing about ties, had collected them like somebody hoarding a thing that would soon be rare and hard to get. I chose a plain blue one, and a gray suit. I tried the suit on, standing in Mrs. Sweeney's spare room, and it fit well enough. Mrs. Sweeney made me wait while she ironed my shirt, and then that evening, after I'd got myself dressed and ready to go, she fussed with me, straightened the tie and brushed my arms and shoulders, her boy, going off to his first party in town. It seemed the appropriate thing to kiss her on the cheek before I left, and I'm afraid I embarrassed her.

"Good Lord," she said, but then she squeezed my elbow. I almost asked what time she wanted me home.

3

BROOKER'S DIRECTIONS were characteristically precise. I had given myself a few minutes to allow for any trouble finding the place, and so I was early. I walked up the sidewalk in front of the building, already feeling stiff and uncomfortable in my suit and my rapist's tie, and Brooker came out on the landing and called to me. He was in shirt sleeves, the sleeves rolled up past his wrists.

"So glad you could make it," he said.

By the time I got up to him he had rolled the sleeves down and was buttoning them.

"I guess I'm a little early."

He ushered me inside and offered me a drink. Anything I wanted. I told him I'd wait awhile, and he excused himself and went upstairs. I sat in the living room, in the middle of his white sofa, my hands on my thighs, my back ramrod-stiff. It wasn't the sort of room you could relax in. There was a fireplace, and a baby grand piano, and on every available surface there were figurines and cut-glass shapes and statuary. The chairs and the love seat and the ottoman were not in the sort of proximity that would make conversation very easy, and the wallpaper was of a dark red hue that was really rather gloomy. I remembered that I had come to look at the place, and in an odd shift of mind I had an image of me sitting there with the whole apartment to myself. Whatever else this room was, it was luxuriously appointed, and I knew I was going to enjoy the luxury of entering and leaving it as I pleased.

Now I sat back a little and breathed a satisfied sigh, while upstairs I heard Brooker and his wife moving around. Twice I heard her heels as she crossed from one room to another, and then she came down the stairs. She was a striking woman in her mid-forties, with wonderful square shoulders and deep, clear blue eyes, and she was wearing a white evening gown that made her skin look marvelously tan and smooth. She offered me her hand (I nearly brought it to my lips), and asked, in a voice that was warm and rich and full of humor, if I would come keep her company in the kitchen while she got things ready for the evening. Apart from being a little breathless at the sight of her, I was now beginning to wonder if I hadn't come more than a little early.

I said, "I must've got the time wrong, Mrs. Brooker."

"Call me Helen," she said, leading me into the kitchen. "And you shouldn't worry about being early—we're just running a little late."

The kitchen was a light-filled, high-ceilinged room that looked as though it might've been transported, brick by brick, board by board, from one of the family farms in Brooker's native Minnesota. She indicated that I was to sit at the table in the center of the room, and then began opening cabinets and hutches, bringing out dishes, glasses, boxes of crackers, knives, and forks.

"Can I help?" I said.

"Absolutely not. I could never stand servants in the house because I wanted to do it all myself, and as you can see I can't even let a guest be polite without launching into an explanation of this—quirk of mine." She paused. "Do you like the kitchen?"

"It's a very nice room," I said.

"Well, and you're going to be calling it home, aren't you."

"For a month. I guess so."

She went about her work, slicing cheese, arranging crackers on the plates, and making dip, and I sat watching her.

"William says your wife isn't with you."

"No."

"Too bad," she said. "Do you miss her?"

"Very much."

"William travels so much. It's just odd that we're both going this time."

"I'll take good care of things," I said.

She waved this away as if there could be no doubt about it, and then without asking what I wanted she fixed me a glass of bourbon on ice. "If this isn't to your taste I'll drink it myself."

"It's fine," I said, and she gave me an odd look, as though my answer had surprised her. I sipped the whiskey, and she went back to setting things in order for the evening's guests, who were apparently arriving now—we could hear Brooker greeting someone out in the hall.

"William will think I stole you from him," she said. "Do you mind if I have a sip of your drink? I don't really want to have a whole one."

I handed her my glass. She took a long, slow sip, then breathed. I have loved the taste of whiskey since I was very young and my father would take me out on the porch at home and let me sip it out of sight of my mother, and I have never seen anyone—nor, I believe, have I myself ever enjoyed a sip of whiskey as much as this stately and beautiful woman did that night in Brooker's kitchen.

"Very good," she said, and smiled, handing the glass back to me. There was something a little hurried about the way she did it, and then I realized that Brooker was coming down the hall. I put the drink down on the table in front of me and tried to look calm as he entered the room, leading Dr. Keller, who did not remember having met me, and who, again, asked if I was tenure-track. We had got past all that and in the next moment Brooker asked his wife if she wanted a glass of bourbon.

"Not on your life," she said.

"I always ask and she always refuses," Brooker said. "I don't know if I like disciplined people."

"Why don't *you* have some?" she said to him.

"No," he said, "I'm off it, too."

Dr. Keller also declined, and so now I was the only person in the group who was drinking. I found this a little irritating, and I made up my mind that I was going to sip the drink very slowly; I might even ask for another. I sat watching Mrs. Brooker put the finishing touches on a plateful of cheeses and cold cuts, while the two men stood talking about diets and diet drinks. Their conversation seemed so banal that I wondered if they weren't trading sides of a sort of running joke, but they were serious: Brooker's full attention was on the college president as he listed his various reasons for preferring iced tea without sugar over the sugarless colas. And then I noticed something else. Helen Brooker was staring at me. She had finished with everything and was simply standing there with her legs crossed at the ankles, gazing at me with all the frankness of a child. When I turned a little and met her gaze, she smiled and offered to refresh my glass.

IT WAS AN ODD EVENING. The other guests arrived, two couples. They were people of Brooker's age and class, and Dr. Keller introduced the men as members of the Board of Visitors of the college.

"This is our writer," he said, presenting me to them. "Professor Brooker was so kind as to invite him here tonight."

The two men shook my hand, and their wives nodded at me from the snowy expanse of the couch. I sat in one of the wing chairs near the fireplace and was promptly forgotten. Brooker had begun to hold forth about the Kennedy years, and I noticed that his wife sat staring at her nails while he talked. She had heard it all before, of course, and she was doing a bad job of disguising her boredom. Finally she got up and carried a couple of empty plates into the kitchen, and when she came back out she had a glass of whiskey. She sat down next to the wives, and when she crossed her legs and let her high-heeled shoe slip to the toe of the dangling foot, my blood jumped. I went into the kitchen to pour my own whiskey, and I think I entertained for a moment the rather puerile fancy that she would make her way to me there, and that she might confess something to me, something I could console her for. But no one came, and in a little while I carried my fresh drink back to the chair by the fireplace.

The others were all drinking iced tea from a tray on the coffee table. I sipped my drink, and watched Helen Brooker sip hers. The talk was general now, and very stilted and hesitant; there seemed no common history for any of them to talk about—or there *was* a common history that all of them were avoiding as a subject for talk. In any case, I grew very tired and so deeply bored that I may even have nod-

ded off once or twice. When Mrs. Brooker stood to go fix herself another drink, I got up, too. I meant to leave, but before I could make
my apologies she took me by the arm and walked with me into the
kitchen.

"You haven't really seen the place," she said.

"It's fine," I said.

"We keep our bourbon in here to discourage our guests." She was
pouring it into her glass. "Billy doesn't like trying to talk to drunks."

"Billy."

"Brooker." She tipped her head slightly to the side. "Doesn't it
sound like a little innocent boy: Billy Brooker? That's what they called
him, you know."

"Who?" I said.

"The Kennedys."

"Did you know him then—when he was with the Kennedys?"

"I worked for him. I was his secretary."

"You must've been very young."

She took a sip of her drink. "Billy's thirteen years older than I am.
He was forty-two and I was twenty-nine. I was just out of a very unhappy marriage, and of course he was—well, he was the famous Mr.
Brooker, though I must say I was really in love with Jack Kennedy
more than anything else. We were all in love with him—the whole
staff. And of course I voted for him because I thought he was so handsome. A lot of women *and* men did that, you know."

"I wasn't old enough to vote, but I guess I would have," I said.

"You were fascinated with him." It was as though she were leading me toward something.

"I liked his speeches."

"He was an awful womanizer, you know."

"That's what they say."

"Are you a womanizer?" She smiled, swallowed some of her
drink, turning to face her husband, who came into the room from the
back door and stood for a moment, looking at her and then at me.

"Hogging the booze," he said.

"Here," said his wife, lazily handing him hers. "If I have any more I'll wind up with a headache."

"Cheers," Brooker said, and drank.

"Have our guests departed, Billy?"

"They've departed."

"I've got to go," I said.

"Why don't you have another drink?" Brooker said. "You haven't really seen the place yet."

So I stayed for another glass of bourbon, which was enough to make me a little bleary-eyed and giddy for the drive back to the motel. Brooker walked me through the upstairs rooms of the apartment, including his wife's reading room, as he called it (it looked like a bedroom), and his study. She excused herself and went off to another room to bed, leaving the smell of her perfume everywhere.

"Your wife is very beautiful," I said to him when she had gone.

"Yes," he said, as if we had agreed on something quite unimportant.

The upstairs rooms were spacious and comfortable-looking, and there was a television room I knew I would spend a lot of time in. I wasn't planning to try to do much writing. In fact, I have always been the sort of writer who works best out of a predictable routine, and with plenty of order and harmony around him. Brooker showed me his study last. It was a small book-lined room with a desk and two straight-backed chairs, and with exactly the harried, busy-paper look you'd expect it to have. "I've been working on something," he said to me, and took one of the pages from his desk. On the wall above the desk were photographs of Brooker among the powerful; and of his wife, wearing something flowing and diaphanous and white, in various balletic attitudes obviously meant to appear candid, and just as obviously posed for. Brooker apparently caught my interest in these photographs, for he put the page back down and touched the corner of the nearest photograph—of Helen standing in a bath of white light, her slender arms almost hidden in the liquid folds of the gown. He moved the frame just so, and then stared at the picture.

"Helen wanted to be an actress for a while," he said. "She wasn't bad."

"She's beautiful," I said, and realized that I was sounding more and more like a love-struck high school boy.

Rather dryly, Brooker said, "Yes, we agreed about that before." And then, giving me a fatherly smile: "I can bear any number of repetitions concerning the beauty of my wife, lad."

We went downstairs, and I declined what was—I was certain—a decidedly halfhearted offer of another drink; in any case, I thought it was time to leave. He stood in the light of the landing and asked if I was okay to drive, and I assured him I was, though I had my doubts. As much as I love the taste of bourbon, I have never been able to drink more than a glass or two without getting very unsteady on my feet. When I pulled out onto the highway there was an immediate blurring of the lines of the road ahead, and I held tight to the wheel, going very slow, feeling more sloshed every second.

Mrs. Sweeney was sitting under her yellow porch light, with her flyswatter and her book. She stood and walked over to me.

"My goodness," she said when I staggered.

I took her husband's tie off and held it out to her.

"I don't want it," she said.

I put it into the suit-coat pocket. "I'm sorry," I said. "I've had a little too much to drink."

"Your wife called," she said. "I waited up to tell you."

"You're very kind," I said.

"They showed pictures," Mrs. Sweeney said. "On the news. They showed him being taken into court. He was covering his face."

There wasn't anything I could think of to say to this.

"It was on the news. They think he killed a lot of little kids and buried them somewhere. I was married to him all that time."

I shook my head, and looked out at the road.

"Your wife called," she said. "I told her I'd wait up."

"Thank you, Mrs. Sweeney—and I wish there was something I could say about all this—"

"It's on the news," she said. "It's a big news story."

"I'll watch for it."

"They're going to come talk to me. The newspeople. They're going to ask me if I knew anything." She shook her head, turning. "You think you know a person."

In the room, I thought of calling Elaine, but what I did was lie across the bed, still wearing the borrowed suit, and, dreaming of a woman twenty years older than I was, I fell deeply, drunkenly asleep.

In the morning I woke to see a shadow move across my window, high up. I lay there with a dry mouth and a headache, watching it for awhile, and finally I decided to investigate. As I came to my feet, I thought I heard Mrs. Sweeney's voice, and then other voices. Outside, across the way, on the grassy hill that led onto the interstate ramp and above which the sun had just risen, men were walking. Their shapes were all blazingly outlined, but I could see that they were combing the ground, searching. Mrs. Sweeney stood in the gravel lot, talking to one man while another filmed her, and there were police cars and news-media vans blocking the entrance to the motel. I went back into my room and turned on the television set, but it was too late for morning news; it was all movies and situation comedies and quiz shows. I started to go back out, and then decided not to. I didn't want to see whatever they would find out there, if they found anything at all.

4

THERE WAS all that work to do on the house, and I was gone a lot during the next couple of days. I had an excuse to be gone, and I took it. One late night I arrived to find Mrs. Sweeney waiting up for me. She wanted to tell me about the interview with the news people, and her voice as she spoke was an exact blend of excitement and horror. The men searching the hillside had found nothing, she said. To think that murdered children might have been buried within yards of her own house; to think that she had been on the nightly news. "I told them," she said. "I made them understand that when Eddie lived with me he never did anything like hurting a little child."

"It's an awful thing," I said.

"I wrote a letter to my son. I don't know how to tell him."

"Would you like me to look at it?" I said.

She seemed puzzled by such a suggestion. "No," she said.

"Well, anything I can do to help."

She thanked me, but something about my offer to read the letter had made her nervous. I think she considered its contents too private even for the eyes of the faraway young man to whom it was addressed. The next day I stayed around the motel—I took a swim in the pool, and basked in the late-morning sun—and Mrs. Sweeney was uncharacteristically cool and distant. When she came to ask if I wanted lunch, I thought she was almost wary of me. I said I wasn't hungry, and thanked her, then went back to my room, certain that removing myself for the moment was the best thing for her peace of mind. In the room I napped and read magazines and watched television. Mrs. Sweeney's husband was big news, all right. The authorities were turning up bodies all over the country. When I called Elaine, I told her about the man whose tie I now apparently owned, and though she feigned interest, I could tell that she was restive, wanted to hang up.

"So," I said, "tell me about your day."

"I studied."

"Anything else?"

"Nothing else."

"No movies? No television? No talk with friends?"

"I said nothing else."

"Is there anything you'd like to talk about?"

"You were telling me about the mad killer-rapist."

"Did I tell you about Brooker's wife?"

"Tell me about Brooker's wife."

"I'm in love with her."

"Wonderful."

"We're going to run away to Paris."

"Terrific."

"We're madly, desperately, spiritually, and physically in love."

"I'm very happy for you."

"Elaine," I said.

"You have my blessing," she said.

"Are you coming out in August?" I asked. "We'll have their place all to ourselves."

"We can play Pretend."

"We can do anything you want," I said.

"All I know how to do is study."

"Are you coming out or not?" I said.

"Not."

"Come on, Elaine."

"Not, I'm afraid, is the truth."

"All right," I said, "why not?"

"Maybe I've decided I don't want to live in Virginia."

I didn't say anything then.

"What if I don't like Virginia?" she said.

"Elaine, you loved it. Remember? You picked out the house. You were all excited about fixing it up. I've been working on it all this time."

"I guess I'm getting cold feet. It's senior syndrome, or something."

"Are you serious?" I said.

"Half."

"You mean it."

"A little, yes."

"Are you telling me you might not come out here at all?"

"I don't know what I'm telling you. Don't badger me."

"I have a place for us both to stay until the house is ready. It's a very nice place, Elaine. It's luxurious, in fact."

"And it's famous."

"I don't understand your attitude about this. Yes, it is William Brooker's apartment, and William Brooker is widely known."

"He's famous."

"All right, goddammit, he's famous. Yes."

"Don't get mad," she said. "I'm too tired for anger over the telephone."

"Elaine," I said, "what's the matter?"

She paused, then sighed. "Nothing."

"No," I said, "what's the matter. Tell me."

"Nothing's the matter. I'm tired, and I don't feel like making any big decisions now, all right? I don't want to think about moving and all that. I'm trying to finish up a degree."

"All right, fine," I said.

She said, "Terrific."

We hung up simultaneously, I think. Then I called her back. We traded apologies and explanations. We were both under a lot of pressure; it was a new job, a new situation. She was so tired and beaten down by the work. She had been having anxiety attacks, and was beginning to wonder what it had all been for. I had upset her by talking about child murders and rape, and now the idea of living in a place where such things happened made her tremble. "I know, things like that happen anywhere, but I still feel jittery about living there and I was feeling jittery about it before you told me this horror story."

"It's just nerves," I said. "It's just getting settled, that's all. Once you get settled you'll see."

But in the silence that followed, I wondered if there weren't something more than nerves bothering her.

"Elaine?" I said.

"I don't know," she said. "I don't want to talk now. We'll talk later."

And again, we hung up almost simultaneously.

IN THE MORNING, I had breakfast in Mrs. Sweeney's small diner-kitchen. There were five or six other people staying at the motel now, and she was too busy to speak to me, except to say that her cook,

Clara, would be coming back on in a few days, and it couldn't be a minute too soon. She made a gesture like a swoon of exhaustion. Outside, cars slowed going by, or pulled in and sat idling while the curious got out to stare and take pictures. Mrs. Sweeney's husband was a national story now—and each day brought new revelations about him: he had been killing people, mostly little girls, all his adult life. He had drifted across the country, killing as he went, years before settling in Virginia with Marilee Wilson. The psychiatrists who were conducting interviews with him found that he was completely without remorse, without any sense of the enormity of his crimes, and when he spoke about his victims he was chillingly direct and simple, a man describing uncomplicated work, something about which there were only the barest considerations of technique. Police officers from seven states would be converging on the small town jail where he was presently incarcerated; they would all be about the business of talking to the killer to clear away open files, unsolved cases. Some were guessing that it might take years for all the crimes to come to light, and estimated that the numbers were well into the hundreds.

Mrs. Sweeney was glad that business was better, but weary of all the questions, and she didn't like being stared at. The day her husband's picture appeared on the cover of a newsmagazine, she closed her shutters and put up the NO VACANCY sign.

"I don't care about the business anymore," she told me. "I think I'll sell the place now, anyway."

This was about a week before I checked out. I hadn't told her yet that I would be leaving before the September date we had initially agreed on. She had come over from her place on the stoop, and headed me off from a night walk. We stood outside my room and watched the lights on the interstate beyond the crest of the hill across the way. "I used to get lonesome for him," she said, "nights like this."

I had the feeling that she was lonesome for him *now*, but I said nothing.

"Were you on your way somewhere?" she said.

"I was going to take a walk."

"It's a pretty night for a walk."

"Would you like to come with me?" I said, and knew immediately that I had embarrassed her again. "I mean I wouldn't mind company."

She mumbled something about having too much to do.

"Well," I said.

"You know what?" she said. "I don't believe him. I lived with him for three years. If he was like they say he was he would've killed *me*, wouldn't he?"

I said that seemed logical.

"But maybe with someone like that, there isn't really any logic to go by."

"That's probably true," I said.

"I'm going to sell this place and move out of the state." She walked off toward her yellow-lighted stoop.

I watched her go into the office, saw her shadow in the window, and there was something so bowed and unhappy and reproachful about the way she stood gazing out at me that I decided against the walk. I didn't want to find her waiting for me when I returned. I was sorry for everything, but I was in fact a little tired of her trouble; I had troubles of my own. I got into my car and drove over to the rental house, and worked for a few hours painting the rooms. While I worked, I thought about Elaine, and then I was thinking about Brooker's wife. It started as an idle daydream, but I found myself putting embellishments on it, and soon enough I was engaged in a full-fledged fantasy. I imagined that she drove by in the night and saw me in the curtainless windows of the rental house, that she came to the door and knocked, and I let her in. We strolled through the house, talking about what I planned to do with it once Elaine and I moved in, and then we said things that led to kissing. I was on a stepladder, with a roller in my hand, dripping paint, and I realized that I had been quite motionless, deep in this fantasy, for some time. I had seen myself removing Helen Brooker's white cocktail dress, sliding the straps down her shoulders, and I had kissed the soft untanned places on her belly. "Are you a womanizer?" she had asked me that night in her kitchen.

Before I was through, I imagined visiting her at the apartment—saw her arriving early from her travels while I was still alone and sleeping in her bed; I played out a small lubricious drama in which I told her that Elaine was staying behind, would not be joining me, and in which Helen Brooker became my mistress, visiting me every day in the rental house, full of appetite for me and the excitement of our illicitness. In other words, I conjured up a woman who bore no real relation to Helen Brooker—a dream woman who wished only to satisfy my whims.

When, a week later, I carried my suitcases up the sidewalk and the stairs to the landing of Brooker's apartment, I kept my eyes averted for fear of catching a glimpse of his wife, as if to see her would be to cause the whole business to come blurting out of me, the confession of a secret and obsessive lust; for I had kept my fantasies about her, had added to them, had suffered them in my sleep, along with crazy shifts of logic in which the mad mass killer Mr. Sweeney appeared, always in the guise of someone quite harmless at first, and then simply as himself, crouched in a kind of striped, shadowy corner, staring out. I had awakened from these dreams with a jolt, and with the sense that I had come into an area of my life that was utterly uncharted and dark. I found myself deciding against calling Elaine, or putting it off, and when she called me I was as uncommunicative and anxiety-ridden as she was. We had a few very unhappy, very gloomy discussions of plans for the end of summer, and we still hadn't established what she would do. For the time being, I was to move into the Brookers' apartment alone.

When I said good-bye to Mrs. Sweeney, she seemed oddly relieved to have me go. Her son was coming home on leave, she said, and it was too bad I wouldn't be able to meet him.

"Maybe I'll come visit," I said.

"That would be very nice," she said. But I think she was only being polite. I was the last of her customers, and she was closing up for good. She had even let Clara go. She told me this almost as an after-thought: it was too bad that someone like Clara had to go off and work for one of the big places, like Holiday Inn. She didn't think a big chain would appreciate someone of Clara's gifts. Everything was so cut-and-dried these days. She went on like this, tallying up my bill, and I knew she was glad I was leaving.

I didn't have to worry about seeing Brooker's wife, for she was al-ready on her way north. Brooker told me this as he helped me inside with my things. He gave me his key, then called a taxi to come take him to the airport. When I offered to drive him there, he said, "Well, I should've thought of that. The taxi's on its way, though."

"Call and cancel it," I said. "I don't mind taking you."

He considered for a moment. "If you're sure about this, lad."

In the car, I caught the odor of alcohol on his breath. He sat star-ing out the passenger window, and I coasted along trying to think of something to say to him. I had hoped we might talk on the way, that I might get to know him better. Finally I said, "Will you be meeting your wife in New York?"

"I'm going to Toronto first. Overnight."

"Will she be at Chautauqua with you?"

"Part of the time, maybe. She has friends in the city—Chau-tauqua's a little too Victorian for her taste."

"Will you be lecturing about the Kennedy years?"

"Some."

"I wish I could've been around for some of that time."

"It wasn't all it was cracked up to be."

"You knew John Kennedy pretty well, didn't you?"

"He was my boss for a while. I knew him, all right."

"He looks so brilliant in all the films—you know, the speeches."

Brooker said nothing to this.

"Everybody who knew him wrote a book about him," I said. "Why didn't you?"

"I decided instead to give lectures. It means more money over a longer period of time. The colleges will pay handsomely for somebody like me to come tell them what they already suspect. After you get famous, lad, you'll be paid handsomely to come read from your work—it's a lot like that. All fiction. Don't tell anyone I said so, but the colleges are full of stupid, limited people, with a very few exceptions. And to be blunt about things, I might as well tell you that it's entirely possible I won't be teaching at our quaint little peaceful school after next year."

"Why not?" I said, breathing the alcohol again. And even so, I thought he would tell me about some grant or other, or plans to spend a year abroad. What he did say was so surprising that I took my eyes off the road a moment to look at him.

"It seems that I'm to be removed—for a few small indiscretions."

I was speechless.

"You must've noticed that I'm inclined to be a bit careless what I say."

If I could've said anything at all, I would have. I sat there staring out at the road and waiting for him to go on.

"The wife and I used to booze it up pretty good. She's got a lot better than I am, of course. But the two of us made a few powerful enemies. It doesn't matter now, you know, because I'm getting near retirement anyway. I guess you're wondering why I'm telling you all this."

"No," I said stupidly, as if I might've expected him to confide in me.

"The truth of the matter is that I did want to salvage something if I could. I mean I hoped that by showing some college spirit I might be able to persuade the Board to reconsider, but I don't think that's going to happen."

"They're *firing* you?" I said.

"Not exactly."

"You're tenured," I said, "aren't you?"

"I never accepted tenure, lad. I didn't want it. I've had a series of special contracts, each year."

I had pulled into the airport terminal. There was a small knot of people at the far gate, and I drove toward it. He already had the door open. "I hope you'll forgive me for deceiving you about—well, about the work. I do like your stories, but I only read them to make this last try, so to speak. I mean I know you thought I was just one of those prescient types who read everything. I searched them out and read them because Helen thought it might impress the Board. I'm afraid it didn't even impress *you* quite as much as I could've hoped it would."

I had stopped the car.

"I guess not," he said, giving me a look.

I got out and helped him with his things, and when he was in line, waiting to board the plane, he shook my hand and told me to make myself at home in his place. I was to use everything just as if it were mine, and he would telephone now and again, if it was all right, just to be sure there wasn't any important mail, or phone calls that needed immediate attention. When I left him there, and started the drive back to town and my new surroundings, I felt as though I had been duped. And I don't mean I was bothered by the fact that he hadn't come upon my work in the course of his normal habits of reading—that had been too outlandish to believe in the first place, and I had indeed been a little embarrassed all along at my own wish to take him at his word; this is hard to explain, muddied as it is by hindsight. In any case, my sense of having been duped had, oddly, to do with Brooker's attitude in the few moments just before I left him at the airport. It was as if I were somehow a creation of his; as if everything I had thought and felt in the few days since I first met him at the faculty orientation party had been produced, orchestrated by him, with calculation and in the certain knowledge that each gesture, each wave of his baton would bring another shade of admiration out of me. I must have looked like an adoring boy at that first meeting.

In any case, I returned to the empty apartment with a very strong sense of dissatisfaction and displeasure concerning Mr. William Brooker. I had decided that if he was a man who deserved my respect, he was not the man of great qualities that I had imagined him to be.

And when, that evening, I took his wife's picture down from the wall and carried it with me into her reading room with its small, flower-fragrant bed, I thought of him with something like the mixture of pity and disdain that an adulterer feels for the man he has cuckolded.

5

*E*LAINE DECIDED not to come until the first of September—the original moving date. I took this news quietly. I had stopped all work on the rental house. I had stopped going out; I was spending each day in the rooms of that apartment, watching television, reading, sleeping, and gazing at what I could find of photographs and belongings of Helen Brooker. I found a box of pictures of her as a girl, and as a bright young student; I found honors and trophies she had won in college, for her work in the yearly stage play, or for her contributions to the literary magazine; I found a stack of lurid-looking paperback books on a shelf in her closet; and, best of all, I found a bundle of old letters and cards in the back of a bureau drawer—birthday greetings, Christmas cards, cards to accompany flowers, and a few thank-you notes, along with letters from her mother, from a sister in Connecticut, and, to my great fascination, from an ardent somebody who kept complaining that she never paid him enough attention. These love notes or complaints were all signed with the initial *W.*

Darling, one of them went, *I suppose you'll laugh when I say this, but someday you'll read what I've written to you and remember me as your one truest friend; and you'll miss me. On that day you won't laugh. And wherever I am, I'll still love you. Always, W.*

Another said, *Helen, I have written a poem called "Sorry." It's about us. You said to keep in touch, and this is the only way I know how. The poem is simple: Could you spend Sunday / or just any one day / with me / she said / "Sorry." It goes on in this vein, so you see, Helen, I am not without humor concerning you and me. Love, W.*

It suddenly dawned on me as I read that *W.* probably stood for William, and that these sophomoric and romantic missives were from the then senatorial staff worker William Brooker, already in his forties and sounding like a nineteen-year-old boy with a crush on his English teacher.

Helen, there's something in your eyes that makes me unable to speak, and the only thing I have is pen and paper. I'm not a poet, but if I were I'd find the words to make you see what happens to me every time you turn your head my way. I love you, Always, W.

This snooping of mine was exactly as undignified and sneaky as it sounds, and I suppose the only thing to be said about it now, once having admitted this, is that it was also a function of a kind of madness that had taken hold of me. At night I had begun to dream about Helen Brooker in a way that left me exhausted in the mornings, and there was always the haunting and shadowy figure of Sweeney, always the terrible fact of his passionless violence in the dreams. I had taken to following the development of the case on the local television stations, two of which were doing specials about him; and there were the continuing newspaper articles. And so in fact, Mr. Sweeney was part of the daytime, too. In the newspaper articles the reporters said Sweeney spoke in a soft, countrified voice about stabbing a girl through the heart, and my own heart shook in my chest, and yet I couldn't look away or stop reading or put my mind on my work. And when I wasn't following the news, I stalked the house for a woman's privacy.

When Elaine and I talked on the phone, our silences grew longer, and the suppressed irritations began to find terms of expression. We argued, or bickered, or teased each other into bickering, and finally she suggested that something was wrong with us which a separation might solve: she wanted to wait through the fall before coming east, if she came east at all. We could see how we felt in six months. I don't know if she thought much would change in that time, but I felt as though we were dissolving the marriage over the telephone, and I told her so. Her response was a very calm denial that this was so; she just wanted a little time. I even offered, near the end of the conversation, to come west; I said I was willing to give up the job. But of course this was a ridiculous idea, and in any case I didn't think I could bring myself to go through with it. If she wanted me to—which she did not.

So after a week in Brooker's apartment, I was fairly crazed: I was sure my wife was divorcing me; I was having a fantasy affair with a woman I had met only once in my life (there was something about being among her things; it was as if I were a ghost, haunting another ghost, and there was always the feeling that I *did* know her after all), and I was monitoring with avid and horrified fascination the story of Mr. Sweeney and his many victims. To put it simply, I was in no condition for what took place at the end of that first week. And to spare you any unnecessary suspense, I'll just say here that what happened was that I had a visitor, a woman I'd never seen before, someone close to my age or younger, who stood in the light of the Brookers' landing and stared at me as if I had materialized out of the summer night.

I HAD BEEN READING Brooker's vaguely plagiaristic love notes *(Helen, nothing is as intensely delicate as you are),* when the doorbell rang, so loudly and so suddenly—it seemed the tolling that calls the guilty to their punishment—that I let out a cry and nearly fell from the chair in which I sat, the letters and notes in a loose bundle on my lap. I almost dropped them all as I came to my feet, and for a confused minute I didn't know what to do with them; I thought this visitor would surely be Helen, or Brooker himself, and that I would be caught red-handed with the evidence of my spying. Finally I jammed everything under a cushion of the sofa and went to the door to peer out at whoever it was. In the dim light of the landing I made out enough of the face to know it wasn't either of the Brookers.

I opened the door.

She stared at me for some time before she spoke. "I am looking for Mrs. Brooker." As I have said, she was my age or younger, and she looked Spanish—her hair was very black, her eyes a facetless black. "I know they live here."

"Mrs. Brooker isn't here," I said.

She looked down a moment, apparently deciding something. Then she simply turned and started back down the steps.

"Excuse me," I said.

She stopped, looked back at me. "You are her son?"

I shook my head no.

"I need to talk to *her*, not him. You tell him that Maria Alvarez came to see Mrs. Brooker. You tell him that."

"Mr. Brooker is in New York State," I said.

"Remember the name," she said, going on, "Maria Alvarez."

I stood out on the landing and watched her cross the parking lot, moving very slowly, almost warily, as if she were afraid someone might spring out at her from behind one of the parked cars. But then it wasn't quite like that, either—for there was an element of discouragement about it, a kind of defeated dignity that made me wonder where she had come from and what she might be going back to. I almost called to her, though of course she probably would not have come back. She got into a small, beat-up Volkswagen bug and drove away, and I went back into Brooker's apartment and took up my invasion of Helen Brooker's personal life.

That evening, Brooker called, and I told him about his wife's visitor.

"Jesus Christ," Brooker said. "Jesus Christ."

I waited.

"Slight Spanish accent?"

"Yes," I said.

"And she asked for *Mrs*. Brooker?"

"Yes."

"Jesus Christ."

"She drove away in an old Volkswagen bug."

"Well, for Christ's sake."

I said nothing. For a moment there was just the faint interference on the line of another, distant conversation.

"Listen," he said. "If she comes back, tell her Mrs. Brooker and I are separated. Okay? We're not living together anymore."

I stood there holding the receiver to my ear.

"Got that?" he said.

"You're separating?" I said.

He took a moment. "Just tell her that. Will you tell her that for me?"

I heard myself say I would.

"Did you tell her when we'd be home?"

"That didn't come up."

"Good."

"She probably won't be back," I said.

"Well, if she *comes* back, you'll remember to tell her Mrs. Brooker and I are separated. We've been separated for some time, you don't know how long."

"Mr. Brooker," I said, "are you asking me to lie for you?"

He took another moment to answer. "Just tell her we're separated. That'll be the truth."

"All right," I said.

"And then call me at this number if she does come back."

"I will," I said to him.

And then he had hung up. I sat for a long time by the phone, not really thinking about anything, and yet feeling low and lonely and sick at heart. Finally I called Elaine.

"Honey," I said, "I miss you."

She had fallen asleep studying, and was groggy and irritable. "Call me back," she mumbled, "okay?"

"Elaine, I'm going crazy here," I said.

"Call me back," she said sleepily, and then the line clicked.

THE AFTERNOON NEWSPAPER, in the third part of a four-part series about Mr. Sweeney, carried a summary of his early life. Apparently Mr. Sweeney had been raised by a self-styled freethinker, a man who believed in exposing children early to the realities of life, particularly the sexual realities: the senior Mr. Sweeney had made his young son take part in his own sexual escapades, had made him watch while he and the boy's mother and a friend of the boy's mother had relations. There were other unpleasant details: in Sweeney's own words, he could never be near a living, breathing Human Being without thinking of murder. Mostly, of course, he had chosen little girls because, he said, they were less trouble; everything was easier. In his early twenties he had been married to a young woman for about a month before he killed her, and in his late forties, after almost thirty years of drifting—during which he had spent stretches in prison for petty crimes and felonies, for vagrancy and public drunkenness, and during which he had also lived for a few intermittent years in Canada and Mexico—he had met and married one Marilee Wilson, a motel keeper, who for three years had somehow kept him happy, though he had continued to wander out in search of victims from time to time. In the words of Mr. Sweeney:

I should've probably killed her when we got separated, and I guess I would have if it wasn't for her changing the motel to my name and her boy being such a pal to me. We done a lot of going around, that kid and me, and I come close to telling him more than once that his stepdaddy weren't no ordinary stepdaddy. She's a lucky one, though. She don't know how lucky. I come close more'n a couple times.

Reading this, I thought of poor Mrs. Sweeney, who would certainly have read the same article, and must now be trembling to think what she had barely missed. And then I was thinking about them as a couple: there must have been moments of tenderness between them, moments when they were happy with each other. Mrs. Sweeney had talked about how she missed him.

I almost never can get really excited about sex with somebody unless they're dead.

I closed the newspaper and went upstairs to Mrs. Brooker's room. There were pictures of her on the bed, and I moved them to the night-stand and lay down. It was warm and bright in the room, the sun pouring through the chinks in the white curtain over the window, and through the curtain itself. I had most of the day ahead of me and I didn't have the energy to move. I thought of trying to write, but I felt empty, and anyway it would take energy to write. I could easily have imagined that I might never have another thing to say. At that moment, nothing seemed further from me than my own dearest and old-est interest. Indeed, the idea of writing stories seemed somehow so much beside the point that thinking about it even in this abstract way made me feel foolish.

I tried calling Elaine again, but there wasn't any answer.

Finally I went out, and drove myself over to the Sweeney Motel. I don't think I intended at first to go there. I remember I thought about riding around the campus, perhaps stopping in on one of my new col-leagues. But the truth of the matter was that I hadn't liked any of them much. They had struck me as a closed group; their conversation in my presence had been full of in-jokes and references to things I couldn't know and therefore could not respond to. (During my years traveling and reading at the colleges I have come to see that this is a rudeness particular to academics, and that my first colleagues were no worse than most.)

So I wound up back at the Sweeney Motel, which was closed now, the windows all curtained and shut and the NO VACANCY sign replaced by a single large wooden plank with the word CLOSED painted on it in black. I pulled in and sat for a minute, looking the place over. Mrs. Sweeney came to her doorway as I got out of the car.

"What is it?" she said.

"Mrs. Sweeney," I said, "how are you?"

"I'm closed," she said. But then she recognized me.

"I just thought I'd—stop by."

She opened the door and stood back for me to enter. I was afraid

I'd come at a bad time, and I apologized, or tried to, but she was already talking.

"My son got his leave canceled. And I know why—I wouldn't come here either if it was me."

The office was a mess. There were newspapers and magazines everywhere; on the television cabinet, glasses and dishes were stacked, and the tables were strewn with clothes. There wasn't anywhere to sit. Mrs. Sweeney cleared a place on the sofa, and then poured herself a tall glass of whiskey from one of several bottles of liquor on the coffee table.

"You want some?" she said.

I declined, and she sat down across from me, keeping her eyes on the TV screen, where a doctor and a nurse argued in an antiseptic-looking hallway. She drank her whiskey, licked her lips. It struck me that I had come there to stare at her, that no matter what I'd convinced myself with when I started out, my motives were no better than those of the merely curious. She was watching me, and I couldn't really return the look, couldn't meet her gaze. "So you're all closed up," I managed.

"Nothing else to do. My son's not coming home. I got people calling me all hours of the day and night. Godalmighty, you know *I* didn't kill anybody. It wasn't *me*, goddammit. I don't know anything. All I know is I was married to the guy three years and I never saw him hurt anyone or anything, and if he wasn't a real exciting man to have around the house he wasn't half bad, either. He left me alone mostly and he never expected much. It wasn't such a bad marriage and now I got to feel like I'm going to grow boils and horns if I miss him a little bit every now and then. People coming here wanting to know did he ever do anything that made me suspicious. I've had three husbands in my life and they all had things about them that you couldn't say was too normal. Who doesn't? Who's normal in private? He didn't seem a bit more strange than anybody else is when nobody's looking." She took a long pull of her drink. "Sure you don't want any?"

"No, thank you," I said.

"I'm going to sell this place and move. Change my name back."

"I'm sorry your son isn't coming."

"He doesn't want to be *seen* in this town again."

I shook my head as if to say how unfortunate this was, but she thought I was disagreeing with her.

"I'm serious," she said. "He doesn't want to be seen. He won't ever come back here. He told me he wouldn't, and I can't say I blame him."

"No," I said, "I can understand that."

She stared at the television. There was a commercial on about sheer panty hose, and then there was one about an airline. She took another drink of the whiskey and then leaned back in her chair. "I don't usually drink," she said. "I don't like the taste of it. I've just been taking it to calm down. You know, I just escaped death. More than once. He was going to kill me."

"I—I saw that," I said.

"Everybody saw it. You know he was with a lot of people here. He knew a lot of people and went to restaurants and fishing and all that, and even sat in church every week—we were regulars, the two of us. And nobody else figured out what he was either, if you know what I mean. You'd think *somebody* would've noticed something."

"It's very strange," I said.

"And I'm not going to pretend I didn't like having him around because I did, and I don't care what they say."

I nodded agreement.

"You know," she said, "you're the last tenant of the Sweeney Motel."

"Why don't you just call it the Wilson Motel again?"

She looked a little puzzled. "Oh, it was never the Wilson Motel. It was the All Nighter Motel."

This harmless piece of information had the effect of putting us both in a kind of musing calm. We might indeed have been mother and son, considering some fact or circumstance that had caught our attention. I reached over and poured a little of the whiskey into a cup on the coffee table.

"Let me get you a clean glass," she said.

I sat back and waited for her. On television a man in a bright T-shirt was biting into a hamburger, and the juices went flying. Mrs. Sweeney came back from her small kitchen and handed me a plastic tumbler, then poured far more whiskey than I wanted into it. We drank. I had an abrupt sense of how truly solitary my existence had become in the weeks since my arrival in Virginia.

"Well," Mrs. Sweeney said, "I sure didn't think you'd actually come back and visit me."

I smiled at her and held up my glass, as if to offer a toast.

"You know, I unplugged my phone. I don't even look at the mail, except to see if there's something from my boy."

Mrs. Sweeney had been leading her own solitary existence.

"I've got plenty of room," I said, "where I'm staying."

She swallowed her whiskey and looked at the television screen. "One time Sweeney killed a cat," she said.

I waited.

"We were on our way to Florida and the cat was in the road and he just pulled right over it—swerved to get it." She took another swallow. "Just—wham. Like that. No cat. A smear in the road behind us. And when I asked him why in the world he'd do a thing like that he said it was because he felt like it."

"So—" I said. "So that was—"

"That was scary," she said. "It scared the hell out of me."

"When was it?"

"Year after we were married."

I drank my own whiskey.

"You know why I divorced him?"

I shook my head.

"The laziness. I couldn't get him to do anything. All he wanted to do was watch television—Westerns. He loved Westerns. John Wayne and Randolph Scott. Horses and dust, and leather saddles and boots, and the cowboy hats. And—and clothes, you know, he loved clothes. He bought stuff he'd never wear even if he could've got around to it.

Shoes and shirts and ties and belts, and pairs of socks. I couldn't get him to do anything around here that needed doing, so finally I just told him to pack his things and get out. Which he did." She was emphatic now. "Which he did. And he went as peaceful as a lamb. Now, you tell me."

I was beginning to feel the whiskey. I put my glass down and stood up. "Mrs. Sweeney, I have plenty of room where I'm staying—you're welcome to come stay there if you want to get away from here." I thought this was the least I could do.

"Isn't that nice of you," she said.

I said, "I mean it."

"Well," she said, rising. The whiskey had had its effect on her as well. She tottered, sat back down. "Stay and watch television for a while."

I didn't really have anywhere else to go, and yet I made my excuses and went out to my car, which was blazing hot in the afternoon sun, and drove back across the campus to William Brooker's apartment, where I intended to lie down and sleep off the effects of what I'd had to drink. As I climbed the stairs to the landing, already sweating profusely in the heat, I thought I caught a glimpse of someone peering at me from the other side of the building. When I looked, there wasn't anything, but I was pretty sure I hadn't imagined it. When I was at Brooker's door, I looked out at the parking lot and saw the Volkswagen bug—the same one, with the same battered fender, the same rusty, gouged finish. Inside, in the cool of the air conditioning, I went straight to the bathroom and took a lukewarm shower, my mind made up to ignore all news and all thoughts of the Brookers or Elaine or poor Mrs. Sweeney, and when I was finished I got into Helen Brooker's bed and took a fitful, erotic-dreaming nap: someone, a woman, a spirit, was leading me into a velvet room.

I woke to the sound of the doorbell. It was dark. There was music coming from somewhere; the doorbell kept sounding, and I hurried down the stairs, trying to get my pants up without missing a step, or tripping over my own feet. "Just a minute," I said. I had no shirt; my eyes were sleep-filled and probably swollen. I opened the door, and of course even half asleep I knew it would be Maria Alvarez.

"Mrs. Brooker, please," she said, in that Spanish-soft voice.

"I should've told you—she's out of town," I answered, peering around the door at her. "They've been gone a few days now." And I was not too groggy to add, "They're separated."

She looked at me, then muttered something I couldn't catch.

"Excuse me?" I said.

"Separated?"

I nodded.

"*Sep*arated," she said, looking out at the dark. For perhaps a minute she simply stood there. "Separated." This time it was as if she were trying to hold back a laugh.

"That's right," I said.

"You know this," she said.

"Yes."

"Separated."

"Do you want to come in?" I asked, holding the door open a little more.

"In there?"

"Yes."

She seemed about to laugh again. "You're very kind, but no."

"I'm sorry," I said.

Her eyes took in the room behind me, and her expression seemed now only curious. "Mrs. Brooker—what is she like?"

"Why don't you come in?" I said.

"Mrs. Brooker is nice?"

"Yes."

"A nice woman. Poor Mrs. Brooker." And now she was laughing, though she tried to stifle it, holding her hand over her mouth. "Separated."

"Look," I said, "what is this about?"

She turned and went back down the stairs, still laughing, and when I followed her partway down she only went faster, until she was on the lawn, almost running.

"Miss?" I said. "Miss?" But she went on. The little, ragged-edged old car roared as she pulled out of the lot and on down the street.

THAT NIGHT, ALL NIGHT, I spent in Brooker's study, looking through his papers, his photographs, his files, for some sign of this young woman who had wanted to talk to his wife. I thought I knew why she wanted to talk to Helen Brooker, and I believed I understood exactly why Brooker had asked me to do what I had in fact done—to tell the lie that he had doubtless known would send the young woman away. Yet it was a fool thing to think I might find what I was looking for in the study of a man like Brooker, even knowing that he had a weakness for alcohol, and therefore might be expected to be careless; and if I did find the incriminating letter or note, I certainly had no plans for it—there wasn't anything at all that I could possibly want with it. No, this rummaging through Brooker's papers was only another kind of undignified snooping, and the fact that I found nothing seemed finally to be a sort of judgment of me, as if my nosiness had earned me exactly what I deserved.

Even so, when I finally lay down in Helen Brooker's bed that early morning, I felt elated, and this is perhaps the most difficult thing to explain; I'm not even quite certain that I understand it now. I didn't know Brooker, really, at all: yet I had at his request relayed a bald lie to a young woman who had believed that lie, and then I had spent most of the night searching for evidence that, I suppose, would merely have proved what I felt I already knew—all of this just as undignified as my nocturnal voyeuristic journeys through Helen Brooker's private things . . . and even so, I felt this sense of elation. I remembered Helen Brooker saying to me about Jack Kennedy, "He was an awful womanizer, you know." And perhaps I was merely feeling the excitement of interest, to have been privy to something Brooker would want hidden.

6

Dearest Helen,

    J. says he likes your eyes best. He especially likes tall, leggy types, very smart, very sexy. All of which you are. I think he has designs on you and so you must be very careful this April. I've been working on a speech for the visit to B. Harbor. Lots of ward types down there. I wish you'd call me once in a while; I mean one could get the feeling you're not letting the absence grow your heart fonder, or words to that effect.

                                          Love, W.

Brooker called late the next morning. I had been up for an hour or so, hiding the signs of my recent strangeness—putting Helen Brooker's photographs where they belonged, her letters and cards back in their bundled order (though I had taken the time to copy down a few things to take with me, things I knew would be of interest to me later, most notably the one set out above, with its reference to a J. that simply must be Jack), and rearranging the casual disorder of Brooker's study. I had mostly finished all this—there were just a few envelopes to be put away—and was taking a short break to watch the morning report. (For the first time in many mornings, no mention was made of Sweeney.)

"Well," Brooker said, through the hiss of long distance. "Did she come back?"

"She came back," I said.

"Jesus Christ."

"I told her you were separated."

"Did she buy it?"

I thought of the first time I had seen him, of the confidence with which he had leaned toward me to murmur his obscenity. And then in an odd shift of mind I had an image of that boy behind the counter at the beach house and restaurant, the day I met Elaine.

"Well?" Brooker said.

"She believed what I told her," I said.

"She bought it."

"Yes."

"When did she come back?"

"Last night. I think she's watching this place."

"Jesus Christ."

"Mr. Brooker, what is she to you?"

"Listen, why didn't you call me last night?"

"It was too late. It was late. What is she to you, Mr. Brooker?"

"She's nothing. Don't pay any attention," he said.

"Well, then what does she want?"

After a moment, he said, "She was a student of mine. She had a problem."

I waited.

"She got the wrong idea of things—the way things were. And now she wants to make trouble for me."

"Did you by any chance have an affair with her?"

"She's just a kid," he said.

I could feel the adrenaline running at the back of my neck. "Yes," I said, "but did you?"

After another pause he said, "Look, I appreciate your help. You *do* have the use of my apartment. I don't think that entitles you to make assumptions about my affairs."

"I think I have to know what the situation *is* if I'm going to be of any more help," I said.

There was still another pause. "I told you," he said. "She got the wrong idea of things. There's something unstable about her that I should've seen—she's of *age*, if that's what you're getting at."

"Does your wife know about her?"

"Jesus Christ," he said, "what is this?"

"She says she wants to talk to your wife—she was asking questions about your wife."

"Look, I can't talk about this anymore. You told her we were separated and you said she bought it—did she buy it or not?"

"I guess she bought it," I said.

"Well, then—fine. If she comes back again will you call me?"

"Do you want to talk to her?"

"Jesus Christ, no. Call me *after* she shows up again, if she does. And if she bought what you told her she probably won't."

"All right," I said.

He muttered, "Jesus Christ," then thanked me for my help, and we said good-bye. The line on his end closed; I listened until the dial tone started.

Outside, the parking lot was ablaze, the sun reflecting too brightly off the cars for me to see much. I went out and walked around the building, hoping that I might find her waiting on one of the landings, or behind one of the parched-looking sycamores in the grassy square across from the main entrance. There wasn't a soul, it seemed, anywhere. All the windows of the building were closed against the heat, and the little park for children was empty; a hot breeze disturbed some sheets on a line that had been strung across one of the landings. Cars going by on the road looked as if they were trailing fire.

IN THE MORNING, there was another article about Sweeney. He had talked to police from surrounding states, and apparently all of his stories were checking out; authorities were finding remains where he said he'd left them. In describing these burial sites, the article said, he often fell into a kind of reverie, and his crimes became nouns. *That one, yeah, that would be a knife. And, let's see, oh, this one's a strangle.*

I read all this with the same, sick fascination, and then called Elaine. She was in bed; she had been down with a cold. "I miss you," she said.

I had the TV on, the midday news, and was lying back in Brooker's easy chair with the telephone in my lap. "Elaine," I said, "I'm going out of my mind."

"Maybe our separation isn't going to work out," she said.

"Are you finished with everything?" I asked. And then I didn't hear what she said, because the local news was showing film of Maria Alvarez standing out on the roof of the college library building. I sat there with Elaine's familiar sleepy voice in my ear and understood what I was seeing. It was Maria Alvarez. Before I could get out of the chair, the picture shifted, everything changed: a crowd of police and firemen were gathered around a broken shape under a blanket in the street.

I pulled the telephone from its table, reaching to turn the TV up, and when I did get the sound up there was only the announcer, a man looking far too calm for what his camera crew had just shown, talking about the morning's tragedy with a series of eyewitnesses, who all reported the same thing. The poor girl jumped. They had seen it all; they were afraid, and their voices shook, and the announcer remained calm, holding the microphone to their mouths.

I don't remember what I said to Elaine. It's entirely possible that I blurted out everything I knew of Brooker and his trouble, speaking, no doubt, with that peculiar clarity that horror sometimes provides an otherwise cloudy mind. But it wasn't long before I was dialing the number Brooker had given me, and having trouble accomplishing it because my hands were shaking so. I don't think I quite expected to get through to him at this hour, and I left a little pause of surprise when he answered.

"Yes?" he said.

"What did you do to her, Brooker?"

"Who is this?"

"Did you tell her you were in love with her?"

He said nothing for a moment. Then, "I can't talk now."

"For God's sake," I said, "I *lied* to her for you. My God, I don't believe this—I told her your lie, and sent her on her way. I helped you do it."

"Now, hold on," he said. "She had a lot of trouble—there were things that had nothing to do with me or any lie. For God's sake, what's happened?"

"Jesus Christ," I said.

"Let's calm down," William Brooker said. "Just tell me what she did."

THAT NIGHT I SLEPT on the sofa in the guest room. In his horror, Brooker had been fatherly and philosophical: there was nothing to be done, nothing *he* could do, at any rate; he was very sorry for the troubled Miss Alvarez, he had tried his best to help her, but in the end he was powerless. He hadn't known her very well, in fact, and perhaps no one ever really gets to know a suicide. Miss Alvarez had wandered into a seminar he had taught as a visiting lecturer the previous fall in Atlanta, and he had seen right away that she was barely holding on. He described his concern for her, his work with her while she was his student; it was all very much a professional relationship, candid and aboveboard, he said; and of course it was quite clear that he was lying. I told him I couldn't talk anymore and hung the phone up. I didn't care what he thought about this, and I don't mean that I was as full of moral outrage as I must have sounded. For the facts of the matter are that something had occurred to me concerning my own part in it all, and I simply wanted no more to do with anyone or anything for a time. What occurred to me was the unpleasant truth that I had held something back in the first minute Maria Alvarez had stood staring at me in the dim light of the landing. She had asked to see Mrs. Brooker and I had said only that Mrs. Brooker wasn't there; I had kept back what I knew about where Helen Brooker was and how long she would be gone, and I had done so, without having to think about it, because of course I understood in an instant what Maria Alvarez had come for, and what she would want with William Brooker's wife. I had, then, already begun the lie that Brooker would later ask me to complete—and this not out of friendship for the man, or loyalty to his interests, but out of something else.

In the days that followed, Brooker called two or three times, wanting to get what details he could. I told him I would not be staying in his apartment anymore, and so there were practical things to consider as well. He didn't say much about his own part in the affair, and yet I was able to piece together a version of it from what he *did* say: Maria Alvarez comes to him looking for what she imagines he can give her; she's pathologically unhappy, but he doesn't see this. He sees her shapely figure and Spanish-dark features, her deep black eyes. He charms her, seduces her, then finds that she is quite mad, quite unable to understand the casual way he means this sort of thing, and he decides it is necessary to evade her. The rest is, of course, an unfortunate chain of events over which he has no control. If only the world weren't the way it is. I had no trouble at all imagining the whole scenario.

What I never imagined had to do with Helen Brooker. She showed up on a Friday afternoon from New York, having set out at the request of her husband, to make certain that things were in order for my departure. (We had no signed agreement, and Brooker was a thorough man.) She came breezing into the living room, where I lay on the white sofa in a bath of letters and photographs—the whole history of William and Helen Brooker. She went into the kitchen and poured us both a bourbon, then came and stood over me, holding my drink out, her eyes not quite settling on what I had in my hands and on my lap. I took the drink, and she sipped hers, still standing over me. "I suppose writers have to be spies," she said. "It must be a perfectly seedy little part of the job."

I put my drink on the end table and began to gather up the photographs.

"Did you find anything of interest?" she said.

I said, "No."

"How unfortunate."

"One of the perfectly seedy little risks of the job," I said.

She took another drink. "Do you suppose I ought to look for a way to get you?"

"I guess you'll do what you want to do."

"You're not even sorry, are you."

"Yes," I said, "in fact I am. I'm quite sorry."

"To think I believed you were charming. It turns out you're just a writer."

I had got everything in a stack, and had put it carefully, as if it were fragile, aside. "I wish I could tell you how sorry I *really* am," I said. When I remember this now, it seems clear that I didn't have much respect for her anymore, and it all had to do with what I thought she did not know about her husband.

"Are you referring," she said, "to Miss Alvarez?"

I looked at her. There was nothing at all in her eyes.

"Of course you are."

"You know," I said.

"William has always been like a little child in a candy store when it comes to women." She finished her drink, and then, precisely as though I were no longer there, put away the papers and letters and photographs. I went upstairs and packed my things, and she followed me, stood in the doorway of the room, her room, watching me.

"This is where you slept?"

"Yes."

"That's fascinating."

"I had to sleep somewhere," I said.

"You don't think much of us, do you? Or of me."

I didn't say anything to this.

"I suppose I should go jump off a building, the way that poor girl did."

"Mrs. Brooker," I said, "you wondered if I was sorry about— about prying the way I did. What about you? What about your husband? There's a young woman dead, Mrs. Brooker. What about that?"

"Your indignation is touching," she said.

We didn't say much else to each other before I left. She stood by with the air of someone who has dealt the telling blow, sipping another drink now and again, tapping the toe of one shoe on the hardwood floor. As I went down the stairs she said, "They all deserve whatever they get." It was as if she were hurling it at me as I scurried away; as if she wanted to chase me with it. There was no anger or pain in her voice—only scorn. And my answer was exactly the kind of stupid, reflexive thing one regrets later, thinking of the smart things one could have said if only one had been able to summon the presence of mind, or the courage, or the calm. I said, "I'm sorry I ever saw you." And of course the fact is that if I'd had an hour to think of something I would no doubt have found nothing better: I was to begin a teaching job in less than two weeks, and I couldn't imagine anything I might have to say to anyone.

I drove around the city for awhile that evening. I don't know what I thought I might see in those quiet streets, the fine old houses and shaded lawns. I suppose I needed simply to get a feeling for the town as something continuous, something—well, ongoing and unabstract, too: children playing in the splashed blue shade of a sycamore; a dog barking from behind a white picket fence.

When it grew too dark to see, I stopped at a package store and bought myself a bottle of whiskey. I intended to get drunk, of course, but I didn't. I went to the rental house and worked all night painting the bedroom and the guest room. Oh, I had some of the whiskey, all right. I had enough to make me sleep in spite of a feeling so desperate and hopeless that, in the morning when I woke and remembered it, I thought of drinking more of the whiskey to keep it at bay. But it was immediately upon me again, and I made myself go about the business of cleaning up the rooms, even as my conviction grew that I would not be living in that house. I had no sense of it—even with all my work on it—as a place where I might be with Elaine, one of a pair of tenants, at home.

A little later, when I headed over to the Western Union office to wire Elaine for the money to fly back to the Midwest, I had my mind half made up to tell her I was coming back for good, that I would not be taking the job after all. In fact, it was Elaine who, that week, insisted that we go through with everything as planned, that we travel east to take up residence in the rental house.

7

THAT FALL, I saw Brooker now and again, from a distance, as I'm sure most people on the campus ever saw him. He left the college that spring, and the faculty bulletin said he was starting his retirement, along with his lovely wife, Helen, in Key West. The Sweeney motel was torn down before the year was out, and I never saw Mrs. Sweeney again. The last thing I heard about her infamous husband was that he was an object of study: the doctors were hoping to find some clue to him.

Elaine and I remained in the rental house for almost two years, and then bought a place, a little bigger, and a lot older, on the other side of the campus. I would never have believed that I might stay at a small college like that, but we did stay more than seven years. All four of our children, two boys and two girls, were born there. Sometimes at night I wake up from a dream that I'm holed up in a place like Brooker's apartment, and then our room feels like a little cave in the dark. If I can't go back to sleep I get myself up and go look at the children. I tuck their blankets over their shoulders, remove their books or toys from their beds; I perform the tasks of a father in the night. Elaine sleeps so soundly that my kiss never wakes her. Our life together is full and perhaps often enough a little too busy; there are times when I think we just miss each other. But that is probably true of any couple.

Whenever I think of that end of summer so long ago, when I took flight from an oppression that might have unhinged me, I remember the slow, lonely hours in the air—the sense that the world below me was little more than a savage place where the weak were fed upon by the strong—and the nervous feeling when I arrived, the fear that my marriage really was over for all my indulgence in those fantasies of betrayal, and our mutual neglect. And the way it felt to see Elaine standing in the white light of the airport terminal, waiting for me.

How good it was to see her.

As I walked up the ramp toward her, lugging my packed suitcase and my unhappy experience like the same great weight, I understood at least that I loved her, and I remember my sense of wonder about this. I remember also that I thought of Sweeney, and of Brooker; that Sweeney and Brooker occurred to me then as though they were, together, the opposing principle—a naked manifestation of the forces that would always be lurking in the darker corners of the spirit. I put this from my mind, and stepped forward to greet her. "Darling," I said. I couldn't believe how familiar and wonderful she looked.

She smiled as if to say we would be all right now.

There was a thing in us both that moved us in each other's direction, that made us recognizable to each other. Whatever our complications, this obdurate fact remained.

"You look beat," she said, and she reached across the little space that divided us.

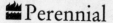 Perennial

Books by Richard Bausch:

WIVES & LOVERS: *Three Short Novels*
ISBN 0-06-057183-7 (paperback)

Three very different stories that illuminate the unadorned core of love—what remains when lust, jealousy, and passion have been stripped away.

THE STORIES OF RICHARD BAUSCH
ISBN 0-06-095622-4 (paperback)

This definitive collection of the best of Bausch's marvelous short stories (including seven new stories) received the PEN/Malamud Award.

HELLO TO THE CANNIBALS: *A Novel*
ISBN 0-06-093080-2 (paperback)

The haunting story of a 19th-century explorer, Mary Kingsley, who became the first white woman to travel to the heart of Africa, and a 21st-century playwright whose research on Kingsley inspires her to break free from the crippling effects of abuse and dysfunction.

**GOOD EVENING MR. AND MRS. AMERICA,
AND ALL THE SHIPS AT SEA**: *A Novel*
ISBN 0-06-092857-3 (paperback)

Set in Washington, D.C., just after the Kennedy assassination. Nineteen-year-old Marshall lives with his widowed mother, studies to be a journalist like his hero, Edward R. Murrow, and fumbles toward manhood in a changing nation.

IN THE NIGHT SEASON: *A Novel*
ISBN 0-06-093030-6 (paperback)

The accidental death of Jack Michaelson has left his wife, Nora, and their 11-year-old son, Jason, nearly destitute and has placed their lives in jeopardy.

SOMEONE TO WATCH OVER ME: *Stories*
ISBN 0-06-093070-5 (paperback)

Bausch offers profound glimpses into the private fears, joys, and sorrows of people we know, and reveals a range of human experience with extraordinary force, clarity, and compassion.

**Don't miss the next book by your favorite author.
Sign up for AuthorTracker by visiting www.AuthorTracker.com.**

Available wherever books are sold, or call 1-800-331-3761 to order.